She waited for him to  front of her, anticipat... hungrily at one anothe... groaned, his arms going... long-awaited kiss.

'Oh, Stuart!' she gasp... ...car it when I don't see you.'

'I meant to stay away from you. Even tonight, when I guessed what that sly old matchmaker was up to, I was determined to keep my distance. I knew if I came near you . . .'

'I'm glad you followed me.' Jane shivered with pleasure as his lips touched her breast. 'God forgive me, but I have wanted to be with you like this.'

'I followed you all, meaning only to see you safely home,' Stuart murmured hoarsely, his hand curving her cheek with a kind of reverence. 'But when I saw you in the water . . .' He gathered her to him, holding her so close that she could feel the pounding of his heart. 'You can't go back to him, Jane. I won't let you!'

Anne Herries was born in Wiltshire but spent much of her early life at Hastings, to which she attributes her love of the sea. She now lives in Cambridge but spends most of the winter in Spain, where she and her husband stay in a pleasant complex of villas and apartments nestled in the hills that run from Malaga to Gibraltar. She likes to swim, walk and lie in the sun weaving her stories of love, passion and intrigue. She writes for pleasure and to give pleasure, owing much of her inspiration to her appreciation of the beauty of nature. If she can bring a smile or perhaps a tear to the eye of her reader, she has achieved her ambition . . .

Anne Herries has written eight other Masquerade Historical Romances—*Devil's Kin*, *The Wolf of Alvar*, *Beware the Conqueror*, *Demon's Woman*, *Raphael*, *The Wild Heart*, *The Spanish Witch* and *The Flame and the Sword*.

THE SLEEPING DEMON

Anne Herries

MILLS & BOON LIMITED
ETON HOUSE 18–24 PARADISE ROAD
RICHMOND SURREY TW9 1SR

*First published in Great Britain 1987
by Mills & Boon Limited*

© Anne Herries 1987

*Australian copyright 1987
Philippine copyright 1987
This edition 1988*

ISBN 0 263 76011 1

*Set in 10 on 10½pt Linotron Times
04–0288–79,400*

*Photoset by Rowland Phototypesetting Limited
Bury St Edmunds, Suffolk
Made and printed in Great Britain by
Cox & Wyman Limited, Reading*

AUTHOR'S NOTE

The Sleeping Demon is the sequel to *The Wild Heart*.
Jane had bravely accompanied her cousin Morna to exile
in New South Wales, helping her to find happiness. This
is Jane's story.

The island of Ti-Ka-Wanna is, of course, fictional, as
are its people and customs. I have presumed it to lie
somewhere in the region of the Friendly Islands.

CHAPTER ONE

THE SHIP SEEMED to skim across the water like a bird, giving Jane the sensation of flying. Lifting her face towards the sun, she felt it warming her, relaxing her. She was free of all the petty restrictions that usually bound her, floating in the cloudless blue of the sky. Then she saw him coming towards her, his stern face seen vaguely through a veil of mist. He was smiling at her in the way that made her whole body tingle, so that she felt almost faint.

'How lovely you look today, Miss Jane,' he said, and the look in his blue-grey eyes sent her heart on a mad race. 'I have been searching for you. I wanted to tell you that I love you . . .'

'Oh, Stuart,' she breathed, moving forward to welcome his embrace. 'Stuart, my love, you've come back to me! I knew you were not dead.'

She went to his arms eagerly, but as they closed round her everything changed. Clouds rolled across the sky and the wind rose, howling wildly as if all the demons in hell had started to scream. Huge waves were crashing over *Sea-Sprite*'s rails, soaking them both to the skin. As her lover's lips touched hers, he was suddenly snatched from her by a terrifying wall of water that lifted him bodily, tossing him carelessly to and fro like a rag doll as it carried him away. She screamed, making a vain effort to catch at his hands—hands that seemed to be held out to her in supplication, begging her to save him. She tried to fight her way through the raging water, sobbing as she battled uselessly against the waves.

'No! No, don't leave me, Stuart,' she cried, her head tossing restlessly on the pillow. 'You can't die . . . You must not . . .'

Suddenly she woke from the dream to find the tears

streaming down her cheeks. Her nightgown was soaking wet, as it had been each time she had had the nightmare, and she shivered. Rising quickly from her bed, she changed into a fresh linen gown and began to strip the damp sheets. She would have to hide them until Morna went into Sydney. If her cousin knew she had suffered yet another night sweat, she would think she was ill and probably insist on postponing her wedding. Jane had no intention of letting that happen. Morna had waited long enough to be married to the man she loved so desperately that she had followed him half-way across the world to save him from the harshness of life as a convict. Besides, these bad dreams were all foolishness! Captain Stuart Smithson had never even glanced at her, except to pass the time of day, and she was not in love with him. She liked him, of course she did, and it was not quite true that he had never looked her way, but at eight and twenty, she should be well past all thought of romance. She knew that he had given her no cause for hope—it was just that the news of the sinking of *Sea-Sprite* and Stuart's likely death had upset her.

It was cruel that he, a strong healthy man with the best part of his life still before him, had been snatched from this world prematurely. Remembering the fever she had contracted during her journey to New South Wales, Jane recalled the kindness shown her by Captain Smithson. Not only had he sent special pastilles to help to purify the air in her cabin, he had come to visit her on two separate occasions, and that despite all his own worries with a sick crew and storm damage to the ship.

She had been feeling very ill the first time, and for once Morna had not been at her side. Captain Smithson had bathed her forehead himself, shaking her pillows and helping her to lie more comfortably. His concern for her comfort had made all the more impression because she had not expected it.

'You are very kind, sir,' she had whispered, feeling the awful pounding at her temples recede slightly for a moment. 'But you must have more important tasks then caring for a sick passenger.'

His smile had set her heart fluttering wildly. There was something about those blue-grey eyes that touched a secret place deep within her, awakening emotions she had not hitherto known she possessed. She had experienced a foolish desire to be kissed by him.

'Nothing is more important than that you should recover, Miss Jane,' he had replied. 'We should all be the poorer for your loss. Besides, I know how much Morna relies on you: she has told me that you have been a tower of strength to her. So you must make haste and get well.'

He took her hand and held it for a moment. His was such a large, brown, cool hand, and she had trembled inwardly, very much aware in that instant of how attractive he was; not perhaps as handsome as the man her cousin loved so desperately, but a strong, caring personality—and there was something more. Something she had been too ill to understand then.

It was on the occasion of his second visit, when she was feeling very much better, that she had realised that the odd sensation in her stomach was because of his nearness and not of the fever. The touch of his hand sent prickles of excitement down her spine, and she felt breathless. No man had ever had this strange effect on her, and it frightened her. Nice women did not react to a man's presence like that; so her mother had taught her long ago. Especially a man she hardly knew, and one who had shown no romantic interest in her whatsoever. It was disgraceful that she should feel this pulsating in her veins. It was wrong. Terribly wrong. She was behaving like a woman of the streets, lying there wanting him to take her in his arms when he had come merely on a visit of compassion.

Shame had made Jane withdraw into herself. She felt crippled by embarrassment, terrified that he might guess what was in her mind. She had hardly been able to bring herself to answer his casual questions about her health.

After he had gone, she had cursed her own shyness, wishing that she had tried harder to hold his attention. She should have said something amusing—something that would have made him see her as a person in her own right and not just as Morna's cousin, but by then it was too late . . .

Sighing, Jane struggled to bring her thoughts back to the present. It made little difference now; Stuart was dead. Perhaps it was better that nothing had come of her foolish infatuation, yet she had a feeling that she might have missed something precious. Was she destined to be alone all her life? She knew that within her there was a great well of love—love that would be wasted if she never married.

Her smile was rueful as she finished making the bed. She did not feel like sleeping and it was too early to begin the morning's chores. Sitting on a stool by the window, she gazed out into the night, watching the moon as it passed briefly behind a cloud, and thinking about the long chain of events that had brought her to New South Wales. When she had been a lonely, unhappy child in her father's rectory, she had never dreamed that she would ever dare to leave the tiny Hampshire village that had been her home, let alone to brave the vicissitudes of a dangerous sea voyage. She had done so because of her love for the young girl who had taken her in after the death of her father. They had shared many adventures, each drawing strength from the other. Life was very strange—and sometimes very cruel.

Sighing again, Jane picked up her hairbrush and began to stroke her thick auburn hair. She glanced at the tips of each shining strand as it hung over her shoulders, realising that the sun had lightened the colour, giving it highlights she had not hitherto been aware of. She normally wore it caught in a severe pleat at the nape of her neck, as it was too bulky to dress in a more becoming style. Since coming to Australia she had considered cutting it short for comfort, but the very idea would have shocked the Reverend Peter Blackwood, and even now

Jane could not bring herself to flout her father's wishes. She had been a dutiful daughter while he lived, despite his coldness towards her, and though living with Morna Hamilton had taught her to be less reserved, she could not quite shake off all the old restrictions.

Her father had never loved her. She had accepted that as a very small child, knowing that it was her punishment for being the cause of her mother's illness. Mrs Blackwood had not died in childbirth, but it had left her an invalid, and though she lingered on for some years, she had not been able to be a wife to her husband again. Jane knew her father had blamed her for the tragedy, hating the plain, pale-faced girl who had robbed him of a once-beautiful wife.

Resolutely Jane pushed the painful memories to the back of her mind. She was being maudlin, letting her thoughts return to the past when there were so many other things she might think of more usefully, such as what she was going to do when Morna was married. She could accept her cousin's offer of a home and go with Morna and Jared to the new land in the Hunter Valley. Or she could stay in Sydney and turn the shop that had been owned jointly by Morna and Captain Smithson into an English-style tearoom, selling her special preserves and cakes. She could live in the rooms behind and be truly independent for the first time in her life. Besides, she had her own reasons for wanting to stay in Sydney . . .

A hot colour stained Jane's cheeks as she realised she was allowing herself to dream again—this time while she was wide awake! It was ridiculous to let herself hope. Even if by some miracle Captain Smithson had not perished in the storm that had sunk his ship, even if he eventually returned to Australia to take up the land that he had hoped to lease, she knew that he would never look at her in the way he had in her dreams. She knew he was in love with Morna. That visit to her sick-bed had been merely kindness. He had never made any secret of his feelings for her cousin, even confiding his hopes to her as they walked together on *Sea-Sprite*'s deck when she was well again. She had wished him happiness, hiding the foolish emotions he had aroused in her. And it was foolish to think like a young girl! She had put all thought of romance behind her the day her father caught her kissing the curate in the vestry. She had been beaten and poor Michael sent away in disgrace.

Jane smiled a little wistfully at the memory. It was the only time she had ever been kissed by a man. She was not beautiful like her cousin. Men talked to her rather as they would to their sisters or maiden aunt. It was surprising how much of their secret selves they sometimes revealed to her all unknowingly. She was a good listener, never poking fun at them or wounding their pride —though she had been known to strike out in defence of her cousin, surprising everyone, including herself.

Shivering, she got to her feet and began to dress. It would soon be light and there was no possibility of her sleeping again. She would take a little walk outside in the fresh air, before the sun came up and it became too hot.

The first fingers of a rosy dawn were stretching across the sky as Jane began her stroll about the homestead. She would be a little sad to leave it, she realised, though of course Dickon and Mary would always be pleased to see her if she cared to visit. Dickon himself had once been a convict, but now he was married, and with Morna's permission was planning to take over the homestead. It had all worked out very well for everyone really, Jane mused, except for poor Philip, of course. Yet the seeds of destruction had always been there in Morna's brother, and he would likely have died young even if they had never come to New South Wales.

Why were her thoughts so sad tonight, Jane wondered. It should be a happy time for them all. Jared had received a pardon from the King and the bitterness of the past few months was ended—or it would be when Jared and Morna were married in two days' time. Lost in her own reflections, she was not aware of the man who watched her from the shadows so that when he came towards her, she jumped. He was a very large man and for one moment her eyes deceived her.

'Stuart—is that you?' she whispered hopefully.

'It's me, Miss Jane,' he said. 'I couldn't sleep, so I came out for a walk. I hope I did not frighten you?'

'Oh . . . Lord Edward,' she said, feeling a sharp cut of disappointment as she saw Jared's English friend. Then she felt ashamed of herself. Teddy Marston had made the long journey to New South Wales especially to bring the King's pardon to Jared, thereby ensuring her cousin's chance of happiness. She should be grateful to him—and she was. 'You startled me a little, that's all. Like you, I found it difficult to sleep.'

'I think it must be the climate,' Teddy said, observing the slight shadows in her face with a little frown. She was not a beautiful woman, he supposed, though his experience in these things was limited; but he found her attractive in many ways. She had a nice smile and her eyes were very expressive, probably more so than she guessed. 'It is so different from what we've been accustomed to at home—though I expect you are used to it now?'

'It doesn't worry me so much these days,' Jane agreed, feeling some sympathy for him. 'You will learn to adjust if you mean to stay here for a while.'

'I intend to see Morna and Jared settled in their new home and then I shall probably return to England, though there's no particular reason why I should. My mother has her own circle of friends, and I've seen my sisters properly married. As for the estate—well, it can run without me for a while. Duty done, what?' He gave her a broad grin, and she laughed.

'I believe you long for adventures, my lord!'

'Yes, you are right. Jared says I should never have resigned my commission in the Indian army, but it wasn't the same without him, and when my father died . . . My mother is fond of telling me that it's high time I found myself a wife.' He pulled a wry face at her. 'Trouble is, I'm not a ladies' man, Miss Jane. The pretty ones don't find me interesting, and the blue-stockings frighten the life out of me, so what am I to do?'

'I'm sure you will find the right person one day, Lord Edward.'

'Perhaps.' He gave a mock sigh, his eyes twinkling. 'Do you think you could bring yourself to call me "Teddy"? "Lord Edward" makes me feel as if I'm in my dotage!'

Her laughter was warm and soft, completely free of mockery. 'Certainly, if you wish it—Teddy—but you must drop the "Miss" in return. I am Jane to my friends.'

'I am honoured, Jane.' He made her a little bow and offered his arm. 'Shall we continue our walk together?'

'Why not?' She took his arm. 'It will soon be time for breakfast, but a stroll will give us both an appetite, will it not?'

There was a welcome breeze blowing in from the sea. Jane stood by the harbour, watching the sea-birds wheel and scream as they swooped low over the water, sometimes scooping up a glittering prize in their beaks. A ship had recently anchored, and boats were bringing cargo and passengers to the shore. It would be their first sight of New South Wales for many of those weary travellers, and she could imagine how good it would feel to them to set foot on dry land after all the long months at sea. On arrival, she herself had experienced all the conflicting emotions of relief, excitement and simple exhaustion.

Having taken the opportunity to ride into Sydney with Morna, Jane had decided to make inquiries from the Captain of the newly-arrived vessel concerning the fate of *Sea-Sprite*. She knew that Morna had already tried to discover the truth of the rumours—for the source of the original story was not one either of them trusted, having come from a man who had been Morna's enemy—and she would not be satisfied unless she heard it for herself. The ship in which she had travelled to Australia with her cousins might indeed have sunk, but that did not necessarily mean that her Captain had perished. He could have been washed ashore on an island, or picked up by another ship. Surely it was possible that someone might have news of Stuart Smithson?

The first small boats had beached and the sailors were beginning to unload trunks and baggage belonging to the passengers. Jane approached a member of the crew, politely asking the questions that had haunted her dreams. He stared at her in a puzzled manner, then shook his head.

'I can't really say, ma'am,' he muttered. 'I heard *Sea-Sprite* sank on her return journey to New South Wales, but I can't swear to the truth of it. You'd best have a word with Captain Bollinson when he comes ashore.'

'Thank you, I shall do so.'

Jane sighed as the sailor turned back to his work. It seemed certain that *Sea-Sprite* had been lost, yet she was not prepared to write her master off. She would come back later and talk with Captain Bollinson. About to move away, her attention was caught by two passengers who had just got out of one of the boats. The man was tall and very thin; the girl of medium height and enveloped by the heavy, full skirts of her gown. Both were dressed in black from head to toe, and they presented a strange appearance against the brilliance of their surroundings—rather like two black crows.

Instinctively Jane recognised the man as a member of the clergy; he was probably a missionary, and that unhappy-looking girl with him was either his sister or his daughter. There was a resemblance about their features that proclaimed the relationship, and a similarity in the pale silver-blond colour of their hair. The girl's straggling locks were just visible beneath her bonnet, while the man had taken off his flat hat to wipe away a film of moisture from his brow. They both looked distinctly uncomfortable in their thick clothes, and Jane felt sympathy for their obvious plight. She hesitated, wondering if she should offer to direct them to the only suitable inn—but perhaps they had relatives . . .

As she watched uncertainly, they began to walk towards her, almost as though intending to approach her. Then the girl faltered, appearing to throw out her hands in despair. A little sigh issued from her lips and she crumpled into an untidy heap on the sand. Even as her companion bent over her, Jane was running towards them.

'Sarah! Sarah, what's the matter?' the man was saying. 'You are making a spectacle of yourself.'

Jane knelt on the beach beside the girl, looking at her white face in concern. 'She has fainted. I am afraid you will have to carry her, at least until we reach my wagon. Then we can drive her to the shop and she can rest for a while.'

'There is no need to concern yourself, ma'am.'

'Excuse me, sir, but I think there is a need.' Jane's dark eyes flashed with anger. 'Your companion is quite clearly exhausted. I assure you that my shop is a very respectable establishment. Your companion's reputation will in no way be at risk.'

For a moment the man's eyes glinted with annoyance, then a smile flickered briefly on his lips. 'I meant no disrespect, ma'am. I may have been rude. I fear my sister has suffered from the journey. We shall be glad of your help, Miss . . .' His brows went up in inquiry. 'I am the Reverend Obadiah Thorne, and this young woman is my sister Sarah.'

When he smiled, he looked younger and less stern. 'I am Jane Blackwood.' Jane got to her feet, dusting the débris from her skirt. 'Please carry Sarah to my wagon. My servant will drive us to the shop. Your sister can rest in the parlour until you are ready to make other arrangements.' She looked up at him, surprising an interested expression in his brilliant blue eyes. 'Have you relatives in New South Wales, Mr Thorne?'

'None we can stay with, though my brother Saul may be here.' He eyed her thoughtfully. 'I shall be glad if you could direct me to a respectable inn?' There was a hint of amusement in his eyes as he stressed the word 'respectable', and Jane blushed.

'Certainly,' she said. 'Please attend to your sister, sir. The crew will know where to send your baggage.'

He nodded, bending down to pick up his sister carefully, though she moaned slightly as he lifted her into the wagon. The driver had seen them coming and hurried to let down the back end, arranging some sacking to make a comfortable couch.

'Thank you, Sam,' Jane said, acknowledging his efforts. 'This is the Reverend Mr Thorne and his sister. Miss Thorne is ill, and I'm taking her to the shop.'

'Yes, Miss Jane,' said Sam. 'I expect it's the heat.'

Jane agreed, giving him a warning glance. Although Sam was a bond-servant, he was accustomed to voicing his opinions at the homestead, and it would not do for him to be too free in his manners in front of the reverend gentleman. Her first impression of this man was that he would expect a servant to know his place. He seemed to be genuinely concerned for his sister, but his first words to her had shown a dislike for anything that was not quite proper. At this moment, she was not sure what to make of him.

'Please ride at the front with Sam, Mr Thorne,' she said. 'I shall sit at the back with your sister in case she comes round.'

'Thank you . . . You are very kind,' he replied, a little stiffly. 'Sarah will be sorry to have given you so much trouble.'

'It really isn't any trouble.'

He frowned. Obviously he felt that they were imposing on her, but there was nothing she could do but smile at him before climbing into the back of the wagon to perch beside the girl. Sarah's colour was returning, and her eyelids fluttered as the buttons of her high-necked gown were loosened. Her tongue moved over dry lips, and she sighed.

'Water . . .' she murmured faintly. 'I'm sorry, Obadiah . . .'

'There's no need to apologise,' Jane said, smoothing the damp hair as she gently removed the girl's bonnet. 'You shall have some water in a little while, Sarah.'

The girl's face creased with emotion, and a tear slipped from beneath her lashes, sliding silently down her pale cheeks. She opened her eyes, looking at Jane in anxious bewilderment.

'Where am I?' she whispered, seeming almost frightened. 'What happened to me? Obadiah . . .'

'You are quite safe, Sarah,' Jane reassured her with a gentle smile. 'Your brother is with us. You fainted and we are taking you to my shop. In fact, we have arrived.'

The wagon pulled to a steady halt, and Sam jumped down to open the flap. He smiled at the girl in his usual friendly way. 'Can you get down, miss, or shall I lift you?'

'My sister is capable of managing alone, aren't you, Sarah?'

A look of apprehension passed across her face. 'Yes, Obadiah,' she said obediently.

Jane cast a scathing look in his direction, jumping down from the wagon herself and giving her hand to the girl. Sarah took it gratefully, her fingers clasping Jane's with obvious reluctance to let go. She smiled slightly as a comforting arm was slipped about her waist and she was led inside a little shop, then through to the cool, shaded parlour at the back. Once she was seated in a chair, Jane brought her a glass of water, which she sipped delicately before setting it down with a sigh.

'Thank you, I feel much better now. I am sorry to have caused you so much bother, Miss . . .'

'Jane. And you were not a bother to me, Sarah. I was glad to do what little I could to help.'

'You were very foolish,' said Obadiah. 'If you were feeling ill, you should have told me before we left the ship.'

'I—I am sorry,' Sarah whispered, her eyes dark with distress. 'I did not mean to disgrace you.' Suddenly the tears were sliding down her face, her thin shoulders shaking as she struggled against the storm of emotion.

'Sarah, do not be ridiculous. There is no need for this display.' He looked helplessly towards Jane, as if he did not know how to cope with the situation.

'Your sister is near to total exhaustion,' Jane said, moving in front of the girl as if to defend her. 'She needs rest and quiet. I think it would be best if you left her with me for a while. Sam will show you the inn I spoke of, and you may come back when you are ready.'

Obadiah Thorne stared at her, the colour sweeping in and out of his cheeks as he struggled to control his surprise. His first impulse was to tell this woman what he thought of her managing ways, but something about her interested him. It was a long time since a woman had spoken to him like this, and such interference would normally have annoyed him. For some reason he found himself drawn to her, despite himself.

His lips twisted in a self-deprecating smile. 'Since you command it, Miss Blackwood, I must obey. I am not quite the monster you and my sister seem to think me. I am grateful for your help. Had Sarah told me how ill she felt, I should have left her on board while I made our arrangements.'

'Obadiah!' Sarah stopped crying and looked shocked. 'You are embarrassing our kind benefactress.'

'No, indeed, I am not embarrassed,' Jane said, her cheeks slightly pink as she saw his look. 'I was advising you, sir, not commanding you.'

'Indeed? My mistake. I apologise.'

'Perhaps I should apologise to you,' Jane suggested, beginning to realise just how outspoken she had been. 'I have no right to interfere in your affairs.'

'No, you have not,' he agreed. 'However, in this case, I believe you had good cause. Sarah is ill and I have been thoughtless. I shall leave her in your care while I make arrangements for our accommodation.' He bowed his head to her. 'Excuse me. Sarah, I shall return for you in one hour.'

He turned and walked from the room, leaving a silence behind him. Sarah fidgeted with her black gloves, glancing up awkwardly at Jane, a faint blush on her cheeks.

'I—I know Obadiah sometimes seems harsh, but he has been very good to me. He raised Saul and me when our parents died, and it wasn't easy on a curate's pay. He has never had the time to—to find a wife or do any of the things other young men do. And Saul was always a trial to him. He ran away to sea when he was seventeen —that's almost eight years ago—and we haven't heard from him since. Obadiah had paid for him to enter college, but he took all the money he could find, and left . . .' The colour deepened in her cheeks. 'So, you see, I try to be all that my brother could wish for. I—I feel that I owe him obedience.'

'Yes, I understand.' Jane frowned as she saw doubt in the girl's eyes. 'I do know how you feel, Sarah, for I had a similar childhood. My father was the Reverend Mr Blackwood, and my mother was an invalid after I was born. I felt I owed him obedience, too.'

'Oh . . .' Their eyes met in mutual understanding. 'Then you will forgive Obadiah if he was rude to you?'

'He was not rude.' Jane smiled wryly. 'I believe I may have been a little presumptuous myself, but you were so obviously upset, and—and I have known what it is to live with a stern disciplinarian. I loved my father, Sarah, and I was unhappy only when I failed to please him.' She sighed. 'I fear that was all too often.'

Sarah gave her a timid smile but made no reply. It was clear to Jane that she was completely under the domination of her brother, and she felt an immediate sympathy towards her. Sarah was very like the girl she herself had been at seventeen.

'Obadiah is to take over the mission on the island of Ti-Ka-Wanna,' Sarah confided, obviously beginning to feel much more herself. 'At least, that's how I think you pronounce it. The Commissioners really wanted him to marry before he came out, but he persuaded them that at his age there was no need to concern themselves that he would . . .' She faltered, realising what she was saying. 'Well, you know . . . He is past forty, after all.'

'I believe the polite expression is "go native", said Jane, her eyes sparkling with amusement. 'Although your brother is not exactly in his dotage, I doubt that he stands in any danger of succumbing to the evils of the flesh.'

Sarah gave a little giggle, her pale face becoming almost pretty as she smiled. 'It is very wicked of me to laugh at Obadiah. He is such a dedicated man, Jane, completely devoted to God's work. He really cares about saving the souls of the poor heathen.'

'I am sure he does.' Jane frowned, thinking that she might have misjudged him. 'Believe me, I do not wish to denigrate Mr Thorne in any way. Yet one cannot always be serious. It is good to laugh, too, Sarah.'

'Oh yes!' Sarah agreed instantly. 'I do hope we can see each other again while Obadiah and I remain in New South Wales. We are staying for a week or so while the ship reprovisions before taking us on to the island. We have heard that Saul may be living here and we hope to receive news of him.'

'I cannot say that I have heard the name, but it may be that he has gone across the mountains to one of the newer settlements. I am sure that the Governor will be pleased to assist your brother if he can, Sarah, and, of course, there are settlers who were here long before my cousins and I came out. Some of them may have heard of Saul.' Jane gave her a thoughtful look. 'My cousin is to be married in two days' time, and I must return to the homestead to prepare for the wedding feast. I know Morna would be happy to have you stay with us; if your brother would permit it, naturally.'

'It is very kind of you to invite me,' Sarah said doubtfully. 'It would be so nice . . . but Obadiah is unlikely to agree.'

In this she was very shortly to be proved wrong, however. Obadiah Thorne returned sooner than he had promised, looking hot, tired and frustrated. He had been able to secure only one single room at the inn, which was a highly unsatisfactory outcome, since he could not allow his sister to stay there alone, and he had been assured that none of the other hostelries were suitable for a young lady. He had been preparing himself to ask a favour of Miss Jane Blackwood, and was clearly relieved to be met with a plea from his sister to be allowed to stay with her new friend.

'It would be far better for you than staying in town, Sarah,' he said with a hesitant smile. 'If Miss Blackwood is sure that it would not be too much of an imposition? I should stay here, of course, and attend to our business.'

'It would be a pleasure to have Sarah's company.'

'Then, I can only say thank you, Miss Blackwood.'

'Oh, thank you, Obadiah!' Sarah cried, her face lighting up with pleasure. 'It will be so exciting to stay on a real homestead.'

'You will behave yourself, Sarah.' He sighed as he saw her face cloud and reached out to pat her face. 'Of course you will. You are a good girl and I am too severe—but you know that I have your best interests at heart, don't you?'

'Yes.' She came shyly to his side, kissing his cheek. 'You are not to worry. I shall not disgrace you.'

He smiled as he relaxed. 'It was fortunate for us that we met Miss Blackwood. Your bag is on her wagon. It was sent to the inn and I thought you might need it. I shall return there now . . .' He glanced at Jane. 'I believe the homestead belongs to Miss Morna Hamilton?'

'Yes. Morna is my cousin. She owns this shop, too, but I have decided to take it over from her and start a tearoom.' Jane gave a self-conscious laugh. 'We were talking of it earlier today. Morna had hoped that I would go with her and her husband to the Hunter Valley, but I have made up my mind to stay here.'

'Your cousin is soon to be married, I think?' He smiled again, and she thought it made him look rather attractive. Perhaps her first impression had been too harsh. 'Forgive me, I made some inquiries—and everyone was talking of the wedding.'

'You had every right to reassure yourself as to my suitability to have charge of a young girl,' Jane said, a hint of laughter in her dark eyes. 'As I was telling Sarah, my father was a member of the clergy.'

Obadiah nodded, looking gratified. 'I have been speaking with a friend of yours, I believe. He speaks well of you. A Mr Harry Robson?'

'Oh—Harry.' Jane nodded cheerfully. 'He and his wife are good friends. You will come to the wedding, Mr Thorne?'

'I do not think so,' he said. 'It would not be right to impose on your hospitality too much. Besides, I have a great deal to do before we continue our journey.'

Jane did not argue. She knew Sarah would be welcome at the homestead, but she was not sure about Obadiah Thorne. He was very strict with his sister, that much was clear to her.

'You will let us know when Sarah is to return to Sydney?'

'Of course,' he assented, a flicker of something in his eyes. 'You will excuse me now. I must return to the inn.'

Jane watched him leave, feeling puzzled. It seemed that he was perhaps not quite the stern disciplinarian she had first thought him. Sarah spoke well of her brother, so he could not be the cold, unfeeling man he appeared to be on the surface, yet she had seen a hint of that same inflexibility in him that had been in her own father. They were indeed much alike, though, since they both had the same calling, that was not surprising. Her father had been a good man in his way, while clinging to the stern principles that ruled his life.

'Was it not kind of Obadiah to agree?' Sarah asked happily.

'Yes,' Jane agreed, wondering just why he had capitulated so easily.

*   *   *

'You look beautiful, Morna,' Jane said, kissing her cousin's cheek. 'I know all brides are supposed to be radiant, but I have never seen one look quite as happy as you do.'

'Perhaps you have never seen a bride with as much reason to be happy,' Morna replied, her eyes glowing. 'Oh, Jane, my dearest, I can hardly believe that Jared and I will soon be man and wife. There were times when I thought it would never happen.'

'Those terrible times are gone, Morna. Forget them. You must not allow anything to spoil your wedding day.' Jane saw the flicker of pain in her cousin's face and guessed that she was thinking of her brother. 'Try to remember Philip as he was when you were children. The seeds of self-destruction were in him, and you are not to blame for his death.'

Morna nodded, tossing back her mane of thick hair. 'I know you are right, Jane. I would have liked him to be here today—but I know he would never have agreed. He hated Jared at the end.' She sighed and pushed the unhappy memory from her mind. She could not be sad for long today! Looking at Jane, she smiled lovingly. 'And how is your little friend this morning? You won't let her come to the wedding in that terrible black dress?'

'No, of course not!' Jane laughed. 'You were right, that blue dress of yours needed only a little alteration. You should have seen her face when she knew it was for her! I doubt if the poor child has ever had a pretty gown in her life.'

'I don't suppose she has.' Morna's eyes were stormy. 'Her brother should be ashamed of himself. She can't be more than eighteen, and it's monstrous to make her wear those awful clothes!'

'I agree, but Sarah is a very meek girl. I had quite a time persuading her to wear the dress. She was afraid her brother would be cross with her. After all, she is only seventeen; scarcely more than a child.'

'Oh, I hate that kind of a man!' Morna cried passionately. 'They seek to kill all pleasure, even when it is as innocent as wearing a pretty gown. I hope you gave her one of my best bonnets?'

Jane smiled as she heard the defiant note in her cousin's voice. Morna would never have allowed her brother to dominate her—but then, she had always been a wilful girl with a generous nature and a wild heart. It was her determination that had brought her through many tragedies, to find happiness with the man she loved so much.

'I only wish Sarah had a little of your spirit, my dear. I believe her brother might respect her more if she dared to stand up to him.' Jane shrugged. 'But I must not encourage her to rebel too much; that would not be fair to her. However, I did give her the bonnet that goes so well with that gown. Unfortunately neither your shoes nor mine will fit her. Sarah seems to have rather large feet.'

'You mean she must wear those black boots?' Morna pulled a face. 'What a shame! If only I had known before I disposed of the remaining stock from the shop. I believe there was one pair of satin slippers that might have fitted her.'

'Well, it can't be helped now. Luckily the dress is a little long and will cover them.' Jame picked up the posy of fresh flowers she had gathered that morning from their garden and handed them to Morna. 'It is time, my love. You do not wish to keep Jared waiting, I think?'

'He would come looking for me if I did!' Morna cried, her eyes alight with happiness once more. 'We must go now. Teddy will be getting anxious, and you know what he is! I think he likes you, Jane. I've seen him watching you when you were not aware of it.'

'Lord Edward is a gentleman,' Jane said, her cheeks pink. 'I hope he does like me a little. He is Jared's friend.'

'You know I meant more than that,' said Morna, 'but I won't tease you. You must make up your own mind about him. I think he would be a kind and indulgent husband, Jane; he has all that money and doesn't know what to do with it.'

'I would never dream of marrying for money!'

'No, of course not,' Morna said at once. 'You know I didn't mean it that way. It's just that I don't like to think of you running that shop alone. Won't you change your mind and come with us instead? You know we both want that, don't you?'

'Yes, I know . . .' Jane sighed. 'I don't want to hurt you, but I should like to try my idea for a while, Morna. I think you should have some time alone with Jared. Besides, I have my own reasons for staying in Sydney.'

Jane's cheeks tinged with pink as the picture of a man's face came into her mind. She was recalling Stuart Smithson as she had last seen him just before the fateful voyage that was to take him to a watery grave. He had been talking of his return to New South Wales, his eyes alight with enthusiasm.

'I've made up my mind, Miss Jane,' he had said. 'I've spoken to the Governor about a lease, and he has assured me that I would be given favourable consideration.'

'But the sea has been your life,' she had replied. 'Do you think you think you could be happy away from it?'

'There is a time in every man's life when he needs to make changes,' he had said with a smile that had made her tremble. 'It's time I started thinking about settling down. I've a mind to marry . . .'

For one breathtaking second she had thought that he was proposing to her, then she saw his eyes move towards Morna, and her hopes died in her breast. Of course, it was her cousin who had made him think of giving up the sea. At that time it had seemed unlikely that Jared would ever get over his bitterness, and she knew that Stuart had believed he stood a chance of marrying the woman he loved . . .

Jane was silent for so long that Morna stared at her in concern. 'I've always known that you liked Captain Smithson, Jane. You are not staying on here in the hope that he will turn up, are you?' She saw the answer in her cousin's eyes and felt a stab of pain. It was no less than she had always suspected, though she had never dared to put the thought into words before for fear of hurting her sensitive friend. 'I am so sorry, my dearest, I thought it might be that. How it must have hurt you when . . . I wish I could offer you some hope of his survival, but everyone I have spoken to says that he must have gone down with his ship. There were a few survivors after all, it seems, though at first it was feared that all hands were lost. According to Captain Bollinson, they all said that Stuart insisted on staying with his ship until the end.'

'I see.' Jane blinked swiftly. It was no more than she had expected, but that did not stop it hurting her. 'I suppose I must accept it . . . But I should still like to try my skill at running the tearoom. I can always join you later if I wish?'

'Of course.' Morna squeezed her hand, wishing that she could do more to help Jane. 'We must go now. Are you ready?'

'Quite ready.'

Jane smiled, holding the pain inside her. She would rather die than spoil her cousin's wedding day, and she had learned long ago how to hide her feelings. They left Morna's room together, discovering Teddy Marston loitering outside the door. He looked at them, his face full of admiration for them both.

'Morna, my dear, you are exquisite! You also look very pretty, Jane.'

Jane laughed and shook her head. 'I have never been that, Teddy, but thank you just the same. I hope we haven't kept you waiting too long?'

'No, of course not, though I was just beginning to wonder if Morna had changed her mind!' He grinned as he spoke, knowing that it was nonsense. 'Jared was impatient an hour ago. We had better not keep him waiting a moment longer for his bride.'

The wedding was being held in the open air at the homestead so that Morna's bond-servants could share in her happiness. The Governor had offered to give a grand reception for her at his house in Sydney, but she had refused, insisting on a simple ceremony that all her friends could attend. Jared had agreed with her, asking his long-standing friend to give Morna to him, and choosing Dickon to be his best man instead. Only he and Dickon really understood why he had done it, but it seemed to please everyone. Dickon's wife Mary had helped Jane to prepare the wedding feast, and many of Morna's customers from the shop were present, with Emily and Harry Robson as the guests of honour. The Governor was to give a little evening party later in the week as a token of his regard for the happy couple.

The ceremony was very simple, just as the bride had wanted, and soon the celebrations were in full swing. Someone produced an old fiddle, and a few of the guests started up a country dance.

Jane noticed Sarah watching them with a wistful expression, and she touched her companion on the arm. 'Will you ask Sarah to dance, Teddy?'

He glanced at her, his brows arching. 'I am not a very good dancer, Jane.'

'You can manage as well as anyone here! Please ask her. I do not believe she has ever been to a dance in her life.'

He smothered a sigh. It would have suited him much better simply to sit in the shade and talk to her, but he was too good-natured to refuse a request from someone he respected as much as he did Jane Blackwood.

'Very well, if you wish,' he said, getting up and strolling towards the pale girl Jane had taken under her wing. There was a pathetic eagerness in Sarah's eyes as he stopped before her, and he felt a rush of sympathy. No doubt she had led a wretched life, and it would not harm him to put himself out for her a little. He gave her a warm smile. 'Would you take pity and dance with me, Miss Thorne? I fear I am not a very skilled performer, but I believe I could manage this.'

'I once learned a few steps from my brother Saul,'

said Sarah. 'Obadiah saw no harm in it when we were children. I have not danced for years, but I would like to try.'

'Then it seems we shall suit one another.' Teddy took the girl's hand and drew her out to join the others. 'Please tell me at once if I step on your toe, Miss Thorne.'

She laughed. The girl was really quite pretty now that the anxious expression had left her face, he thought. Her skin did not look as sallow as the dull black of her usual gown made it appear, and the blue of her new dress matched her eyes. Jane had helped her to curl her fine hair into ringlets, winding it tightly into rags the previous night, and it was surprising what a difference it made to her face.

Sarah actually felt attractive for the first time in her life, especially when Lord Edward smiled at her. She thought him a fine figure of a man, just the kind of gentleman she had always hoped might one day sweep her up in his carriage and carry her away. He was so handsome, in her opinion, and such a big, strong man. Yet there was kindness and sensitivity in his face. His large hands were gentle as they touched her, making her feel that he was a caring person. She responded to his friendly teasing like a rosebud opening to the sun, finding it very easy to be relaxed and natural with him, forgetting all her fear of Obadiah's displeasure if he should ever discover that she had danced with a stranger. Of course, Lord Edward wasn't really a stranger—he was Jane's friend—but that wouldn't matter to her brother. He had allowed her to dance with Saul when she was a child, but she knew that he did not really approve of such frivolity—especially something as free and easy as this gay country reel.

Watching them together, Jane was pleased with the success of her suggestion. It would be wonderful if something were to come of it, she thought. She believed Teddy was rather a lonely person beneath that cheerful façade, and Sarah would respond well to being

spoiled. It would surely be the ideal match . . . Her
pleasant thoughts were suddenly shattered as she saw
the tall, thin, black-clothed figure striding towards them.
Obadiah! What on earth was he doing here? He had said
that he would not be coming. She would never have
risked letting Sarah dance if she had thought . . . He was
angry! Seeing him seize his sister's wrist, Jane gave a
little gasp of dismay. He exchanged a few sharp words
with Teddy, then began to stride away, forcing Sarah to
accompany him. She went meekly enough, but her
distress was obvious.

'Forgive me for causing you embarrassment,' Jane
said as Teddy hastened to her side. 'What did Mr Thorne
say to you?'

'He merely said that Sarah was not permitted to
dance. I did try to reason with him, but she gave me such
a beseeching look that I didn't know what to do.'

'You were right not to try and stop him. It was my
fault.' Jane pursed her lips. 'I must go after them.
Perhaps I can persuade him not to be too harsh with her.'

'I should let them go . . .' Teddy began, but Jane was
already hurrying after them. 'You'll only get hurt, my
dear . . .' He sighed as he realised that she could not
hear him. 'Damn! I danced with the girl only to please
you!'

Jane did hear him call, but she knew she must go after
Obadiah Thorne. He had placed his sister in her care,
and she was at fault. She had known instinctively that he
would not wish Sarah to dance, but the wistful look on
the girl's face had touched Jane's heart. It was so unfair!
He had no business to keep his sister under such strict
control. She was young and she could be pretty; she had
a right to some happiness in her life! It was not too
late . . .

She caught up with them as they reached the house.
'Mr Thorne, please wait. You must not blame Sarah for
what happened.'

He turned on her, his eyes blazing. 'I am well aware
who is to blame for all this! Sarah, go and change into

your own clothes. You look like a hussy and I am ashamed of you!'

'I wasn't doing anything wrong, Obadiah.'

'You will allow me to be the judge of that. Now, do as you are told.'

Her eyes were dark with distress and she was shaking. 'Yes, Obadiah.'

Jane watched as Sarah went into her room, closing the door quietly. Memories of her own childhood came flooding back to her, and she felt her anger mounting. She stood in front of Obadiah, her eyes flashing with sudden temper.

'You—You fiend!' she cried. 'How could you speak to that poor child so cruelly? She was merely dancing with a friend of mine—a very respectable man!—doing nothing that could offend any reasonable person. How dare you come here and make a scene at my cousin's wedding? You are insufferable! You are so wrapped up in your own conceit that you think you alone are able to judge what is right and what is wrong. God himself would not frown on an innocent girl's pleasure.'

'You do not know what you are talking about. There is bad blood in that girl. If I do not teach her what is right, she will go the way of her mother.'

'I don't care what her mother was!' Jane snapped, beyond all caution now. 'Any intelligent person can see that she is a meek, dutiful child, but you—you are set on breaking her spirit. Soon she will be too frightened to sneeze in case she upsets you. Do you want to drive your sister into a lunatic asylum, Mr Thorne? If you continue in this way, that is what you will do. She is very near to breaking-point already.'

'I suppose you are an expert?' he asked coldly.

'I saw my own mother go into a decline because she was terrified of her husband.' Jane drew a deep breath. 'I implore you not to be so harsh with Sarah, sir. If you care for her even a little . . .'

'My sister is all I have, Miss Blackwood.' His face was suddenly drawn and haggard. 'I do not wish her to be frightened of me, but I am as I am. The truth is that I do not know how to behave towards a young woman. When she was a child it was easier . . .' He sighed. 'I believe I need a wife, Miss Blackwood.'

'As a mother for Sarah?' Jane nodded, her anger fading as she saw genuine concern in his eyes and a kind of bewilderment. 'Yes, I think that might be the answer for both of you. A caring woman could be the bridge between you. She might be able to show you that there is no harm in a girl enjoying herself quite innocently.'

There was a sudden eagerness in his face. 'I knew you would understand! I want only the best for Sarah, but I need help to keep her from straying. I need a wife, Miss Blackwood. I need you! *You* are the woman you described to me just now. You are the woman I would have as my wife. To stand beside me and do God's work among the heathen. You are the one, Miss Blackwood, I see it clearly now. God's hand is in this . . .'

Jane gasped, her face turning pale. 'Oh, no, Mr Thorne! You cannot have thought I meant myself?'

'I know you did not mean it as you spoke,' he agreed at once. 'You are far too sensitive a woman. But the thought was put into your mind by him who watches over us. Don't you see, it is the perfect answer to all our problems? You cannot really wish to work in the kitchens of a tearoom all your life? You are a lady, Miss Blackwood, and it is not fitting.'

'But I wish to do it,' Jane protested, feeling overwhelmed by his enthusiasm. There was a crusading expression in his eyes, and she realised that he really believed he had received a sign from God. 'No, it is out of the question. I could never marry you.' He could not seriously expect her to accept a proposal of marriage from a man she had met only twice?

'Oh, I understand your reservations completely,' he said, his manner one of perfect reason. 'We are still strangers, and any woman must feel as you do, but we should come to know one another in time. You have a fondness for Sarah. I have seen it in your eyes, and you would not have defended her so nobly if it were not so. Can you not see how much better it would be for her if we were all together as a family?'

'Yes, I can see that,' Jane said slowly, feeling a little confused. 'But you would not commend that as a reason for marriage?'

'Many women marry for less worthy objectives,' he argued. 'How many spinsters marry a widower for the sake of a comfortable home and an end to loneliness? I think we could be comfortable together. Perhaps you dream of love? It might be that we should find some warmth in the relationship . . .'

Jane's cheeks were hot as she looked at him. He really was asking her to be his wife. His arguments even made sense. Many women were happy to marry simply for the sake of a home—but she had never been inclined to such a course. Yet she felt herself being swayed by his arguments. Why? She had seen elements of charm in him . . .

'Even if I were to consider the arrangement for Sarah's sake, I would never be able to bring myself to—to submit to my conjugal duties, Mr Thorne. It would never be a true marriage in that sense.' What was she saying? She could not be considering the idea. It was madness!

He brushed aside her statement in his mind, pleased by her maidenly reserve. It confirmed his first opinion of her. She spoke just as any decent woman should in the circumstances.

'Naturally I would not expect such a commitment from you—at least until we knew each other better. Even then I would make no demands upon you that you would dislike. I have never found that side of my nature a problem, Miss Blackwood. All I should ask of you would be friendship, and the qualities of caring and compassion that I know you possess in abundance.'

'It would be a permanent arrangement, Mr Thorne. I should not change my mind . . .' Jane broke off as she realised what she was saying. No, this was nonsense! Her intuition warned her to have nothing to do with him. She must not be swayed by his persuasion, even though it would put an end to her fears of dying a lonely old maid. Surely it was better not to marry than to take a man she did not love for her husband? She was so confused. 'No,' she said at last. 'I cannot. It would not be right.'

Even as she denied him, the door to Sarah's room flew open and the girl came out, running to throw her arms round her waist and looking up pleadingly.

'Oh, please say yes, Jane,' she begged with tears in her eyes. 'You are the only real friend I have ever had. It would make me so happy if you were to be Obadiah's wife.'

Jane hesitated, her heart torn by the girl's look. Was it selfish of her to turn down Mr Thorne's offer without even considering it? How could she know that this was not indeed a sign from God? Oh, she did not imagine that he was calling her to carry his message to the heathen, but perhaps he was asking for her help on Sarah's behalf? She gazed at Obadiah uncertainly. Had she misjudged him at the start? It was obvious that he was a caring brother, so would he not also be a caring husband? Might she not find a kind of happiness as his wife? After all, she was not likely to experience a passionate love affair at her age. What had she to lose if she agreed? Only her freedom, a little voice whispered, and the dream that Stuart Smithson would one day learn to care for her. But Stuart was dead, and Sarah needed her so desperately . . . And there was a deep need of something within her. Perhaps God was giving her a chance of happiness.

'Please tell me that you will think about it,' Obadiah said, smiling, as he took her hand. 'I know I am older than you, Jane, and a stern, plain man, but I would try to be a good husband.'

He was strange, unpredictable and obsessive about his beliefs, but she believed that there might be another side to him. Perhaps his coldness was a mask behind which he hid his feelings for fear of being hurt. It might be that she could teach him to be a kinder, warmer person . . . She hesitated, and was lost.

'Give me a little time,' she whispered faintly. 'I must think about it more carefully . . .'

CHAPTER TWO

'YOU'VE MARRIED that man?' Morna stared at her cousin in dismay. 'Jane! I don't believe you. What on earth made you do it? You don't even like him, and I know how wretched your father made you feel for years.'

Jand flushed, dropping her eyes. 'I loved my father, Morna.'

'You loved him, but did he ever care for you? Obadiah Thorne is the same kind of a man. You told me so yourself, and we've all seen how he treats his poor sister . . .' Morna nodded angrily. 'Of course, that's it! You will ruin your own life for her sake.'

'It's not quite like that. I think I may have misjudged him at the start. It's true that he is a little harsh with Sarah, but underneath I think he truly cares for her.' Jane sighed as she saw her cousin's look. 'Please try to understand. I want to help Sarah, but that is only part of my reason for marrying.'

'I don't understand, Jane.' Morna stared at her. 'I thought you wanted to stay here in case Captain Smithson returned? I was under the impression that you cared for him.'

Jane flinched, feeling the sting of tears behind her eyes. 'I do care for Stuart. It is because of him that I am marrying now, don't you see?'

It was so difficult to put into words. In her mind, Jane could picture that last dinner with Captain Smithson. She saw him smiling at her across the table as he complimented her on the meal she had cooked.

'My mother was an excellent cook, Miss Jane,' he had said, 'but you are magnificent! Some day you are going to make a lucky man very happy.'

Jane had merely smiled and shaken her head, but after

he left the homestead, she had not been able to forget the look in his eyes as he smiled at her. She knew he was not in love with her, but he liked her and appreciated her for what she was. Might it not be that one day he would really look at her and see her as a woman in her own right? She had never wished to marry, believing that it would not suit her, but he had planted the idea in her mind, and she had realised that there was something lacking in her life.

She looked at Morna now, her eyes beseeching her to understand what she could not put into words. 'I—I need something more. I think perhaps. . . .'

'But you could have married Teddy,' cried Morna. 'Surely he would have been a better choice if you wanted to marry?'

'Lord Edward does not need me,' Jane said, frowning. 'I believe that Obadiah may. Oh, I do not have to explain all this, Morna. He is my husband now, and I intend to make the marriage work if I can. I had hoped you would accept that, but if you cannot . . .' She turned to leave, but Morna called her back.

'No, don't go. I'm sorry. I did not mean to quarrel with you. It's just that it was such a shock.'

'I know.' Jane looked out of the parlour window at the dusty street that wound past the shop. 'When Obadiah first asked me I refused him, but a night of reflection made me see that perhaps it was right for me. You yourself said that I should marry. I—I believe that I can help Obadiah, and I know that Sarah needs me. Surely that makes it worth while?'

There was such a look of appeal in her face that Morna could no longer resist. Swiftly they moved to embrace one another, tears springing to their eyes.

'Wish me happiness, Morna?'

'Of course I do. I only wish you had chosen Teddy. I'm sorry, Jane, I can't pretend to be pleased. I love you too much.'

'And I love you.' Jane sighed deeply. 'Believe me, my dearest, I have not done this lightly. I do not expect to be wildly happy, but I hope to find contentment in helping others.'

'You are a fool. Such a wonderful, soft-hearted fool! You knew I would not let you do it, and that's why you kept it so quiet.'

'Obadiah made the arrangements. His ship leaves tomorrow, so there was no time to waste. I wanted to ask you, but I thought it best not to invite you.' Jane's lashes flicked down to hide her expressive eyes. 'I have done what I thought was right. You see, this marriage is not . . . I have told Obadiah that I cannot . . .'

'And he has accepted it?' Morna's brows went up as she guessed what Jane could not say. 'I see. Oh, Jane, I'm afraid for you.'

'You must not be.' Jane smiled a little oddly. 'Now that you are married, my life had no real purpose. Now, perhaps, I can make a new life for myself.'

Morna stared at her uncertainly. Had she been selfish in expecting Jane to settle for a comfortable life as her companion? She did not believe that there was a chance of real happiness for her cousin with Obadiah, but she and Jane had come closer to quarrelling than ever before, and she must not stand in her way. They must not part with anger between them. She smiled at her lovingly.

'Then we must say farewell for the moment, dearest. Yet I shall pray that we will meet again and . . .' Morna held her hands tightly. 'You know that there will always be a home for you wherever I am. You must promise that you will come to me if ever you need help?'

'Where else would I go?' Jane smiled, and kissed her cheek. 'But please do not worry about me. Although I do not love Obadiah, I respect him, and I believe that he is sincerely dedicated to his work. I do not believe that I shall be unhappy.'

If only she were truly certain she had done the right thing, Jane thought, holding her velvet pelisse tighter round her as she stood on the deck of *Brixham Princess*.

Pride had made her hide her doubts as she said goodbye to her cousin, but now that the coastline of New South Wales had been left behind, they niggled at the back of her mind, especially when she looked at the tall, cloaked figure of her husband. Her husband! Had she really married Obadiah? It had all happened so quickly that she had found herself being swept along by his enthusiasm. He was a very determined man, and despite his sometimes harsh manner, there was a certain boyish charm in him now and then which was very appealing.

Now that she was married, Jane meant to make the most of her new-found influence. Already she had persuaded her husband that it was bad for Sarah's health to wear such thick clothing. The result was that the girl had been permitted to leave off some of the layers of heavy petticoats. She had also been allowed to keep a few of the gowns Morna had given her, though Obadiah insisted that she remove most of the lace trimmings. Even so, the gowns were far prettier than anything Sarah had ever owned.

As Jane watched him conversing with Captain Bollinson, he became aware of her gaze and came over to her. He gave her the grin that seemed to belie his stern character. She thought that perhaps, when he was young, he had been a very different person. What had changed him?

'You are a better sailor than my sister, Jane. I wish you could persuade her to come on deck. It would do her more good than lying on her bed.'

'She has a headache at the moment, but you are right. I shall make her take a walk later, when it is cooler.'

He nodded, a slight frown creasing his forehead. 'I have been speaking to Bollinson about our accommodation arrangements. I had hoped we might be able to share a cabin, but you and Sarah must continue together for the duration of the voyage. As you know, I am forced to share with Mr Stretton. I fear he is a gambling man, and a little too fond of his wine . . .'

'I am sorry you are obliged to endure his company, but

I really could not submit to the intimacy of sleeping in your cabin, sir. Please do not forget the terms of our agreement: this marriage can never be more than a formality.'

'I am aware of your feelings, Jane. Once we are on the island it will not embarrass either of us, but this rather unusual situation does make me appear something of a fool. For a man who has only just married to . . .'

'As you have already ascertained, we have no choice, Obadiah.' The colour rose in Jane's cheeks. 'There are only two passenger cabins, and surely you do not expect Sarah to change places with you?'

'Facetiousness does not become you.' There was a note of extreme displeasure in his voice. 'I was merely regretting the situation.'

'I am sorry.' Jane sighed, and laid her hand on his arm. 'You and I have made a strange bargain, Obadiah, and it will need patience on both sides to make it work. I shall try to be a good wife to you in my own way.'

'I have no doubt of your sincerity, my dear. This is God's will. He will show us the way forward.'

Jane did not reply as she turned to gaze out across the water. She had almost made him angry, and she guessed that it was because she had insisted on sticking to their bargain. It was clear that Obadiah had hoped she would change her mind, but at the moment she could not contemplate the idea of being a true wife with any degree of equanimity . . . Perhaps, in time. She was not yet too old to have children . . . A little shiver went through her and she brought her thoughts to another direction.

Was it really God's will that she should join this man in his crusade to convert the people of a tiny island in the middle of the South Seas? What would they be like? They must have their own culture and their own religion, so did they truly want foreign missionaries telling them how to behave and what to believe? It seemed that they did, for there was an established mission on the island, and Obadiah was replacing the incumbent of the mission house, whose wife had died some two years ago. He had requested a recall at the time of her death, but it had taken some time to arrange. Not every young clergyman was burning with a desire to convert the heathen. The life of a missionary was often hard, and many found their health ruined by the harshness of the climate or the hardships they were forced to endure. Especially the women.

Even before she had decided to accept Obadiah's offer, Jane had realised that she might never return to England. It was possible that both she and Sarah would succumb to a fever and die on the island. Perhaps it was the thought of Sarah's suffering that had decided her, though her own inner loneliness had contributed to the impulse that had made her agree. Was it possible that she might eventually find happiness with her husband?

The happiness of loving someone who would love her in return had so far been denied to her. Her father had sent away the only man who had shown an interest in her as a woman. It was probably not such a great tragedy, she admitted with a wry smile. She and Michael had both been too young really to know their own hearts, but it had hurt her at the time. Now it was too late. She would never know that special kind of love—but might she not find some warmth in the relationship?

The island lay shimmering in the sun before them. A fringe of golden sand beyond the calm lagoon, and then the dark haze of greenery and the overshadowing presence of the volcano. It was an enchanted place, beautiful and peaceful, but with a haunting mystery.

'I suppose it's the volcano,' Sarah said, as Jane joined her at the ship's rails. 'It's the sleeping monster within that makes the island seem forbidding.' She shivered despite the burning heat of the sun. 'I've wished sometimes that we could go on sailing for ever and never arrive . . .'

'I'm nervous too,' Jane replied, giving her hand a reassuring squeeze. 'Despite all Obadiah has told me about the mission, I can't help feeling that we are intruding. What right have we to bring our way of life to this place?'

'I know what you mean. Oh, look!'

A group of islanders had gathered on the beach to greet the ship. The men were naked to the waist—and so were the women! Some of them were wearing what appeared to be a grass skirt, while others had a piece of brightly-coloured cloth wound around their waists. The men had ornaments made from feathers, pieces of bone and shells, while the women wore necklaces of shells or garlands of exotic flowers about their necks. The flowers helped to cover their naked breasts, but both Jane and Sarah avoided looking too closely at the figures on the shore, their own cheeks pink.

A large flower-decked boat with long, curving prows had been launched from the beach. The men dug deep into the water with flat-bladed paddles as they sped towards the supply ship. Among the colourful islanders, the black-coated missionary looked somewhat incongruous. He was sweating profusely as he climbed aboard, followed by a tall, proud-faced islander. Advancing towards Obadiah, he mopped his brow with a big handkerchief and then held out his hand.

'Richard Grenshaw,' he said. 'I'm glad to meet you, sir. The Queen is waiting to greet you at her village, but her brother has honoured you by coming to meet you. Don't try to shake hands with him or you might get more than you're expecting! Just bow your head and smile. He understands English, but he won't always speak it.'

Obadiah's brows went up. 'I shall greet him in a moment. First, you must meet my wife and sister.'

'First, you must meet Kumi,' Richard Grenshaw insisted. 'Kumi is a bad man to have as your enemy.'

'Very well.' Obadiah frowned. 'How do I address him?'

'He is Prince Kumi, second only to Queen Ma-Llalla in importance. Now, sir, I'm afraid he's already becoming impatient.'

The two men advanced towards the tall islander. Having overheard their conversation, Jane watched the meeting apprehensively. She was sure that Prince Kumi had also understood what had been said, and she thought there was a moment when his eyes flashed with anger or perhaps contempt. Somehow she felt that he had taken an instant dislike to Obadiah. The greetings between them were very stiff and formal. It was a moment or two before Richard Grenshaw beckoned to the two women, his smile a little forced.

'Prince Kumi would like to meet the ladies,' he said, after the islander had spoken rapidly in his own language.

Sarah's indrawn breath was an indication of her nervousness, but Jane grasped her firmly by the hand, drawing her forward. Prince Kumi was a daunting figure, but it would be foolish to show fear. If they were to live on the island, some kind of a relationship must be established from the start. Stopping a few feet short of the Prince, Jane dipped in a respectful curtsy, then she lifted her eyes, meeting his penetrating gaze steadily.

'Welcome to Ti-Ka-Wanna,' he said, his voice deep and surprisingly warm. 'I am Prince Kumi. I come from Queen Ma-Llalla to bring you to our village. You will sit by my side in the canoe.'

'On behalf of myself, my husband and my husband's sister, I thank you, sir.'

The Prince's dark eyes flickered towards Obadiah, showing open contempt now. He spoke rapidly to Richard Grenshaw and then turned to climb down to the flower-laden boat.

'Prince Kumi is surprised that you are the missionary's wife,' Grenshaw explained with an apologetic glance at Jane. 'He insists that you sit beside him in the place of honour.'

'Jane will do nothing of the sort!'

'I must, Obadiah.' Jane gave him a warning look. 'The Prince knows that I am your wife. I am sure that he will respect that relationship.'

'Prince Kumi is very interested in the idea of Christianity,' Grenshaw said. 'He has not quite made up his mind yet, but the islanders all respect the relationship between a—a husband and wife. He would not dream of stealing another man's woman. You will be quite safe with him, Mrs Thorne.'

'I am certain of it.'

Ignoring Obadiah's scowl, Jane went to the ship's rails. A rope-ladder was hanging over the side, and to reach the boat below, she had to descend it. It would be quite impossible to do so without giving the man staring up at her an excellent view of her petticoats. Her embarrassment was tempered by the realisation that he would in all probability be too amazed by the amount of clothing she was wearing to take much notice of anything else he might glimpse. In any case, she had no choice. She eased her foot over the ship's side and felt her ankle grasped by a firm hand. Glancing down at the Prince, she caught the glimmer of a smile as he set her foot safely on the first rung. He had waited to help her.

Knowing he was there gave her the necessary determination to make the descent with the minimum of fuss. She would give this proud, rather fierce, islander no reason to scorn the missionary's wife! Safely on board the ceremonial canoe, she smiled slightly and nodded in response to his enquiring look. She was not sure, but she thought she detected a hint of respect in his eyes. It vanished as he looked up and saw that Obadiah was making the precarious descent, followed by an obviously nervous Sarah. Despite the girl's fear, they both reached the boat safely and were followed by Richard Grenshaw. As the islanders began their swift, rhythmic paddling, they chanted a song in their own language.

'It is a song of welcome,' Richard Grenshaw explained to Jane, leaning forward to whisper in her ear. 'They say you are blessed by the gods and will bring good fortune to their island.'

'I hope we can bring some . . . benefit.' She saw his sharp look and lowered her voice. 'H—Have you found the people receptive to God's word, sir?'

'Queen Ma-Llalla has made me most welcome . . .' He looked awkward, obviously finding it difficult to answer. 'She is willing to accept our ways up to a point, but they have their own customs. It is a case of give and take on both sides. We cannot expect them to desert all their old ways overnight.'

'How long have you been here?'

'Five years.' He sighed, and mopped his brow. 'Queen Ma-Llalla was very fond of Beth; they understood one another. When my wife died, the Queen was very good to me.'

'It must have been rather lonely for you after Beth died?'

Richard Grenshaw's cheeks grew hot as he avoided her gaze. 'Yes, it was, at first . . .'

Seeing his embarrassment, Jane did not press the conversation further. She suspected that he might have found consolation with one of the island women, and she hoped that Obadiah would not discover his secret too soon. Such a liaison was strictly forbidden by the Commissioners, and her husband might consider it his duty to send back a report on his predecessor's misdemeanour.

The boat had reached shallow water. Jane was surprised when the islanders jumped out and suddenly lifted the canoe bodily, carrying it up the beach, thus saving the ladies from getting their feet wet. It was a thoughtful gesture, and she was sure it had been done at Prince Kumi's special command. He was busy issuing orders to those around him. The islanders were clearly very curious about the newcomers, but stood back respectfully as their prince gave his hand to Jane. He led her up the beach, indicating a garlanded litter. It seemed that he had decided she was to be carried to the village in style, but seeing that there was no similar conveyance for the others, she held back, feeling reluctant to be singled out.

'You must do as he asks,' Richard Grenshaw whispered. 'Otherwise he will be offended.'

'But why me?' Jane asked, puzzled. 'Obadiah is the missionary.'

'On this island, a woman is always queen. Her consort is a prince. When I brought Beth here, I soon learnt that I had to work through her. Queen Ma-Llalla will not listen to your husband unless she approves of you. I'm sorry, but it's their way.'

'Obadiah will not be pleased. I'm sure he does not realise how important that custom is to the islanders.'

Richard Grenshaw smiled. 'No one who hasn't lived with these people can hope to understand. Fortunately, Queen Ma-Llalla is a very tolerant lady. She forgives me much.'

Jane laughed softly. Richard was a very modest, likeable man, and she could understand how he had managed to live on the island for five years among these people. He would seek to persuade gently, taking his failures without bitterness. She was not sure that Obadiah would be as patient.

Deciding that a friendly relationship with the natives was their first priority, Jane took her seat on the litter. She was lifted to shoulder height by several powerful islanders, and the Prince gave the order for the little cavalcade to proceed towards the village. He walked beside her litter while the others were left to struggle on behind as best they could, Sarah finding it difficult to cross the soft sands, which seemed to drag at her long skirts. In the end she had to hitch them up above her ankles, causing Obadiah to frown. However, he was aware of her predicament, and kept his thoughts to himself. The going was a little easier once they entered the lush mass of trees, trailing creepers and flowers, though Sarah had to watch where she placed her feet. It was a little cooler, however, and the track through the forest was well worn by many feet. The journey was relatively short, taking them perhaps half an hour to reach the Queen's village, which was situated beside a small stream that flowed down from the mountainside.

Here the forest had been cleared to allow for the

building of quite a large village. The huts were strongly constructed and thatched with palm, seeming to consist of one large room only. Most of their living appeared to be done out in the open. From her vantage-point, Jane had an excellent view of all that was going on: women cooking, weaving baskets, plaiting grass or cleaning shells. Soon, though, all this activity ceased as the excited villagers clustered around the newcomers. There was much gesticulation and a buzz of voices as Jane was lowered to the ground. She thought that the voices sounded happy, and everyone appeared to be smiling at her. Some of the women giggled, trying to touch her until they were shooed away by Prince Kumi.

At one end of the village was a much larger hut, and Jane guessed that it belonged to Queen Ma-Llalla. Arranged on the ground in front of it were long lines of palm leaves, on which a vast array of food had been set out. Just outside the Queen's house, a kind of rude couch had been decorated with flowers and leaves, and there were smaller seats of a similar sort to either side. It was clear that the missionaries were to be honoured with a banquet.

The villagers followed behind as their prince led the way. When everyone had gathered about the dais, an expectant hush fell over them. It was a moment or two more before the fringe of knotted grass over the doorway was drawn aside and a woman came out. She was very large, tall and well-fleshed, with a deep honey-gold complexion and black hair. Although she must have been well into middle age she was strikingly handsome, her eyes bright and inquiring. She was wearing a colourful tunic that covered her ample charms, while leaving her shoulders and arms bare. A coronet of flowers was her only ornament, but she looked completely regal, and no one needed to be told that this was Queen Ma-Llalla.

'This is she you dreamed of, Gracious One,' Prince Kumi said, pushing Jane forward. 'She says she is the missionary's wife.'

Queen Ma-Llalla studied Jane as she dipped into a graceful curtsy and then straightened up, meeting the older woman's gaze. She nodded thoughtfully, then a warm smile spread across her face.

'You are welcome here, Wise One. We have been awaiting you for many moons. It is good that you have come.'

'We are all very happy to be here, Your Majesty.'

The Queen glanced at Obadiah and his sister. For a moment the warmth left her face, but then it returned as she waved her guests to their seats.

'You will sit beside me,' she said, her steady gaze returning to Jane. 'By what name shall we know you?'

'I am called Jane, Your Majesty.'

'Jane? Yes, it is well. You shall call me Ma-Llalla. To others, I am the Gracious One.'

Jane smiled, understanding that she was being favoured by the Queen just as Richard Grenshaw had predicted.

The Queen seated herself on her couch, indicating that the others might also sit. At this sign the villagers took their places, cross-legged, in lines at either side of the food, while some of the men remained standing to serve the Queen with food and drink. Prince Kumi himself brought Jane a large shell with several delicious-looking pieces of meat, fish and fruit. The milky-coloured liquid had an odd flavour and was served in little cups made from the shells of the coconut, but the drink was not simply the milk of that fruit, and Jane could feel it warming her throat as she sipped it carefully.

The Prince watched as she tasted the food, smiling as he saw her face register approval. 'You find it good, yes?'

'Very good, Prince Kumi.'

Several large platters had been placed within the Queen's reach. She stretched out her hand regularly, eating with evident relish and encouraging her guests to do the same. Jane and Sarah obeyed, both finding the succulent dishes to their liking, but Obadiah ate sparingly, his face frozen. This was quite clearly not what he had expected.

Jane's thoughts were distracted by the sound of giggling. She turned round to glance over her shoulder, and saw a group of children peeping out of the Queen's hut. A cry of delight escaped her. 'Oh, what beautiful children!'

'Would you like to meet my blessed ones?' Queen Ma-Llalla asked, a look of maternal pride in her eyes as she beckoned to the first child. 'This is Sumi, my first son; Kalli, my eldest daughter, is a year older, and these are Talla, Oona, Manalla . . .' She introduced them one by one. 'This is Beth, my little one.' She stroked the black curls fondly. 'Is she not worthy of love, Jane?'

'She is beautiful,' Jane said, smiling as the tiny child peeped from behind her mother's couch.

What happened then was so sudden that, afterwards, she was to think of it almost as a dream. The child snatched a piece of fruit from her mother's dish, popping it into her mouth and swallowing. Somehow it lodged in her throat, choking her. She rolled her eyes in fear, obviously finding it impossible to breathe. While her mother whimpered with fright, staring at Beth in helpless anxiety, Jane leapt to her feet and seized the child, thumping her hard in the middle of the back. Beth coughed and spluttered, and Jane stuck her finger in her mouth to clear the obstruction at the back of her throat. A hard lump of fruit popped out and she began to cry noisily, huddling against her mother for comfort.

Queen Ma-Llalla embraced her, then passed her to the waiting arms of Prince Kumi. Rising to her feet with surprising agility for one so large, she reached out to Jane, crushing her in a great enveloping hug. Then she rubbed her nose against Jane's in what was plainly a show of affection before hugging her once more.

Breathless and overwhelmed, Jane was eventually released and allowed to sit down again. Although no words had been spoken, it was obvious that her action had earned the Queen's gratitude, but she herself felt only relief that Beth appeared to be perfectly well and was restored to the company of her brothers and sisters. The children were shooed away by an indulgent Prince Kumi, who was obviously very fond of them, and the feasting went on. Everything appeared to be just as it had been, and it was not for several minutes that Jane realised that the islanders were watching every move she made. They ate when she ate, and drank when she drank, seeming to strain after her words every time she spoke. At first she found it a little disconcerting, then realised it was a mark of respect; a way of showing their gratitude for what she had done. At last the Queen rose to her feet. She made a sign to Kumi, and then beckoned to Jane. 'You will stay here with me for three moons while Kumi builds you a hut. The others will go now to the mission.'

Jane hesitated, knowing that Obadiah would be annoyed by the Queen's demands. 'I am honoured, Ma-Llalla, but my place is with my husband.'

'Kumi will build you a big hut next to mine. Your man can visit you there when you wish for mating.'

Hot colour rose to Jane's cheeks. The Queen could not know how tempting her offer was, but it could not be accepted. If Jane was to have any influence over Obadiah, she knew she must live at the mission with him and Sarah.

'I shall stay here for three moons if you wish it, Ma-Llalla, but then I must go to the mission. It is our way.'

The Queen looked into her face, then she inclined her head. 'You have chosen. I give you your wish, but Kumi will build the hut. You will return to us when the time comes. Go with this man. I shall send for you when I am ready.'

The others had all realised that it was time to leave, and Jane joined them as the Queen disappeared inside her hut. She glanced at Richard Grenshaw uncertainly as he led them from the village.

'I hope I have not offended the Queen by refusing to live within the village?'

'No, I don't think she really expected you to agree. She asked my wife to stay here, but Beth refused, too.'

'Your place is at the mission,' Obadiah growled. 'Is it far, Grenshaw? I'm anxious to see what you've achieved. Is the school built yet?'

'No, not yet.' Richard seemed awkward. 'The Queen prefers me to go to the village. She likes to oversee the children's lessons. In fact, most of the women come to listen.'

'That is excellent, but what of the men? How many have you managed to convert?'

'Only a handful, I'm afraid. They are waiting for Kumi to make up his mind, and, as I told you, he has not yet decided.'

'I thought the Queen's word was law?'

'It is, but she has decreed that her people must choose between the old ways and the new religion for themselves; Queen Ma-Llalla is very tolerant. She allows her brother to make most of the decisions, though she can be stubborn if she is angry. I remember once . . .' Richard ceased speaking as his companion uttered a surprised cry. 'I'm afraid this is it. The islanders did the best they could, but it's not quite what you're used to . . .'

The mission house differed from the villagers' huts in so much as it was square instead of round. Consisting of several small rooms divided by grass walls, it was built in an almost straight line. Actually quite large by the islanders' standards, to a European eye it was just a rude shelter from the sun, and certainly not what Obadiah had expected.

'Is this the sum of five years' work?' he asked, obviously disgusted. 'Where is the church? Why haven't you built a decent house? There's plenty of wood.'

Richard Grenshaw mopped his sweating brow. 'Excuse me, I think it's a touch of fever. I've never been much good with my hands. I have to rely on the natives for building work, and they just don't see the point of labouring over something they don't consider necessary. It's as easy to worship God under a palm tree as inside a dark, stuffy building.'

'That isn't important,' Obadiah grunted. 'A church becomes special to its congregation because people go there to worship God. It is his house. No wonder Prince Kumi has no respect for Christianity! You have given him nothing to make him understand why it is the only way for those who wish to be saved. How can you expect these ignorant people to understand if you do not show them the way?'

'It is you who do not understand, sir. These people believe that life is important. Death is only darkness . . .'

'Then it's time they were told the truth! I see I have much to do here.'

'Obadiah, do you think we could go inside?' Jane said quickly. 'Sarah is feeling exhausted, and I should like to rest for a while.'

Her interruption was timely, the men having come close to more than an argument. Obadiah was silenced, and Grenshaw became very apologetic, turning his attention to seeing the ladies comfortably settled in what was to be their new home. His own personal possessions had already been packed into two trunks, waiting for transfer to the ship.

Inside the house, he had managed to accumulate a few pieces of simple furniture, some acquired from the supply ship, which visited once or sometimes twice a year, other pieces roughly hewn by his own hand. He apologised to Jane again for the inadequacy of his hospitality, but she shook her head.

'It is sufficient for our needs, sir. We have brought many household items ourselves, and we must learn to adjust to a new way of life.'

'We shall manage,' Obadiah said coldly. 'But there will be many changes here. I came to this island to bring civilisation to the heathen, and that's just what I intend to do.'

'I thought you came to bring God's word?' Jane asked, feeling apprehensive as she saw the look in his eyes.

'God's word and a decent way of living go hand in hand, Jane.' He gave her a reproving look. 'It is for us to show these ignorant people how to behave. I have already seen that discipline is sadly lacking. The women's dress is shocking. Even you must admit that, my dear.'

'It is a little embarrassing at first,' Jane agreed. 'However, I think it would be wiser to go slowly to begin with, Obadiah. There are other, more important, considerations.'

'Such as?' He raised his brows.

'Why, the church, of course. Before you try to change their way of life, it might be best to build a place of worship.' Jane held her breath as he frowned. Oh, let her ruse to deflect his thoughts work! She could just imagine what trouble it would cause if he started dictating to the islanders too soon. Perhaps in time they could learn to know one another better, but it would be foolish to antagonise the Queen from the beginning.

'Yes, you are right,' Obadiah said at last. 'Adam and Eve were naked in the Garden of Eden. It is for us to show these simple people how to behave. We shall start by building the church.'

Jane heaved a sigh of relief. It would take some time to complete such a task, and by then Obadiah might have learned something of the islanders. At least it would give them all a breathing-space . . .

It was much cooler now that the sun had gone down. A pale moon had taken its place, casting a silver shadow across the sands. The island seemed very quiet, with only an occasional bird cry and the whisper of the ocean to break the silence. It was very beautiful, Jane thought, as she stood gazing out towards the ship. Beautiful, but strange and a little frightening, especially the great volcano that dominated the centre of the island. Richard

Grenshaw had told her that in the old days the natives had thought of it as a god, laying gifts of flowers at the top of the crater to appease the slumbering demon within.

'It has been silent for the last five years,' he said. 'I believe the islanders think my magic is stronger than the god's. I haven't seen any tributes lying there for some time now.'

Jane had wanted to listen to his stories of the people, realising that there was much they could learn from this gentle man, but Obadiah had insisted on being shown around his part of the island while it was still light. Sarah had retired to her room with a headache, leaving Jane alone. So she had come out to wander on the stretch of golden sand at the mission end of the island, enjoying her first moment of true peace since her marriage. It was so good to be alone for a while . . .

The sound of singing destroyed her feeling of peace. She stiffened, appreciating its incongruity in the stillness of an island paradise. This was no rhythmic chanting such as she had heard earlier in the day, but a sea-shanty sung in English, in a loud, raucous voice. Spinning round towards the sound, she saw three figures lurching across the beach. At least the man was certainly lurching and weaving in a drunken manner, while the two island girls giggled and attempted to keep him from falling face down into the sand. They seemed highly amused, and all three were obviously enjoying themselves.

It must be one of the sailors from *Brixham Princess*, Jane surmised, her lips twitching at what was a comical sight. She had not thought that any of the crew were to be allowed on shore, except for unloading the stores and collecting Richard Grenshaw's trunks, but apparently one of them had escaped Captain Bollinson's eagle eye. The man was obviously very drunk, and would no doubt be in trouble when his disobedience was discovered. Captain Bollinson was anxious to deliver his remaining passenger at another larger island some distance away and return to New South Wales; if this truant were not careful, he might be left to cool his heels on Ti-Ka-Wanna until the supply ship returned in several months' time. Jane wondered if she ought to try and warn him, but she hesitated, feeling it might be unwise to approach him in his present state. Perhaps it would be better to speak to Richard about it.

About to turn away, something made her stiffen, an odd tingle running through her as she realised that there was a certain familiarity about that unsteady figure. He was a little closer now and she thought that there was something in his build that seemed to remind her of . . . Yet it was impossible! She was dreaming. It could not be . . . But there was a definite likeness . . . No, it wasn't, it could not be him!

'Stuart!' she whispered, and the earth seemed to tremble beneath her feet. 'But you—You're dead . . .'

She was rooted to the spot, unable to move as the merry little party came nearer. She was dreaming again. She had to be! This was all part of some terrible nightmare, and she would wake up to find herself drenched to the skin once more. Then she saw his face quite clearly in the moonlight, and she knew that it was not a dream. It really was Captain Smithson. He was alive! A feeling of utter joy swept through her, and she began to run towards him, forgetful of everything but the fact of his return from the dead.

'Stuart—Captain Smithson,' she cried. 'It is you! It is! They all told me you were dead, but I never believed it . . .'

The drunken man had stopped walking. He stared at her, blinking his eyes stupidly as he tried to focus on the woman running towards him. Then he shook off the restraining hands of the island girls, taking a few tottery steps towards her, his blurred gaze seeing the woman he wanted to see.

'Morna,' he muttered thickly, stretching out his arms. 'Morna, my love, you've come to me . . .'

Jane halted before him, her heart twisting with pain as she heard his feverish words. He thought she was

Morna. He was still as much in love with her as he had always been. What an idiot she had been to think in her first overwhelmingly joy that he would want to see *her*!

'No, Captain Smithson,' she said, her voice sharp with pain. 'It's not Morna. I'm her cousin Jane . . .'

The light died out of his eyes and he blinked, peering at her as if through a mist. 'Miss Jane?' he asked, looking like a startled owl. 'Well, I never! So it is.' He grinned at her foolishly, then began to crumple at the knees, sinking gently into a heap on the sand.

'Oh, Stuart,' Jane whispered chokily, her own hurt draining away as she witnessed the pain he had unknowingly revealed before he collapsed. A sad, tender smile curved her lips as she knelt beside him on the sand, touching his cheek. 'What has happened to you?'

Looking at the dishevelled and slightly disreputable figure of Captain Smithson, she felt an urge to gather him up in her arms and comfort him as a mother would a child: it was the age-old instinct of woman to give unselfishly without thought of reward. She had no idea of how he came to be on the island, but it was quite obvious how he had been spending his time. He had always been a smart, upright man with a pride in his own appearance, that was one of the first things she had noticed about him. Now his clothes were stained, his hair straggled untidily over his shirt collar, and he had not shaved for some time. It was not uncommon for sailors to grow a beard, but the growth on Stuart's chin was ragged and unsightly. It was clear that he had lost all self-respect.

Jane became conscious of the two island girls. They had stopped giggling and were looking at her with wide, anxious eyes. Getting to her feet, she brushed the débris from her skirt, fighting for calm, and realising that her own behaviour left much to be desired. She was the missionary's wife. For a few minutes she had forgotten that Obadiah existed, but now she remembered who and what she was.

'This man is my friend,' she said, her cheeks a little pink. 'I—I thought he was drowned in a storm at sea. I am so happy to know that he is still alive. It was such a surprise to me . . .'

The girls nodded, smiling now, and one of them said, 'Captain Smithy come from sea. He long time in little canoe. He very sick. We make well again. Now he live with Mallami and Kara. We take good care of him. Mission lady Jane come visit soon?'

'Perhaps.' Jane smiled a little wistfully. The islanders had such a warm charm, and the girls were so pretty, that she could hardly blame Stuart for indulging in a free and easy life. Yet it hurt to know that he had made no effort to send news of his whereabouts to his friends in New South Wales. He must have known they would all worry about him. 'Can you manage to get him back to your hut, or shall I fetch help?'

'We manage.' The girl's white teeth gleamed as she laughed. 'Captain Smithy fall down many times. We sit, wait till he wake up, then we go to hut.'

'I see.' Jane frowned, realising that it was typical of the islanders. The air was warm and the sand was soft. No harm would come to Stuart if he lay where he was all night, so the girls would simply sit beside him until the effects of the wine began to wear off. 'Well, I shall leave you to do as you think best. Good night, Mallami —Kara.'

'Sleep in peace, Mission lady Jane.'

Jane smiled to herself as she walked away. Obviously the islanders had decided she should have a title to denote her status: mere 'Jane' was not impressive enough for them. She was beginning to be enchanted by these people; they had an almost childlike capacity for happiness and an innocence that made her want to protect them. Yet why should they need protection? Unless it was from Obadiah . . .

The thought took the smile from her lips. A great surge of revulsion went through her as she remembered that she was now his wife. How could she have married a man she did not even like? It was madness! Yet, if she had not done so, she would never have come to the island, and might never have known that Stuart was still alive. Surely, had she waited a little longer, he might have returned to New South Wales, and she would have been free! Why had she not waited? Why had she let Obadiah persuade her into an unnatural marriage?

A wild desire to be rid of the bonds that tied her to her husband swept over her. Everything had changed so suddenly in one single instant. She had married Obadiah of her own free will, partly, it was true, because of Sarah, but also because she had seen something attractive in him. She realised that nothing had really changed because of her discovery tonight. Sarah still needed her. She believed that Obadiah, too, needed her help, despite his sometimes overbearing manner. Captain Smithson did not need or want her, so why did she feel as she did?

She closed her eyes, the tears slipping beneath her lashes as she recalled the afternoon when Morna had told her that Stuart's ship was lost. For one terrible second she had wanted to die, too. She had thought that that must be the worst moment of her life, but now she knew that it was possible to suffer even more, and it was all her own fault. No one had forced her to marry Obadiah. It had been her own decision. She was trapped in a web that she had spun for herself. What could she do? Her mind went round and round. One part of her wanted to shout her joy aloud for all the world to hear. Stuart was alive. Alive! She could hardly comprehend it. It was wonderful—an answer to her prayers. Even though she would never be his, it filled her with happiness to know that he had not perished in the sea.

'Oh, thank you, God,' she murmured. 'Thank you for letting him live.'

She knew that she would never mean anything special to him. She could not replace Morna in his heart, neither could she give him a reason to return to his old way of life. If he was content to live with Mallami and Kara, she had no right to attempt to reform him. She would not even try. It was very sad to see how low he had fallen, but he would not thank her for trying to save him from himself. He would probably think her an interfering old maid. No, not any more. She smiled wryly. She was married now. A wife—and yet not a wife . . .

A little shudder ran through her. She could never be a true wife to Obadiah now. The meeting with Stuart had at least made that much clear. The thought of her husband's hands touching her intimately made her shudder. She was not sure that she would have enjoyed that side of marriage with any man. Her mother had found it so distasteful that she preferred to be an invalid, and perhaps Jane was cast in the same mould, though she had sometimes thought that with Stuart . . . She recalled that moment in her cabin when she had felt the beginning of physical desire . . . Realising where her thoughts were leading, Jane felt ashamed of herself. She was betraying the vows she had taken such a short time ago. Even though it was not a true marriage, they were still binding. She had promised to be a good wife to Obadiah, and she must abide by that promise. She must keep her word because she was not the kind of woman who gave an undertaking lightly. If she betrayed her husband, even in her own thoughts, she would lose her self-respect . . .

'Jane! Jane, where have you been?' Obadiah's voice broke into her reverie, making her turn to look at him. 'I was worried about you.' He came towards her, smiling. 'I have neglected you for far too long, and I fear I have not been in the best of moods all day. Will you forgive me?'

He was gazing at her intently, and Jane felt a twinge of guilt. She had always known she was not in love with him. It was not his fault that she now wished to be free. She could not allow the fact of Stuart's being alive to affect her attitude towards the man she had married. Obadiah was doing his best, and she could do no less. She was smiling as she went to meet him.

'It is the most amazing coincidence, Obadiah! You will hardly believe it when I tell you what has happened . . .'

CHAPTER THREE

THEY HAD FINISHED unpacking at last, and Jane breathed a sigh of relief as she looked round the room, feeling more at ease now that she had some of her own things about her. It was still a very primitive form of housing, and she could not help agreeing with Obadiah when he grumbled about Richard Grenshaw's lack of ambition. If a permanent mission was to be established on the island, they would need to build better accommodation. Cooking, washing and sanitation had all proved to be something of a problem in the last few days. It was a week since their arrival, she realised, and their predecessor was somewhere on the high seas . . .

A week since she had made the discovery about Stuart. Jane sighed as she trailed her hand lovingly over the smooth surface of her mother's sewing-box. A week in which she had lain sleepless night after night, torn between her desire to see him again and the wish to be fair to her husband. Obadiah had not made things easier for her, his manner becoming increasingly irritable as the days passed. She glanced up as the grass curtain that served to keep out insects was swished aside and her husband came in. He was sweating, and his pale skin looked an uncomfortable red, the penalty of staying too long in the sun.

'Kumi is here asking for you,' he said, plainly annoyed. 'It seems that the Queen has sent for you again.'

Jane felt a surge impatience. It was hardly her fault that the Queen preferred to talk to her, but Obadiah had not ceased to resent it.

'I've tried to explain that you are the missionary,' she said, 'but she insists that I am to teach the women and children. She says that the men will hear you preach on Sundays.'

'I suppose I should be grateful for the extra time it will give me to build the church.' His voice was heavy with sarcasm. 'I am fortunate that you decided to accompany my sister and me—Sarah has done nothing but complain of the heat, and the Queen refuses to listen to a word I say.'

Jane was tempted to tell him that it was his own fault that Ma-Llalla would not listen, but she contented herself with a frown as she defended Sarah. 'Your sister has helped with the unpacking and the washing,' she said, a flash of anger in her eyes. 'You know she isn't strong, so how can you expect her to work in this heat?'

'How fiercely you defend her!' He moved closer, his hands reaching out to grasp her shoulders. 'You are a good woman, Jane. I hope you know how much I admire you?'

Jane moved away, trying to control her feelings. Perhaps it was her fault, but of late she had found it harder and harder to keep the peace between them. She knew he had suffered some disappointment over the mission, but he had made both her and Sarah suffer for it.

He came up behind her. 'You know I want this marriage to be successful, don't you?'

She dug her nails into the palms of her hands as he touched the back of her neck. 'Please don't do that,' she said tensely.

'I find you very attractive, Jane. I should like to be a true husband to you.'

She turned on him then, her eyes glittering. 'No, Obadiah. You promised you wouldn't . . .'

'But we are not strangers now . . .'

Her nerves were stretched to breaking-point. It had taken all her strength to carry on as if nothing had happened after her discovery the other night; now he was suggesting . . . It was unfair! He had agreed to the bargain they had made. She could never do what he wanted, especially now!

'I must not keep the Queen waiting,'' she said, holding back her anger.

'I suppose not. Will you speak to her about the men helping to build the church?'

'I'll try.' She smothered a sigh, feeling a prick of guilt. 'Do not work too hard, Obadiah.'

'Thank you for your concern. As a matter of fact, I thought I might visit Captain Smithson. I have been thinking about what you told me, and I believe I may be able to help him. Besides, his behaviour is a bad example to the natives. It is for us to show them a civilised way of life, not to corrupt them.'

Jane bit back a sharp retort. She wished he would not meddle with things that did not concern him, and regretted her impulse to tell him of her meeting with Stuart. Perhaps it was imagination, but she fancied she had noticed a change in his moods since then: there had been a sharper note in his voice, and she had seen him looking at her oddly.

'I must go,' was all she said.

Donning a wide-brimmed straw bonnet, she went outside to meet the Prince. He greeted her with his slow, warm smile, apparently not in the least concerned that she had kept him waiting for several minutes. After greeting her, he lapsed into silence as they walked together to the village. It was not however an uncomfortable silence, and sometimes he pointed to a brightly-coloured bird or an exotic flower, nodding sagely as she exclaimed in delight. Kumi did not need to be told that she had fallen under the island's spell.

Her daily sessions with the women and children were a pleasure shared by all. Kumi attended quite often, as did many of the other men, though they watched from a discreet distance. The islanders were eager to learn all she had to teach them of the outside world, and though she always began her lessons with a moral tale from the Bible, she usually ended up by telling them stories about her life in England. The women had been shy at the start, but now they asked so many questions that she found it difficult to satisfy their curiosity.

This morning she produced a tattered copy of an English ladies' fashion magazine, containing drawings of gowns that had been modish when she left London. It had caused much amusement amongst the island women, especially an illustration of a polonaise gown that had an overskirt bunched up behind to reveal a trailing underdress. They simply could not understand why anyone should wear so many garments. Jane's own dress of a pale blue silk in a very plain style was much admired—and touched—by curious fingers. The Queen asked her if she could show them how to make such a dress, but she laughed and shook her head.

'I am no seamstress, but Sarah sews beautifully. I know she would be glad to give lessons at the mission house.'

Queen Ma-Llalla looked at her long and hard. 'She will not come to the village as you do?'

'Sarah is not always well. She could not sit in the sun for long periods.'

'Then we shall build her a shelter.' Queen Ma-Llalla said, nodding wisely. 'And she shall be carried back to the mission.'

'I am sure Sarah can manage the walk,' Jane murmured with an inward smile. She had hoped that Sarah's sewing lessons might be the beginning of the mission school, but it was obvious that the Queen's mind was made up. She preferred that the missionaries should come to her village, and that was of course her right, no matter what Obadiah might think.

The morning's lessons at an end, Jane left the village alone, refusing the Prince's offer of an escort. There was nothing to harm her on this peaceful island, and she wanted a little time alone. She wandered in the direction of the beach, stopping to stare at the calm waters of the lagoon, her thoughts whirring in her head. It was proving more difficult to put the meeting with Stuart

Smithson out of her mind than she had imagined . . .

'Miss Jane? It is you! So I wasn't dreaming the other night.'

Had she conjured him up from her subconscious? Jane turned as she heard Stuart's voice, her heart leaping wildly as she saw him walking towards her across the sand. Immediately she was aware of the change in his apppearance: the straggly beard had gone, and some effort had been made to wash the stains from his clothing. Now he looked much as she had remembered him, and he was smiling at her as he did in her dreams. Her head spun a little, and she felt a tightness in her breast.

'I have been looking for you,' he said. 'When Mallami told me the mission lady claimed to be a friend of mine, I thought she must be mistaken. I can't believe my own eyes! What . . . How did you come here? Morna isn't with you, is she?'

'No . . .' Jane drew a shaky breath, knowing that her news must hurt him. 'Jared received a pardon from King William some months ago. Morna and he were married soon after.'

His eyes clouded briefly, then he seemed to subdue his pain. 'So she has her wish at last. I am glad. I wish her only happiness.'

'She is very happy, but she did grieve for you, Captain Smithson. We all did. Was there no way you could have sent word to—to Morna?'

'I should have done so by the last ship,' he admitted gruffly. 'When you saw me the other day I had been indulging myself because I could not face the arrival of more English people. Believe me, I have my reasons.'

'Did you not wish to return to New South Wales on the supply ship? I am sure Captain Bollinson would have let you work your passage.'

'I could, but young Charles Heatherton doesn't want to leave the island yet, and I shall not go without him.'

'I'm sorry . . .' Jane was bewildered. 'Who is Charles Heatherton, and why can you not leave without him?'

'That is none of your concern.' Stuart's tone sharpened with annoyance as anger flared in him suddenly. 'Any more than it's that blasted missionary's. Who asked him for his opinion? The lad has enough troubles without his interfering . . .' He glared at her as if he thought she was to blame.

'Please do not say any more! I think you should know that Obadiah Thorne is my husband.'

Disgust showed in his face. 'You're married to him? I can scarcely believe it. You were always a sensible woman, or so I had thought.'

'You are discourteous, sir.' A flash of anger lit her eyes. 'Once, I believed you were a gentleman, but I see you have forgotten your manners. I know there is some excuse, living in the way you do . . .'

'And how do I live, ma'am?' he demanded furiously. 'Oh, I know what you thought when you saw me with those girls the other night. I am sure you ran back to your pious husband and told him that I was in danger of losing my immortal soul! I suppose that's why I received a visit this morning.'

'Naturally I told him I had seen you, but I said nothing of your soul, immortal or otherwise. As far as I am concerned, you are welcome to do exactly as you please.'

He swept her a mocking bow. 'Thank you, Mrs Thorne.'

Jane flushed as she heard the scorn in his voice. 'I see that nothing I can say will convince you that I really have no interest in you or your morals, Captain Smithson.'

'Then perhaps you will ask your husband to keep his nose out of my affairs in future?'

'Obadiah does what he thinks right. I neither encourage nor discourage him. Now, if you will excuse me, I must return to the mission.'

He felt an unreasonable fury at her attitude. Who was she to look down her nose at him, or to judge him? He did not know why her opinion of him should matter, but it did.

'Those girls you saw me with . . . It wasn't what you thought. I know I had been drinking, but . . .'

'Please do not bother to explain. I really do not wish to hear the details of your life, Captain Smithson.'

'You think I've gone native, don't you?' He felt an urge to take her by the shoulders and shake her. 'Well, Miss Prissy, you're quite wrong.'

'I'm not prepared to be insulted, sir.'

As she tried to pass him, he caught her wrist. 'Don't run off. Perhaps I had no right to speak to you like that.'

'No right at all,' she agreed bitterly. 'Let me go, Captain Smithson. I think we have no more to say to one another. I see that you are not the man I thought.'

He released her, flinching at the scorn in her voice, and watching as she walked swiftly across the sand, her head high. For a time he stood gazing after her, puzzled by his anger. Why had he resented that look in her eyes? She had lovely eyes, especially when they flashed with fire like that, and he wondered why he had never noticed them before. She wasn't a beautiful woman—not compared to her cousin—but there was something about her . . .

Suddenly he laughed out loud at himself. 'It's getting to you, Smithson,' he murmured, mocking his own thoughts. 'The island is turning you soft! Any English woman would seem attractive at this moment.'

He was starved of companionship, that was it. The island girls were beautiful, warm creatures, but they giggled at everything he said or did. He needed stimulation, intelligent conversation—a damned good argument! A grin twisted his lips. He had had that once already this morning when that stupid fool of a missionary started on at poor Charles. It had taken all his time to keep from striking the idiot. Surely he could see that the young man was sick? Charles had been very ill for a long time, and was only now beginning to recover physically. The trouble was that the lad remembered nothing after . . . Oh well, perhaps it was for the best. Why should either of them want to leave the island? They neither of them had any reason to return to civilisation.

'So I told him he had no business letting that young seaman go native,' Obadiah ranted across the dinner table. 'Loss of memory is no reason to let go of all moral standards. What Charles Heatherton needs is spiritual guidance and . . .'

'I should think he needs the attention of a doctor and the love of his family,' said Jane. 'Staying on the island will not help him to recall his memory.'

'Exactly!' Obadiah gave her an approving look. 'Had I known of his presence before Richard Grenshaw left, I should have insisted he took charge of that young man and returned him to England.'

'Perhaps he doesn't wish to go back yet,' Sarah put in suddenly, causing her brother to stare at her in surprise.

'What do you mean by that?'

'Only that he may be afraid of leaving the island. It must be very strange to have no recollection of the life you left behind, don't you think?'

'Sarah has a point,' Jane admitted, wondering if Charles Heatherton's reluctance to leave was the only reason Captain Smithson had made no attempt to return to New South Wales. 'If the young man remembers nothing of his life before he was shipwrecked, the island must seem like his home.'

'Even so, it is for his friends to see him returned to England for his own good.' Obadiah stuck his fork savagely into a piece of fat salt bacon. 'However, the point I was making is that I want both you and Sarah to stay away from Smithson. The man is mad. He almost attacked me this morning.'

'Captain Smithson is quite sane,' Jane said irritably, forgetting that she too had been angry with him earlier. 'I have no intention of seeking him out, but I shall speak if we meet. I have known him for some time, Obadiah, so I cannot ignore him.'

He was a little surprised at her tone. 'I suppose not.

You may speak to him if you feel it necessary to be polite.'

'Thank you.' Jane sipped a glass of water, needing a moment to calm herself. How dared he be so pompous? His dictatorial manner made her want to scream, but she held her nerve and the moment of frustration passed. Obadiah had not changed; the change was in her. She forced herself to smile at him. 'Are you pleased that the Queen has asked for Sarah to teach the women to sew? It is the first step towards a new attitude to their clothing. When they have made something pretty, they will want to wear it.'

'I thought I could show them how to make a simple smock,' said Sarah. 'Something with no sleeves that will be cool to wear.'

'That sounds ideal,' Jane smiled encouragingly at her. 'Don't you agree, Obadiah?'

'As long as it covers them decently.' He finished his meal and pushed the plate away. 'Excuse me, I have work to do. Sarah can go with you to the village if she wishes.'

He left the house, and the two women looked at each other in delight. Both had wondered if he would insist on the lessons taking place at the mission, and they could hardly believe he had given in so easily.

'You've changed my brother,' Sarah said, looking at Jane in awe. 'I have never known him to be so—so . . .'

Jane could have supplied the right word, but she refrained. She was trying very hard not to lose her patience with Obadiah. After all, it had been her own choice to come here with him. It was not his fault that she could not bring herself to care for him. She knew he had tried to please her in his own way.

Gathering the dishes to take them outside to the wooden tub they used for washing, Jane felt the pain twist inside her and she blinked hard as the tears stung her eyes. She was such a fool! Dreams of romance were for young girls, not for a woman of her age. Besides, the man she loved dreamed of someone else . . .

*   *   *

'Hold the pen like this,' Jane said, guiding the Queen's hand with her own. 'Now form the letters this way. That's right. There, you have written your own name.'

'Queen Ma-Llalla.' The older woman smiled in triumph. 'Beth showed me, but I had forgotten. It is not good to forget, Jane. Soon more and more ships will visit our island, and if we do not know the ways of the strangers, they may take advantage of our ignorance.'

'You have not been cheated by the Commissioners, I hope?'

'No. Richard Grenshaw gave us what we asked for for our copra.' The Queen's brow wrinkled in thought. 'Kumi likes the fiery liquid that warms men's bellies, and my people are happy to accept pretty beads and cloth for their work. But I dream of bad things. Bad men will come one day soon to destroy us.'

'Surely not!' Jane looked at her in surprise. 'Why should they?'

'I do not know this. I had hoped that you would know.'

'Me? How can I know, Ma-Llalla? You have the copra, but it is only a small amount, not enough to encourage men to come here to rob you. Yet your island is rich in its supply of natural wealth. I suppose if the wrong people came to the island to provision their ship . . . But if they did, you would give them what they wanted, wouldn't you?'

'There is food enough to spare.' The Queen sighed, obviously still troubled. 'Yet they do not come for this. There will be death and pain when they come. I have seen it.'

Jane touched her hand. 'We must all pray that it will not happen, Ma-Llalla. I shall ask God to protect you and your people always.'

'Will your god be pleased if we build the church?' The Queen looked at her intently. 'Have we offended by our neglect?'

'No, of course God is not offended,' Jane said quickly. 'Yet a church is God's house. By building it, we show him that we love him—and we ask him to bless us when we enter it.'

'Then you may tell your man that we shall help him to build his church. Tomorrow the men will start to fell the trees.'

'Obadiah will be so happy,' Jane cried. 'God bless you for this, Ma-Llalla!'

The Queen stood up, solemnly embracing her. 'Go and tell him now. I dreamed again last night—more vividly than ever before. Tell Missionary Thorne that we shall hear him preach to us on Sunday. The women, children and men shall all hear of God's words.'

'Yes, of course, I'll tell him. It will please him very much.'

Leaving the village, Jane felt oddly subdued. She had achieved something that had seemed almost impossible, yet she experienced no elation. Queen Ma-Llalla was very worried about her dreams. It was her fear that had made her accept the idea of a church, not Jane's powers of persuasion. Had she given Ma-Llalla the impression that the building of a church would somehow protect the islanders from harm? If so, it was unintentional and quite wrong. There was no magic in a wooden building, even if it was a church. Supposing the Queen's dreams really were a premonition of some terrible tragedy? Supposing . . .

'Jane, please wait a moment. I must talk to you.'

Jane halted as she heard the man's deep voice, feeling a tingle of apprehension. Turning, she saw Stuart standing in the shade of a tree. She halted, undecided. She was tempted to walk on and ignore him, since he had been so rude to her, yet she found herself moving in his direction. He gave her a rueful smile.

'I am surprised you don't tell me to go away and never darken your path again,' he said, a wry grin quirking his mouth.

'Perhaps I should. You certainly deserve it.'

'Yes, I know. I owe you an apology. I don't understand why I was so angry.'

'I was angry, too.' She smiled, despite herself.

'I should not have insulted you—or your husband.'

'Perhaps you had good reason as far as Obadiah was concerned. He means well, but he sometimes says more than he should.'

'Even so, I should not have taken it out on you. And perhaps he had a point. I have been thinking things over since we talked . . .' He looked at her awkwardly. It was suddenly very important that she should listen to him. 'I should like to explain how I came to be on the island, and what made Charles the way he is. It doesn't necessarily excuse my behaviour, but it might exonerate me a little in your eyes. Have you time to walk with me for a while?'

She hesitated, knowing that she ought to refuse. She had no business to walk in the sun with this man, yet her heart rebelled. Where was the harm in it?

'Yes, of course, if you wish.'

She felt a little shiver of pleasure as he fell into step beside her. What was it about him that made her happy just to be with him? She did not understand it, but it had been so from the first time they talked on board *Sea-Sprite*. They walked in silence for a while, and it was as though the fact of being together was enough for them both at the moment; then she turned to look at him, her brows rising.

'I believe Mr Heatherton has lost his memory?'

'Yes. He did not even know his own name until I told him. I believe it was the shock of what happened to us, or perhaps the blow on the back of his hand.'

'You are not speaking of the sinking of *Sea-Sprite*, I think?'

'No. Charles was not a member of my crew, but of the vessel that picked me up after my own ship went down . . .' He was thoughtful and Jane waited, understanding his silence. 'It was extremely lucky that the lookout spotted me. She was a trader bound for China, carrying a fortune in gold.'

Looking up at him, she saw the glimmer of anger in eyes that were more grey than blue just now, and she knew that he was fighting some strong emotion. 'What happened?' she asked softly. 'Mallami said that you had been at sea in a rowing-boat for a long time when you finally reached the island. What happened on board that trader, Stuart?'

He looked down into her melting brown eyes and somehow a little of his anguish fell away. She had called him by his first name, and he liked it.

'Gold is a severe temptation to any man, especially when too much of it is in one place for weeks and months on end. The crew got to thinking about it, and one night they mutinied. Charles and I stood with the Captain against them. The Captain was killed, but the lad and I were put in an open boat with water and rations for a week. It must have been nearly three times that long before we sighted the island. A man could go mad in that time, Jane. Charles was delirious, and I wasn't much better when the islanders spotted us. They saved our lives, and they've made us welcome ever since.'

'I see.' She gazed up at him, her heart full of an emotion she dared not put into words. 'I can understand why your friend is reluctant to leave, but don't you want to go home, Captain Smithson?'

He could not guess at the fight going on inside her, but he sensed a kind of withdrawal in her and frowned. 'I have no home. I lost everything when *Sea-Sprite* went down. I had sold all I owned to purchase that cargo. I lost a great deal that belonged to Morna, too. I suppose that's why I didn't try to get in touch—I was ashamed of letting her down.'

'But why?' Jane exclaimed. 'Morna would never have blamed you for something that was not your fault. She was concerned only that she—we—had lost a friend.'

'I'm sorry if I caused her—or you—unnecessary pain,' he said with a wry twist of his lips. 'I never imagined that my death would bother anyone as much as that.'

Suddenly the passion flared in her eyes and she looked at him angrily. 'Then you are a fool, Stuart Smithson! Perhaps you do not deserve that we should care, but we do. In fact I would never have m——' She broke off, flushing as his gaze intensified. 'You still have much to live for. You surely cannot intend to waste the rest of your life here?'

A touch of humour quirked his lips. She was a damned attractive woman when she was roused to passion. By God! who would ever have suspected the fire beneath the ice? She had seemed such a meek little woman on board ship, but something had changed her. Or perhaps she had merely hidden her true nature behind a mask of docility? He was suddenly very curious about the real woman.

'But you intend to spend your life here, Jane? Somehow I don't see you as one of those earnest women who devote their lives to good works. Just why did you marry Obadiah Thorne? I do not think it was because you fell desperately in love with him.'

There was a devil in his eyes, Jane thought, an imp of Satan that sought to tease and torment her. She had seen the latent mockery lurking beneath the surface once or twice when they were on board *Sea-Sprite*, though he was a very private man and did not often share his thoughts with others. He was essentially a strong, silent character, perhaps because of the long months and years he had spent at sea. Yet she had sensed something very different behind the mask of stoicism, feeling that the real Stuart was often lonely. Perhaps it was this that had first touched a chord in her; there was so much love in her for the right person . . . But she must not allow herself to think like that. It was much too late.

Lifting her eyes to meet the enquiring gaze of her companion, she knew that she must not betray herself. There was a new awareness in him; he was really seeing her now, looking at her with the eyes of a man who was interested in what he saw. It was because he had been on the island for several months, she understood that. He would not notice her if Morna were standing beside her—and who could blame him? She was not a beautiful woman, and there was no reason for him to be attracted

to her. Even so, it was a potentially dangerous situation.
She found him far too attractive for her own peace of
mind.'

'No, I do not love Obadiah,' she said truthfully. 'Yet I
respect him for what he tries to do. His sister is devoted
to him, but she is not strong. I married him because she
needs me, and because I thought I might be able to help
him in his work.'

Her reply was so honest that the devil died within him.
She was a real woman, he saw that now, capable of
caring for others unselfishly, even at her own expense.
He could not mock that. He had not realised how strong
she was until this moment. It was a quiet strength, often
overlooked because of her modesty. She had seemed a
pale shadow beside Morna Hamilton, but now he per-
ceived that she was so much more than her cousin's
shadow.

'Obadiah is a fortunate man,' he said, his tone oddly
wistful. 'I hope he appreciates it?'

She looked away from his admiring gaze, feeling a
sharp pang of regret. If only he had shown some interest
in her before, when there was a chance that they might
find happiness together! She would never have married
Obadiah if she had thought there was the least possibility
of being Stuart's wife. If only he had sent word that he
was still alive . . . But of course it was too late. She was
not a woman to betray her vows lightly, even though
they were meaningless. She had to end this immediately.

'I believe he does,' she said, sounding much calmer
than she felt inside. 'He is a decent man in his own way.
He will be waiting for me, and I have some good news for
him. The Queen has decided to help him to build the
church, and I must tell him. I must go to him now.'

For a moment more his eyes held hers, almost to try to
prevent her, somehow, from leaving. It was as if both of
them were fully aware, for the first time, of what they
might have had. As if both knew that something in-
finitely precious had been carelessly thrown away. Then
Stuart moved to one side and she walked on past him,

her eyes temporarily blinded with tears. Blinking them away, she lifted her head proudly, subduing the desire to turn and run back to his arms. She must not even think of such a thing! She was married to Obadiah, and she would not betray him . . .

'Jane, how do you know when you're in love? Really in love with someone?' Sarah asked, laying down the loose shift she was embroidering as they sat together in what passed for the parlour. 'Does it make you feel weak and dizzy?'

'Lots of things make you feel like that,' Jane replied with an amused glance at her companion's face. 'Including too much sun. Have you been overdoing things, my love?'

'Oh, Jane!' Sarah giggled happily. 'I know you're teasing me. It's so pleasant to be able to laugh with you. Saul used to tease me, too, before he ran away. Obadiah doesn't laugh very much.' She sighed, staring down at her sewing for a moment. 'When we lived at the rectory, Lady Connolly used to say that he was too serious for his own good. She was his patron, you know, and very kind to us both. I often used to visit her at the Hall . . .'

'You must miss her.' Jane saw the wistful look in the girl's face, and smiled. 'Now what brought all this on? Are you pining for one of the beaux you had to leave behind?'

'I never had a beau!' Sarah protested, laughing again as she saw the mischief in her friend's eyes. 'Oh, you are wicked! Seriously, how does one know—about loving someone?'

Jane put aside her book, studying the girl's face. She felt uneasy as she saw the new sparkle in Sarah's eyes. Something had happened to bring this about. Surely she had not fallen for Stuart Smithson? He was far too dangerous for a young girl!

'Why do you ask?' she enquired carefully.

'I—I think I may be in love.' Sarah looked at her shyly. 'Oh, don't look so anxious, Jane. I haven't done anything silly. Charles is so gentle. He wouldn't dream of doing anything improper.'

Relief surged through Jane. Charles Heatherton was not much more than a year or so older than Sarah. She had seen him wandering about the beach searching for shells and looking rather like a lost child. Obadiah's sister would be safe enough with him.

'I should hope not indeed!' Jane said with mock severity. 'Have you lost your heart to him, Sarah, or is it merely sympathy you feel?'

'I'm not sure,' Sarah replied honestly. 'I do feel pity for him. It cannot be very pleasant not to know who you really are, but I sometimes feel . . . Oh, I don't know! Do you think it would be very wicked if I let Charles kiss me?'

'Not wicked, no. It might not be very sensible, though. Young men can be carried away by their feelings. At home a kiss might not mean very much, but here on the island things are different. You know Obadiah would not approve, don't you?'

'He never approves of anything!' Sarah exclaimed, a resentful note in her voice. 'If I may not let a man kiss me, how will I ever know whether I love him enough to marry him?'

'When the time comes you will know, Sarah, I promise you that.'

'And should I let him kiss me if I'm really sure?'

'That is your choice, my love. I cannot tell you what to do with your life, nor would I wish to. I only ask that you think carefully before you decide.' Jane smiled at her and got up. 'Put away your sewing now and help me to prepare Obadiah's dinner. He will be back very soon.

'What is a church bazaar?' Queen Ma-Llalla asked, puzzled by the unfamiliar term. 'You were telling us of the cushion you made for the Christmas bazaar, but what is this thing?'

Jane smiled, her gaze flicking momentarily across the compound to the man who sat with his back leaning against a tree and his eyes closed. He gave the appearance of being totally uninterested in the proceedings, but it was curious that he was always somewhere near by whenever the islanders gathered to hear her stories. As she looked at him, he opened his eyes and grinned at her before settling down once more.

'A bazaar is a kind of . . .' She had been going to say 'market place', but that would be equally mysterious to the islanders. 'It's a kind of feast where people trade the goods they have specially prepared; they meet, eat and drink together. A church bazaar is held so that the profit can be given to the poor people in the village.'

'It is a very strange custom,' the Queen said. 'Here, everyone helps to gather the food and there is enough for all to share. I have heard that in England some people have no food at all, while others have much more than they need. Why do they not share everything as we do?'

How could she explain, Jane wondered. Here in this paradise where the bounty of nature supplied all the people's needs, it was impossible to find a parallel to illustrate a culture that differed so greatly from their own. Yet she patiently endeavoured to do so, describing the large towns where the inhabitants worked to pay for the food and materials they needed, and telling of how the farmers laboured long and hard in the fields to supply those needs. Her story was interrupted many times by the Queen, each question involving detailed explanations. Consequently, it was long past her usual time when she was finally allowed to leave. There was no sign of Sarah, and Jane thought that she would have finished her lessons and returned to the mission more than an hour go.

She had hardly left the village when she heard Stuart calling to her. Stopping to wait for him, Jane knew that she had expected him to follow her, had hoped for it, even. Since he had started to attend the morning sessions she held each day, she had known deep inside that it was merely a matter of time before he spoke to her.

They were both of them hungry for some form of contact; each of them needing release from the growing tension within.

'You've so much patience,' Stuart exclaimed with a laugh as he reached her side. 'I thought the old lady had you foxed this time for sure!'

The sparkle in his eyes made her heart race. It was so good to be near him again!

'She isn't old,' Jane reproved him. 'I admit I some-times think she tries to confuse me, but it's really because she wants to learn all she can about the outside world. She's afraid of what may happen to her people as more and more strangers discover the island. And it's bound to happen now that a mission is established here.'

'Mallami told me about the Queen's dreams.' Stuart made a harsh sound in his throat. 'It would only take a visit from Jack Thorne or some of his cronies to turn the nightmare into reality . . .'

'Did you say Jack Thorne?' Jane looked at him in surprise.

'Yes.' He gave her an odd look. 'Yes, the name struck me too when I met Obadiah, but there can be no connection. Jack was the leader of the mutiny—and a very unpleasant character.'

'Obadiah has a brother called Saul. He ran away to sea after stealing money from his own family. But it couldn't be he, could it?'

Stuart saw the concern in her eyes and cursed himself for a fool. He had not intended to tell her of his suspicions, but there was a definite likeness between the missionary and the man he had sworn to kill if ever they met again. Even so, there was little likelihood of either of them ever discovering the truth. Jack Thorne was probably somewhere in France or even America, en-joying his ill-gotten gains, and would never come to this tiny island. It did not matter.

'I doubt there is any relationship,' he said carelessly. 'The name must be common enough.'

'I suppose so,' she agreed uncertainly. 'Obadiah could

gather no news of his brother in New South Wales, but if he had changed his name to Jack . . .'

'Let us forget him—I should not have mentioned the rogue,' Stuart grunted. 'He's not worth wasting your breath over. Let's talk of something else.'

'Yes . . .' Jane stopped to pick an exotic bloom. 'Why don't you write to Morna? I have paper and ink. You could send your letter when the next ship calls.'

'That won't be for months.' He scowled as he saw the look in her eyes. 'Don't bully me, Jane! I'll write when I'm ready, and I'll leave the island when the time is right. I'm not still under her spell, if that's what you think.'

'Aren't you?' Why had her heart begun to behave so foolishly? She looked up at him, trying to read his expression. 'I'm pleased for you, if that's true.'

'What will it take to convince you?' he asked, his eyes narrowing as they searched her face. Then they seemed to flare with an inner flame as he reached out to take hold of her shoulders, pulling her against him almost roughly. 'Maybe this will help?'

She resisted for a moment, but then his lips were on hers, tasting slightly salty as they gently caressed and moulded her mouth. At first she was stiff and unyielding in his arms, not knowing how to respond to the new sensations flooding through her. What was this fire in her veins? Why did she feel so weak with longing? Her lips seemed to soften and open beneath his kisses, her body melting into his as her resolve dissolved and she gave herself up to the sheer pleasure of being kissed. His hands were moving down her back, over the rounded shape of her buttocks, pressing her to him with a sudden urgency that shocked her. She felt a sharp jolt of fear at the intimate contact and jerked away, her eyes flying open in alarm as she became aware of the throbbing maleness of him.

'No! I cannot . . .' she whispered breathily. 'Please do not . . .'

He recognised the virginal fright in her eyes and stared at her, unable to believe what he saw so plainly. She could not still be a virgin? She had been married for several months—surely . . . Yet it was there in her eyes. 'Jane . . .' he murmured, half laughing as he felt the triumph surge through him. She had been no true wife to Thorne: he would stake his life on it! He was not sure why it made him feel like shouting aloud with sheer joy. 'I didn't mean to frighten you. I wasn't trying to seduce you . . . Or perhaps I was? I thought you wanted me too, but you haven't been with a man, have you? I should have guessed that pompous idiot wasn't a real man!'

'No, you mustn't say that. You mustn't sneer at him,' Jane gasped, feeling confused and shaken. 'It was never —never intended to be a true marriage. I—I told you, I don't love him . . .' As soon as the words had left her lips she knew that she had betrayed herself. He must be able to see the truth in her face. 'I have to go . . .'

She turned away, but he caught her wrist, holding her firmly so that she could not escape. She could feel his eyes on her face, burning into her, reading her secret thoughts. He would know that she loved him. At last, unable to bear his silence a moment longer, she glanced up at him, surprising a strange expression on his face. An expression she immediately took for pity. He had guessed her secret and he was sorry for her. The humiliation burned in her, making her speak without thinking.

'You don't have to feel guilty,' she said, the pent-up emotion of years pouring out of her. 'I don't want your pity, Stuart. Jeer at me if you will. Yes, I know it's laughable—the classic example of the plain girl falling for the man who loves her beautiful cousin. Well, I won't hide my face in shame! I've loved you for a long time. I don't expect you to love me, so you need not be embarrassed.'

'Jane . . .' he faltered, feeling stunned by her revelation. 'I don't know what to say.'

'Then don't say anything. It isn't necessary.' She smiled at him, her eyes bright with the tears she had held inside for so long. 'I always knew that you loved Morna.

How could you know her and fail to care for her? She is everything any man could want. I adored her from the first moment we met; she was so generous—so full of life. I never blamed you for loving her, Stuart. Please don't hate me for loving you.'

His fingers had slackened about her wrist as he struggled to accept what she was saying. Why had he never guessed what was in her mind? Why had he been such a blind fool? 'But, . . . you married him,' he said in a strangled voice. 'Why, Jane? You threw your life away for nothing. I don't understand . . .'

Her eyes met his unflinchingly. It was too late for pretence now. 'You were dead. What did my life mean to me?'

He was silent, made dull and stupid by the shock of her words. She had cared for him that much? His mind reeled as he tried to take it in.

Jane stared at him, mistaking the reason for his silence. She bit her lip, turning away quickly before the tears could fall and shame her more. She was a fool to have told him! She should have run away and let him think what he liked. Walking swiftly across the sand, she heard him call her name but would not look back. She felt the hot shame wash over her. She was ridiculous! Only a weak fool would have blurted it all out like that! His lovemaking had meant nothing to him—no more than a pleasant interlude to while away the time. He had thought she wanted a love affair! How could she have behaved so wantonly that he thought that of her? No wonder he had laughed at her when she reacted like a child!

Hearing a sudden sound, she glanced over her shoulder and saw that Stuart was trying to catch up with her. She began to run, the fear making her desperate now. She could not bear to see the pity in his eyes. How amusing he must find her confession of love! The pain twisted inside her, causing her to gasp for breath. She could not—would not—look at him. She was too ashamed.

There was a flurry of sand behind her, and she gave a cry as she sensed his next move. He lunged at her, catching her round the waist and bringing her down. She struggled wildly, hitting out and sobbing in anger as he held her pressed firmly beneath him.

'Let me go, you monster! Let me go!'

'No! Not until you hear what I have to say.'

He looked down into her stubborn face, and smiled. Her hair had come loose, straggling about her neck and shoulders as it escaped its net. It was thick, with a slight wave, and he had a sudden urge to bury his face in it. He felt his pulses quicken and knew that in another minute he would lose his head. Giving her a rueful smile, he got up and pulled her to her feet. She had quietened now, and was waiting for him to speak.

'I can't let you go like this, Jane. I don't pity you—far from it! I'm not embarrassed either. Stunned might be more accurate. I had no idea you had such feelings . . .' Fire burned in her cheeks, and he chuckled. 'I'm also very flattered and grateful that you care for me . . .'

'But you're still in love with my cousin?' Jane's eyes were stormy. 'I told you that I don't expect anything . . .'

'You also said that you were plain, and that's a lie.' He grinned at her, refusing to be frozen out by her scowl. 'Nothing would suit me better than to tell you that I'm madly in love with you, and carry you off on my white charger—if I had one! But I won't lie to you, Jane. I wanted to make love to you just now, that's true enough, but I'm not sure what I feel about you at this moment.'

'That's honest, anyway.' Jane glared at him, wanting to tear him limb from limb for inflicting this pain on her. Why could he not just have let her go? Did he expect her to be flattered because he wanted to make love to her? It was all so ridiculous! Suddenly her mouth curved with wry amusement and the anger drained out of her as she saw the humour of the situation. She was making too much of it all. 'You were always a man for plain speaking: I think that's what I first liked about you. Most men would have lied and made what they could of the opportunity . . .'

'Oh, Jane,' he murmured, feeling the desire move in him hotly as he saw the self-mockery in her eyes. There was something special about her that made him very much aware of what he might have had. 'What a fool I've been! Why didn't I see how attractive you were when you were there under my nose? I must have been blind!'

'Or blinded by love?'

'Ay, I'll not deny I loved her,' he said gruffly. 'You would not want that?'

'No, of course not. You owe me nothing, Stuart.'

'I owe you nothing.' He lowered his gaze to study her intently. 'Except honesty, perhaps. I find you attractive, Jane, and you must know I want you. Maybe that's all there is.'

It hurt when he admitted it like that, but she had always known he did not love her as she loved him. There was no use in crying for the moon. 'It doesn't matter, Stuart. In any case, it's much too late for there to be anything between us.'

'Not if I could be certain that I could make you happy. Your marriage is no marriage. It could be annulled, and we could . . .'

'No! No, I gave Obadiah my word. I won't break it.'

'You made a mistake . . .'

'And I cannot rectify it.' She looked up at him earnestly. 'Don't say any more, I beg you. You must understand that we can never be more than friends. I should not have spoken to you as I did. I never intended that you should know.'

'But I do know, and I think there may be a chance of happiness for us, Jane.'

'The happiness of being friends, Stuart. There is no harm in our meeting sometimes to talk. If that isn't enough for you, I shall walk away now and never see you again.'

He saw that she meant it, and the protest died on his

lips. What could he say to persuade her when he was not sure of his own needs or desires? This feeling he had for her was not the same as he had had for Morna—that had been a quicksilver thing that inflamed his senses, making him feel like a child on a swing reaching for the stars. This burning in his loins was of the earth rather than the heavens: perhaps it was only that, the physical need of a man for a woman. Yet he could satisfy his lust with Mallami if he cared only for physical pleasure. That he had not already done so was the cause of much speculation among the island women. Mallami had offered him the services of a young boy when he had refused her body, reacting in surprise when he roared at her angrily. She could not understand why he held back from something so natural to her people as mating. Perhaps it was the very fastidiousness of his own nature that had kept him single so long; for him, a woman must be more than just someone warm to reach for in the night . . .

'Then we're to be friends, Jane.' He smiled as he saw the relief in her eyes. She could not bear that they should be irrevocably parted any more than he could. Whatever this attraction between them, it was stronger than he had previously imagined. Perhaps the earthy need in him now was a truer love than the adoration he had felt for Morna. He would have worshipped at her feet if she had let him, but he wanted to talk to Jane, to turn to her when the doubts possessed him. Certainly he would rather slit his own throat than hurt her. If she ever came to him, it must be of her own volition.

'Yes, we shall be friends.' She gave him her hand, and he held it between his own like a precious jewel. 'I must go now. Obadiah will be wondering where I am.'

He let her go reluctantly, grudging the part of her life that must belong to her husband. These snatched meetings on the beach could never be enough for him. He wanted to know her. To understand what made her laugh—and what made her cry. Yet he knew that this was the only way. They were all caught up in a strange fate that was somehow bound up with the island. It must be so, he reasoned; why else should they all have been brought together in this place?

As if in answer to his thoughts, there came an odd rumbling noise, and the earth seemed to move slightly beneath his feet. It was over so swiftly that he might have imagined it, had he not seen the sudden activity in the village. The islanders poured out of their huts, heading for the beach. They were shouting, and pointing at the mountain. He heard their frantic cries, and frowned, waiting for a sign that the volcano was really about to erupt. But he could see nothing—no sign of smoke hung over the crater and there was no sudden belching of fire.

'The Sleeping God awakes!' Kumi cried in warning. 'You go to beach, Captain Smithy. You safe there. I go to mission to warn Jane.'

'No, I'll go myself,' Stuart said, startled into action. 'If I hurry, I can catch her. She can't be far ahead.'

'Tell her we all sleep on beach tonight. If god angry, he send down hot rain, and forest burn. We all die if we stop here.'

'I'll see that she gets to safety.'

He started to run in the direction Jane had taken as another tremor shook the earth and a tree toppled over behind him. Kumi could be right: the whole damned island could explode at any moment. A feeling of terror swept through him. If anything happened to Jane . . . All at once he was laughing at himself. What a fool he had been, dithering over his precise emotions as though he were a Greek philosopher! If what he was experiencing now meant anything, he was pretty well besotted by the woman!

The laughter died in his throat as he heard her call his name. She was in trouble; he knew it before he saw her lying trapped beneath the branches of a fallen tree. God! If she was hurt, he would never forgive himself. He ran to her, tearing at the débris pinning her to the ground like a madman until he could lift her body from beneath it. He held her as she half swooned, then her eyes flickered open and she smiled at him.

'I hit my head as I fell. I'll be better in a moment. I must get back to Obadiah and Sarah . . .'

'Thank the Lord you weren't killed!' he grunted harshly. 'I'm taking you to the beach, where you'll be safe; then I'll find Sarah. No arguments, Jane. This time, I'm having my own way.'

She chuckled weakly, closing her eyes as the faintness overcame her again. Stuart's arms tightened protectively about her, his lips brushing against her hair. Then he turned, and found himself staring into the cold blue gaze of her husband.

CHAPTER FOUR

'WHAT ARE YOU doing with my wife, sir?' Obadiah started forward angrily. 'If you have harmed her . . .'

'Don't be a fool, man!' Stuart snapped. 'She was trapped by a fallen tree and hit her head. I'm taking her to the beach for safety.'

'I'm here now. You can leave her to me.'

'I'm damned if I will! Why don't you go and help your sister? Kumi says everyone should sleep on the beach tonight.'

'I expected Sarah to be with Jane. Obviously that is not the case.'

The two men glared at each other, neither willing to give way. Stuart's mouth twisted with contempt. 'I'm hardly likely to ravish Jane with the rest of the population looking on! The whole damned island may blow up at any moment. Don't you think you should find Sarah?'

Obadiah's face tightened with fury. He looked as if he wanted to strike the younger man, but even in his anger, he realised that Jane was in no immediate danger and he was anxious about his sister. She ought to have returned over two hours ago. It was unusual and he had thought she must be with Jane. Now this impudent rascal had the effrontery to tell him his duty!

'I shall hold you responsible for my wife's safety,' he grunted, turning to stride off in the opposite direction.

Jane moaned slightly, her eyelids fluttering. 'Was that Obadiah?' she asked.

'He's gone to look for Sarah,' Stuart said. 'I'm taking you to the beach, my darling. You'll be safe there, I promise.'

She leaned her head against his shoulder, feeling dazed but content to be where she was. 'Where can Sarah be?' she murmured faintly, her head spinning.

'She must have left the village a long time ago.'

'I expect she's with Charles,' Stuart replied. 'I think they spend quite a bit of time together . . .' He broke off, his face strained as he saw that she was barely conscious. 'Jane, are you hurt badly? I'll never forgive myself if . . . I shouldn't have let you go.'

She smiled and looked up at him. 'I'm so sleepy . . .'

He held her closer, knowing he must get her to the beach quickly. The last tremor had not caused an eruption, but he dared not take any chances, although he felt that he must not let Jane lapse into unconsciousness. There was no means of knowing how much damage that bang on the head had done. He shook her shoulder gently. 'Don't go to sleep,' he said. 'Damn you, Jane! I refuse to lose you now that I've finally found you!'

Charles was climbing just ahead of Sarah when the first tremor shook the island, and he stumbled. They were almost half-way up the side of the mountain, and the movement of the rock beneath their feet was more violent than further down. Sarah was thrown to the ground, a feeling of sheer terror surging through her as she heard the roaring sound from somewhere deep inside the volcano. She screamed, clinging to a clutch of protruding roots as if needing support from somewhere, even though she was in no real danger. He looked back at her, his usually vaguely dazed expression changing to one of full awareness. He was a thin man, his thick blond hair streaked with sun-bleached white, his eyes a curious green-flecked hazel. The sun had turned his skin to a light gold, giving him a healthy appearance despite the hollows in his cheeks.

'It's nothing to worry about, Sarah,' he called. 'Just a slight tremor. Stay there and I'll come back to you.'

It had been his idea to climb the mountain. He had waited for her to leave the village, suggesting the expedition to the rim of the crater because she had previously shown some interest in the volcano. He had discovered an easy route to the top weeks—or was it months?

—ago, and he had persuaded her to attempt it, despite her caution. Now he wished that he had merely taken her for a walk along the beach. His mind was quite clear now as she began to scramble down to her ledge, fully alive to the danger they could be in if the volcano erupted. His bare feet found footholds in the loose earth and shale disturbed by the tremor, and he had almost reached the girl when the second tremor occurred; it flung him several feet, and he struck his head on a rock, sliding past Sarah and landing on a ledge just below her.

'Charles!' she screamed. 'Oh, God save us! Charles, are you hurt?'

There was no reply from the sprawled figure below. She eased herself to a better position, looking down at him in dismay. What was she to do? He seemed to have lost consciousness, and could be of no help to her. A wave of panic swept through her. She was not used to coping with dangerous situations alone. Obadiah always told her what to do. How could she manage by herself? She was not strong . . . A fit of violent shaking overcame her, and she lay on the ground with tears running down her cheeks. Oh, where was Obadiah? Why had she stupidly disobeyed him to climb the mountain with Charles? She had known it would make him angry.

The shaking stopped as she remembered just why she had risked her brother's displeasure. It was because she wanted to be with Charles. Because she cared about him. Her heart had been touched by his suffering, and it gave her pleasure to see him smile. She had discovered that she had the ability to banish that vague look from his eyes. When he was with her, Charles came alive. Suddenly she knew that his safety meant more to her than her own. He had been so ill, and now he might be badly hurt. She had to get down to him somehow, but it was not easy to let go of the tree roots. She was whimpering with fright as she began the descent, made dangerous by the loose earth and stones beneath her shoes. Her long skirts hampered her, catching on a jagged branch and almost bringing her down. She hesitated, then bunched them up, tucking the excess material into the waistband so that her bare legs were revealed. That was better. It was as though the act of defiance had steadied her, giving her the strength to go on. Now all that mattered was that Charles should be alive when she reached him.

He was lying very still, his eyes closed. She touched his cheek, feeling a little surprised at the satin softness of his skin. How beautiful he was, she thought, rather like the pictures of a young Greek god she had seen in the library at the Hall. Lady Connolly had allowed her to use the room whenever she wished. She had been surprised and disapproving when Obadiah had told her he was giving up the living and taking Sarah to an island mission in the South Seas.

'But Sarah is too delicate for that kind of a life,' she had argued. 'I am very fond of her. Why don't you let her stay here as my companion?'

Of course Obadiah had refused. He would never have countenanced such an idea, even though Sarah had pleaded with him. She wondered what Lady Connolly would think of her now. But all that seemed to have happened in another life. It was so long ago, and so far away. This was real. This was what mattered to her now. She bent over the young man, her tears dropping on to his face.

'Oh, Charles, don't be dead,' she wept. 'Please speak to me!'

To her surprise, his eyes opened and he grinned at her. Before she could gather her wits, his arms closed around her and he pulled her down on top of him.

'I knew it would work,' he crowed in boyish triumph. 'You were afraid for me so you came to help me . . .'

'You—You wicked tease!' she cried, struggling furiously in his embrace. 'You made me think you were hurt, so . . . Oh, I hate you!'

'No, you don't! You love me,' he said, and kissed her.

She broke free of his embrace, her eyes flashing with temper. 'How could I possibly love someone as cruel as you? You didn't care that I was frightened.'

'Of course I cared, but I knew that you had to conquer your fear for yourself. If I had tried to help you, you would have screamed and held on to those tree roots.'

'I don't believe you. You are unkind, and I don't want to see you again! I'm going home!'

'Sarah . . .'

She heard him calling to her, but she would not look round. He was selfish, childish—and she did not love him! She had been foolish to let him persuade her to come all this way. Obadiah would be looking for her, and he would be very, very angry when he found her!

Jane stirred as the cool hands touched her forehead, stroking back her hair. She moaned, opening her eyes to find several anxious faces staring at her. She remembered Stuart bringing her to the beach, but she must have fainted again. Sitting up, she put her hand to the back of her head, feeling a twinge of pain, though there was no blood and the skin was unbroken.

'What happened?' she asked, struggling to overcome the blank in her mind. 'Oh, I remember . . . I fell and hit my head.'

'Tree fall on you,' Kumi said. 'Captain Smithy find you, bring you here.'

'Yes . . . I remember that. There was a tremor . . .' She glanced towards the volcano anxiously as if expecting to see it belching fire and lava. It was silent, without even a plume of smoke.

'The Sleeping One angry,' Kumi said. 'He warn us what will happen if we turn away from him.'

'Surely it was only the volcano,' Jane spoke without thinking. 'You cannot believe it means that God is angry with you?'

'Not your god. The god of our people.' Kumi's face was stern. 'For all time we pray to him; we take him tributes; he not angry. Now Ma-Llalla say your god has stronger magic, so we build church for him. But the Sleeping One is angry. He warn us what will happen if we forget him.'

'That's nonsense! It was a natural occurrence—nothing to do with magic at all.' Obadiah's scornful tones made Jane glance round in alarm. He should not dismiss Kumi's beliefs like that. 'It's all over now. I doubt there will be an eruption. Are you better, Jane?'

'Yes, thank you.' She took the hand he offered as Kumi moved away, catching a glimpse of the anger in the islander's face. 'It was just a little bump on the head. Where is Sarah? Is she with you?'

He frowned, obviously very annoyed. 'No, my sister seems to have vanished. No doubt she will come back when she's ready. Anyway, the excitement appears to be over. We might as well go home.'

Jane looked at him curiously, seeing the hard lines about his mouth. Something had obviously upset him, and she did not think it was only Sarah's disappearance. Could it be because he had seen her in Stuart's arms? Did he imagine . . . Colour stained her cheeks, and she could not look at him as she said, 'Kumi said we should stay on the beach tonight, just in case.'

'I have no interest in what Kumi says.' His gaze flickered momentarily towards the Prince. 'I believe we shall be safe enough at the mission. Come along, Jane.'

Jane allowed her eyes to wander around the beach, looking for the commanding figure of Stuart Smithson. He was nowhere to be seen, and she felt a sharp prick of disappointment. Had she imagined that moment when he held her in his arms and called her his darling? He had certainly carried her to the beach, but her memory of the rest was a little hazy. It all seemed to have happened in a dream. She remembered clearly enough what had happened a little earlier that afternoon. She had blurted out her feelings for him like an idiot—and he had done his best to save her from embarrassment afterwards. He had not said he loved her, only that he wanted to make love to her . . .

'We are leaving now, Jane.'

'Yes, Obadiah,' she replied, unusually meek. Was his

mood because of what he had seen, or had she betrayed her thoughts in some way?

She felt rather than saw him glance at her. His cold disapproval was evident as he walked beside her, making no effort to help her. Not that she needed it, of course. Yet she could not help thinking that he might have shown some concern. Glancing at his profile, she saw that he was angry, and felt a spurt of rebellion. It was not her fault that a tree had fallen on her. Besides, she had never promised to love him. The bonds of her marriage seemed tighter than ever before and she knew a desperate longing to be free. Why should she ruin her life by living with a man she did not love? She had sworn that she would not betray him, but she knew that she did so with every breath she drew. What point was there in a marriage that had been a farce from the beginning? It was merely a mockery of something that ought to be sacred. She had been a fool to agree to it, and she ought to ask Obadiah to release her before it was too late. Surely it was better that they should part.

They had almost reached the mission when they saw Sarah coming towards them from the direction of the forest. She looked tired and dishevelled, her hair straggling down her back in damp wisps where it had escaped from the neat coronet she usually wore. At the sight of her, Jane started forward eagerly, but Obadiah's hand clamped over her wrist, restraining her. Looking at him in surprise, she saw his lips were set in a hard line and her heart sank.

'No, do not go to her,' he said coldly. 'Sarah has some explaining to do. This time, you will not protect her, Jane.'

'But . . . You can see that she has had an accident of some kind!'

'If she had come home when she left the village, no harm would have befallen her.' His hard eyes raked his sister's face as she approached them. 'Where have you been all this time?'

Sarah stared at him, her heart pounding wildly. She

was tempted to lie, as she had sometimes in the past when she feared his anger, but something rebelled inside her, and she lifted her eyes boldly to meet his.

'I was climbing to the crater with Charles when the tremors started. It was frightening, and he had a fall—so we came back.'

A muscle twitched in his cheek. 'Have you lost all sense of propriety, Sarah? I am ashamed of you.'

'I have done nothing wrong, Obadiah,' she said, her face pale. 'Perhaps I shouldn't have . . .'

'There is no perhaps about it. Going off for hours with that man without telling anyone . . .' His icy gaze chilled her. 'Your behaviour disgusts me. I had thought I could trust you, but it seems I must set a watch over you. You will not see Charles Heatherton again.'

'That's not fair!' Sarah exclaimed hotly. 'Charles is my friend. 'Oh!' She gave a cry of pain as he struck her across the face, staring at him with hurt eyes. 'Obadiah!'

Jane rushed to her side, placing her own body between the brother and sister. 'You shouldn't have done that,' she said. 'Sarah was just upset. I am sure she knows she ought not to have gone off alone with Charles, and she will apologise in her own time.'

'She deserved her punishment,' Obadiah replied harshly. 'By defending her against me, you encourage her to sin again.'

'I don't believe she has sinned. It was a thoughtless action, Obadiah, nothing more.'

'It may be nothing to you that she has damaged her reputation; you seem to care little enough for your own!'

'Oh, I see what this is all about! Surely you won't punish Sarah because you are angry with me?' Jane gave him a scornful look. 'Or do you mean to forbid me to speak to Captain Smithson too?'

'I should prefer it if you saw him as seldom as possible.'

'Perhaps you think that I have been meeting him in secret? Perhaps you imagine that he is my lover?'

Jane was very angry, and something in her face

warned Obadiah that he had pushed her too far. A look of uncertainty replaced the ice in his eyes, and he moved one hand towards her in an awkward gesture.

'No, I cannot believe you would . . .' He glanced towards his sister. 'I should not have hit you. Go indoors, Sarah, and we shall talk again later. I am sorry if I have misjudged you, but you were very wrong to behave as you did.'

'Yes, Obadiah.' She walked away, her head hanging in a subdued manner.

For a moment neither Jane nor Obadiah spoke, then he moved towards her. He gazed down at her, his face seeming to twitch oddly. Before she could collect her thoughts, he bent his head and kissed her, his arms going quickly round her in a clumsy embrace. His lips were cold and demanding on hers, making her recoil in instinctive revulsion. She broke away from him, breathing hard.

'No, Obadiah,' she cried. 'I cannot. You know I cannot!'

'This is nonsense, Jane.' His eyes glittered with something that she vaguely recognised as lust. 'You are my wife. I have the right to kiss you.'

'Not like that,' she whispered, feeling sick as she saw the way his nostrils flared and the tiny beading of sweat on his brow. 'I won't be a wife to you in that way. I won't!'

'Sometimes I think Satan sent you to torment me,' he muttered thickly. 'This reluctance to fulfil your marital duties is unnatural. I have been more than patient with you, Jane, but it is time you saw your duty to me. I am your husband.'

'No . . .' She backed away from him in disgust, her mind, body and senses rejecting what he was saying. 'I should never have agreed to marry you. I did so only for Sarah's sake. It was agreed between us; you know it was! I'm warning you, Obadiah, if you try to touch me again like that, I shall leave you.'

'You don't mean that!' He looked stunned and

disbelieving. 'I refuse to accept that as your final word.'

'Oh yes, I do mean it,' she said, holding out her hand to keep him at bay. 'You had better make up your mind to accept it now. I am going to join Sarah, and we'll call you when the meal is ready.'

'Jane, I want to talk to you. Come back here.'

She heard his call but she would not look back. Only concern for Sarah kept her from running away this very minute. She was shivering, the sickness churning inside her as she remembered the feel of his mouth pressed against hers. It had been unbearable! She could never, never be a true wife to him. She knew it would destroy her. She would die a little inside every time he touched her. From the beginning she had known it was improbable that their relationship could ever be a true one —now she knew it was impossible. She could not let Obadiah make love to her when her heart and body cried out for the touch of another man. Somehow she had to force Obadiah to keep the bargain they had made. The alternative was unthinkable!

'You look sad,' Queen Ma-Llalla said, looking at the shadows beneath Jane's eyes with concern. 'Are you unhappy here with us?'

'No, I am only happy when I am with you,' Jane replied, flushing beneath the Queen's intent gaze. 'I—I cannot explain. Forgive me.'

'You do not love Missionary Thorne. I have always known this was so. Why do you not come to the village and live with us? He will not harm you here.'

'He—He hasn't attempted to harm me.' Jane sighed. 'My place is with him, Ma-Llalla. It would be wrong of me to desert him.'

'It is as you wish.' The Queen shrugged. 'You will be welcome here when you are ready.'

It was impossible to explain what was troubling her, Jane thought. Obadiah had not tried to force his kisses on her again, but she sensed that he deeply resented her refusal to share his bed. He had changed towards her, speaking only when it was impossible to ignore her. Even Sarah had noticed, and commented on his new mood.

'I am sorry if you quarrelled with Obadiah over me, Jane,' she said. 'I've apologised to him, but he refused to discuss it.'

'No, it wasn't over you,' Jane said, squeezing her hand to comfort her. 'Don't blame yourself. It is my problem, and I shall have to cope with it as best I can.'

'You married him for my sake. I shouldn't have asked that, Jane. I didn't understand what it meant for you. It was selfish of me, I see that now. I've ruined your life.'

'No, my dear, you mustn't think that. It was my own decision. You were a part of the reason for my agreeing to the marriage, but I was confused and lonely. I thought it might work out for all of us. I believed that I could make Obadiah see that his attitude to you was too harsh, and for a while I believed that it was happening. But there seems to be some inner core that I cannot reach. Your brother is two people . . .' She laughed self-consciously. 'That sounds ridiculous, I know, but he can be charming when he chooses. I think that his anger just now is more with me than with you. He has begun to realise that I can never be a true wife to him and I think he resents it. He wants more than I can give him. It was unfair of me to enter into this arrangement . . .'

'He knew. He agreed to it, too.'

Jane nodded, a flicker of anger in her eyes. 'It seems that he believed I would change my mind. Now he is feeling cheated because I have not.'

'I shall never marry unless I love my husband,' Sarah said with sudden decision. 'And I shall marry the man I love, no matter what Obadiah says!'

Jane looked at her anxiously then. 'Be careful, Sarah. If you disobey your brother again I may not be able to protect you. I fear my influence with him is not what it once was.'

'Charles will take care of me.' Sarah's face was

defiant. 'He loves me, Jane. It was harsh of Obadiah to forbid us to meet. But I shall be careful, so don't worry about me.'

Naturally, Jane could not help being anxious about her, but even this was not the true cause of the ache in her heart or the sleepless nights that had brought the shadows to her face. It was more than two weeks now since the volcano had given them all such a fright —unwarranted, it seemed, since there had been no further tremors—and she had not seen Stuart once in all that time. He had stopped coming to the lessons each morning, and it was clear that he was deliberately avoiding her. In her mind, she knew that it was because he was embarrassed by her confession of love. She ought never to have told him what was in her heart, but surely he had seen it in her face?

What a wasteful muddle she had made of her life! Yet she could have accepted all the rest if only she could have seen Stuart now and then. Surely it was not too much to ask of life? She was so desperately unhappy . . . She admitted it to herself at last. The evenings spent in Obadiah's company were almost unbearable. How could she have let him persuade her into a marriage she had known was wrong? She ought to tell him that she would be leaving when the next ship called. She ought to go away and start a new life on her own. It was time that she began to live for herself—to understand who and what she really was. Yet she had promised to help Obadiah with his work, and he would find it difficult to communicate with the islanders without her. How could she simply walk out on him? She felt she owed him something—and there was still Sarah to be considered. Perhaps she was just being weak and selfish . . .

'You and Sarah come to feast tonight?'

Jane dragged her thoughts back to the present, staring at the Queen in a daze. 'The feast? Is it some kind of a celebration?'

'It is the Feast of Love.' The Queen smiled slyly. 'Tonight the young ones choose those they wish to love with. It is a time of joy and happiness for all.'

'Oh . . .' Jane's cheeks were slightly pink. 'I'm not sure that Obadiah would approve of us being present.'

'Do not tell him why we feast. You come with Sarah. Be happy. Maybe you find a new man tonight?'

Jane laughed and shook her head. 'I'm afraid it isn't so simple for us. No, I don't think we dare come, Ma-Llalla, though we should both enjoy it very much. Obadiah would never allow us to attend something he would think of as a pagan ceremony.'

Queen Ma-Llalla was silent, but her eyes were thoughtful. 'You go to mission now,' she said, smiling to herself. 'Maybe you come tonight. I see what Kumi say . . .'

Jane stared at her suspiciously. 'What do you mean, Ma-Llalla? You're plotting something.'

The Queen waved her away. 'You go now. Tonight you be ready . . .'

It was useless to protest, and Jane was amused by the Queen's manner. She was like a child planning a birthday surprise. To refuse her outright would be too harsh, but of course there was no question of her and Sarah attending the feast. Obadiah would see to that! A little surge of resentment went through her. Why must they always do what Obadiah wanted? He had no God-given right to dictate how they lived!

Stuart watched as Jane walked slowly across the beach, feeling a strong desire to join her. He thought that she looked unhappy, and he felt anger against the man who was her husband. A man like that should never have married! He thought that there was something unnatural about Obadiah . . . Or maybe that was merely because of the feeling of mutual dislike between them. There could be no harm in simply joining Jane for a walk, he argued with himself, wanting to see her smile. Yet he knew that he would not be satisfied with walking with her. He wanted more, much more. It was for this reason that he had stayed away from the village when he knew she would be there, putting temptation out of reach.

Did he want her only because she was out of reach? he asked himself. Would he have given her a second look if they had met again in New South Wales? He recalled the day he had visited her in her cabin at sea when she was recovering from her illness. She had shrunk away from him then like a timid mouse—but the woman he had kissed the other morning was no mouse. She had responded to him with an eagerness that was a sign of a passionate nature. Had she really changed so much, or was it that he had not understood her before? He thought now that she was a woman with very strong emotions, but for some reason she had been afraid to show them until now. Had her reserve been caused by fear of betraying her love for him?

Her revelations on the subject had shocked him at first, but then he had felt a natural pleasure. It was good to be loved and needed, yet it made the situation more difficult. He could hardly have a casual love affair with her . . . Besides, she was not that kind of a woman. Maybe it was best that he stayed well away from her . . .

The sound of the island drums was intoxicating, Jane thought. She felt an urgent longing to witness this feast of love, but knew it was impossible. Its very name would be offensive to Obadiah. Glancing across the dinner table, she saw the irritation on his face, and wondered why she had ever thought him attractive. He was certainly not in the best of moods and had complained several times since the wild music had begun.

'I wish they would stop that,' he muttered. 'I'll wager there's something odd going on tonight.'

Sarah looked up, about to speak; then she remembered and checked herself. 'I expect it's merely one of their customs,' she said with an air of innocence. 'After all, we've only been here a few weeks. We can't pretend to understand . . .' She broke off as the grass curtain at the doorway was swished aside and Kumi entered.

He looked directly at Obadiah. 'You come quick,' he said. 'Child is to be born. Mother may die. She good Christian. She fears to die without you to bless her.'

'Then I shall come at once,' Obadiah responded, an eager expression replacing the irritation. 'Thank you for coming to fetch me, sir. Please wait one moment while I collect my things.'

As Obadiah went into the room he used as his study, Jane looked at the Prince in concern. 'Can I be of any help?'

'No, you not needed,' he replied sternly. 'Only Missionary Thorne.'

She stared at him, feeling slightly hurt by his brusque dismissal of her offer to assist at the difficult birth. She believed that she might have been of more use than Obadiah but did not protest, beginning to clear the dishes instead.

Obadiah emerged from his room, armed with his Bible and wearing his black coat and hat—just as if he were preparing to visit a sick parishoner in England. It was comical, Jane thought, and yet a little sad. He meant so well, but he was not willing to bend even a little. In a way she respected him for holding so strongly to his own principles. He smiled at her, his manner more friendly than it had been for a long time.

'I may be gone all night, Jane,' he said. 'Do not trouble yourself to wait up for me.'

'As you wish,' she replied, and saw his look of satisfaction.

He followed Kumi from the room, and walked across the sand towards the forest. The missionary's shoulders were square and straight, and Jane knew it had pleased him that the woman in labour had asked for him. That was a little strange—as was the fact that they were heading in the opposite direction to the village. Her eyes narrowed in suspicion and she almost called him back, then she shook her head, feeling sure that the Queen would not trick Obadiah in this way. Or would she? Was it not exactly the kind of prank a child might play?

Hearing the giggling behind her, she swung round to see two dusky beauties staring at her mischievously. One of them placed a finger to her lips.

'You come village now,' she whispered, giggling again. 'Sarah come too.'

'So it was all a plot!'

Jane bit her lip, hesitating as she tried to decide what to do. She really ought not to be encouraging Obadiah's sister to disobey him, but what harm could come of it? If they stayed only a short time, he need never know. Besides, he had not actually forbidden them to go, and the Queen would be offended if they refused after all her trouble. Anyway, it would be a change. Her decision was made as Sarah came hurrying out of the house dressed in the gown she had worn to Morna's wedding. From the look in her eyes it was clear that she was determined to go to the feast, and Jane had not the heart to deny her. Why should they not have some fun?

The island girls obviously thought it was a great joke; they chatted excitedly to Sarah, telling her about the special dances they were to perform and how they expected to be chosen by the most handsome of the men. Watching her laughing with them, Jane was aware of just how much Obadiah's sister had changed in the past few weeks. Her skin had lost that unhealthy pallor and her eyes were much brighter. She was a very pretty girl, Jane thought fondly, and it was good to see her looking so happy. The night air was warm and scented as they strolled along, and the magic of the occasion was not lost on Jane. Surely this island was as near to Paradise as anyone could imagine, she thought.

A huge fire was burning in the centre of the village, and there was the tantalising smell of roasting meat. An abundance of fresh fruit, meats and fish had been prepared in advance so that everyone could join in the celebrations. Chains of flowers hung about the necks of both men and women, and the newcomers were each presented with garlands when they arrived.

The drums ceased for the moment, and it seemed that

the villagers were waiting for their guests to begin eating. Jane and Sarah were shown to the places of honour beside the Queen, sitting on flower-decked couches prepared for their comfort. Once they were settled, everyone began to help themselves from the laden platters.

'So you come to feast after all,' the Queen said, her eyes sparkling. 'Missionary happy. You happy also, yes?'

Jane shook her head in mock reproof. 'Is there really a woman in labour, Ma-Llalla?'

She nodded slyly. 'She pray to God and weep much. Maybe child born tonight. Maybe child come tomorrow . . . or next day.'

'You are very naughty,' Jane said laughing. 'But thank you.'

Ma-Llalla's plump body shook with gentle amusement. It seemed a very good idea to her to make everyone happy while getting her own way. She did not much like the stern missionary, who was so different from those who had first brought the new religion to her island, and she suspected him of being unkind to Jane. If her plan worked, those she cared for would be much happier. And tonight was a time for loving. All those who chose a lover on this special night were assured of fertility. Jane was a special woman and she deserved a real man, not that cold-eyed missionary she claimed as her husband. There was another man on the island, a man whom she believed could make her friend very happy . . .

Stuart could scarcely believe his eyes as he looked across the clearing and saw the two Englishwomen. What on earth were they doing here, he wondered, feeling apprehensive. They could have no idea of the kind of ceremony they were about to witness. He himself had found it vaguely shocking the first time he had attended a feast of love. What was the missionary thinking of to allow his wife and sister to be present?

It was only a moment or two before he realised that Obadiah was not in the village. Of course! This was some mischief brewed by Ma-Llalla and her brother, he guessed, understanding now why she had gone to some lengths to make certain that both he and Charles attended tonight. She was a wily one! He smiled wryly as he wondered just what she was hoping for. Did she imagine that, as he watched the ritual lovemaking when the drums reached a wild crescendo, he would lose control, seize Jane and take her into the bushes as the island men did with their chosen partners? He chuckled inwardly as he admitted her cleverness. It would be easy enough to be swayed by the atmosphere, for there was magic in the soft scented air and the intoxicating music that seemed to heat men's blood, but he had not gone out of his way to avoid temptation only to let a moment's madness ruin all their lives.

Jane had made it clear that she wished to remain faithful to her husband, and he had no right to try to persuade her otherwise. Even if he took her away from the island, he had nothing to offer her: everything he owned had gone down with *Sea-Sprite*. How could he ask any woman to share the hardships of life on a simple seaman's pay? It might be years before he was able to support her decently. Besides, it would cost a great deal to have her marriage annulled, and he could not let her face the disgrace of living as his mistress, an outcast from her own class. The whole situation was much too complicated; he had come to see that clearly in the past few days. It was better if he stayed away from her . . .

The drums had begun again now that everyone had eaten their fill, and the dancing was about to start. A fine display of spear-waving and warlike gestures from twenty of the strongest men opened the ceremonies. Then, the men having shown their bravery, it was the turn of a score of very young and beautiful girls to take their place in the firelight, their dusky skins shimmering like gold in the reflected glory of the flames.

So far it was all quite innocent and enjoyable with

nothing to disturb the English ladies' peace of mind, but as the beating of the drums gradually became wilder and wilder, some of the warriors jumped to their feet to dance frenziedly with the girls of their choice. Then, all at once, the men formed a circle around a couple who were gyrating wildly to the pounding of the drums, their faces wearing a strangely intent look as if they were no longer really aware of what they did.

'I think it's time we took Sarah and Jane home, don't you?'

Charles's urgent whisper broke the pattern of Stuart's thoughts. He stared at him for a moment, then nodded. 'You take them,' he muttered. 'You don't need me.'

'Surely . . .' The younger man hesitated as he saw the spark in his companion's eyes. 'I thought you liked Jane?'

'Damn you, Charles! It's none of your business. Get them out of here before they realise what's going on.' He got to his feet and walked away from the clearing, leaving Charles to stare after him in dismay.

Jane had already sensed what might be the outcome of the ritual dance. She touched Sarah's arm, bending to whisper in her ear that it was time for them to leave.

'Oh, must we?' Sarah said, her eyes straying to where the two Englishmen had been sitting. 'I haven't even spoken to Charles yet. Besides, I am enjoying myself.'

'We must go now,' Jane said firmly, standing up. 'I think Charles is coming to speak to you now. Perhaps he will walk some of the way with us.'

She was disappointed that Stuart had departed without speaking to her, but she was determined that her feelings should not show as she said good night to the Queen. As she had expected, Ma-Llalla tried her best to keep them from leaving, but Jane would not be swayed. The dance was approaching its climax, and it would not be proper for them to remain.

Her purpose was helped by Charles Heatherton's insistence that he would see them home. Now that he was to leave with them, Sarah was no longer reluctant. They were outside the village by the time the music reached fever pitch, culminating in a high shrieking sound that issued simultaneously from all those still present. A sigh of relief was on Jane's lips. They had left just in time! She was not really shocked by the knowledge of what was going on behind them: it was simply another way of life, a different culture from their own. Yet it was not something she wished to witness, and it would be very wrong of her to expose Sarah to such a pagan display. It was obvious that Charles had also been anxious to protect the girl from something that would embarrass her, and she found his concern admirable. She thought as she watched the young couple together that there was something rather beautiful about the way love was developing between them. It was an innocent, almost childlike, relationship as they hovered on the brink of romance.

Their steps grew slower and slower as they neared the mission house, and it was clear that they wished to be alone, though neither said anything to her. Her gentle heart was touched. Why should they not have a moment to themselves? Charles obviously respected the girl too much to think of overstepping the line.

'I should like to walk on the beach for a while,' Jane said. 'You two go on. I shall not be long, Sarah.'

She turned away, walking unhurriedly along the fringe of silvered sand. The drums were silent now, and there was only the peace of the velvet night and the gentle ripple of the lagoon. How tempting the water looked at night, deep turquoise in colour with the occasional crest of silver as a breeze kissed the surface. Suddenly she was seized with a longing to feel the cool water on her limbs. She had often watched the island girls frolicking at the edge or diving further out in the lagoon for pieces of coral, envying them their freedom, but knowing that she could never behave as they did. Yet why should she not paddle her feet at the edge for a while? Who was there to see her?

Slipping off her shoes with a gurgle of delight, she ran into the shallows, splashing happily like a child. It was so wonderful! Far better than she had ever imagined. Her laughter rang out as she experienced the sheer ecstasy of it. Her long skirt was soon soaking wet, clinging round her ankles until she hitched it up above her knees. She had never felt like this . . . never known such a sense of freedom . . . The splashing sound behind her made her turn, her heart quickening as she saw the tall, powerful figure coming towards her through the water, his trousers clinging wetly to his legs. She waited for him to reach her, smiling as he paused in front of her, anticipating the inevitable. They stared hungrily at one another for a long moment; then he groaned, his arms going about her as their lips met in a long-awaited kiss.

It was a deep, demanding kiss that seemed almost to tear Jane's heart from her. She trembled, her body arching against him as his mouth took hers hungrily, sliding down the slender curve of her throat to end in frustration where the modest frill of her gown prevented his searching kiss from its sweet conclusion. When she felt his fingers at the tiny buttons, urgently seeking entry to the pulsating swell of the firm breasts beneath, she stiffened momentarily, afraid of this new emotion, then relaxed, allowing him to have his way. A slight moan escaped her as his hand caressed her smooth flesh, seeming almost to burn her.

'Oh, Stuart!' she gasped. 'I—I cannot bear it when I don't see you.'

'I meant to stay away from you. Even tonight, when I guessed what that sly old matchmaker was up to, I was determined to keep my distance. I knew if I came near you . . .'

'I'm glad you followed me.' Jane shivered with pleasure as his lips touched her breast. 'God forgive me, but I have wanted to be with you like this.'

'I followed you all, meaning only to see you safely home,' Stuart murmured hoarsely, his hand curving her cheek with a kind of reverence. 'But when I saw you in the water . . .' He gathered her to him, holding her so close that she could feel the pounding of his heart. 'You can't go back to him, Jane. I won't let you!'

'I have to.' She pressed a finger against his lips as he would have protested. 'No, you must hear me out first. I shall ask him to let me go. He must know in his heart that our marriage is an empty sham. If I talk to him sensibly, he will agree to a separation.'

'And if he won't agree?'

'He must!' She trembled in his arms. 'Is it so very wrong to want a little happiness? I didn't mean to betray him, but I couldn't help myself.'

'No, it isn't wrong,' he said, his kiss silencing her. 'You tried to do what you thought was your duty, Jane, but it was never meant to be. If you really want to tell him yourself, I suppose I must let you.' He smiled tenderly, touching her cheek. 'Come on, let's get out of the water. You're shaking.'

She was not cold, but there was no point in telling him why she was trembling. If he guessed that she was nervous about the confrontation with Obadiah, he would insist on being with her, and she could not let him do that. She owed Obadiah a private meeting; he would be humiliated and angry. Very angry. The thought of the scene that must follow her confession sickened her. She had always hated quarrels. Although she had braved his fury for Sarah's sake on several occasions, she instinctively knew that this would be much worse.

Stuart's arm went round her waist as he glanced down at her. 'You're not frightened of him, Jane? He wouldn't hurt you?'

'No, of course not.' She controlled her fluttering nerves and smiled at him. 'Obadiah does have a temper, I'll admit, but he wouldn't harm me.'

'Well, we'll give him no cause to lose his temper,' Stuart said, fastening the buttons of her bodice. 'I lost my head just now, but I can wait, my darling. I can wait until you come to me.'

'It—It might be for the best.' Jane gave him a grate-ful look. 'If I can tell him truthfully that we are not lovers—that I have not betrayed him . . .'

'Yours is the right way,' he said. 'A moment ago I thought only of my needs, my desires, but that was selfish. Free yourself of this marriage, Jane, and then you will come to me with a clear conscience. We shall find a way to leave the island and start a new life together. I haven't much to offer you, but I'll work for you, and one day . . .'

'Hush,' she whispered, touching her lips to his briefly. 'We'll manage—together.'

He held her then, his hand stroking the nape of her neck in a soothing action. It was an embrace that was meant to comfort without passion. A man and a woman, each drawing strength from the other.

'I must go,' she said, withdrawing from him reluc-tantly. 'If Obadiah should return before me . . .'

'I'll be waiting for you tomorrow when you leave the village.'

'I love you,' she whispered, unafraid to say it now.

She was suddenly gloriously happy, her steps lighter than air as she walked back to the mission. She had never before experienced the kinds of sensations that had flooded through her while Stuart held her tonight, never expected to feel such pleasure in a man's embrace. She had thought herself cold, but now she knew that it was only that she had never met a man she could really love until the stern-faced captain of *Sea-Sprite* had walked into her life. If Fate had been kinder, she might have been his wife long before this; but it did not matter, he wanted her now. He wanted her and he cared for her. Perhaps not in quite the same way as he had loved Morna, but she did not expect that. She was not a child to cry for the moon. She would take what he offered, seizing her chance of happiness now that it had finally come. Suddenly all her doubts and confusion had gone. Why should she feel guilty? She had never promised to love Obadiah. She had tried to help him as much as she could. He was a sensible man. He would understand why she had to be free . . .

Sarah's scream broke into her thoughts. The girl was in trouble! What could have happened? She began to run towards the sound as it was repeated again and again, halting only when she was close enough to see what was going on. Obadiah and Charles were struggling on the ground, and, oh Lord! poor Charles was receiving a beating. His face was already cut and bleeding. No wonder Sarah was hysterical!

'Stop this at once!' Jane cried, losing her temper. 'Obadiah, if you hit him again, I'll take a broom to the both of you!'

Her words seemed to bring the two men to their sense. They broke apart, breathing hard and looking at her shamefacedly. At least Charles had the grace to look ashamed. He wiped the back of his hand across his mouth, giving her a defensive grin as he got to his feet.

'I'm sorry, but he was going to hit Sarah.'

'Your interference has not saved her, you impudent whelp!' Obadiah growled, dusting the débris from his clothes as he straightened up. 'I told her she would be severely punished if she disobeyed me again, and . . .'

'It was my fault,' Jane said quickly. 'Queen Ma-Llalla invited us to her feast, and Charles saw us safely home. I left them alone for a few minutes, that's all.'

'That's all?' Obadiah rounded on her furiously. 'You deliberately left them alone together, knowing that I would disapprove! Just what was your purpose, madam?'

'I could see no wrong in it. They are innocent children, Obadiah.'

'Innocent!' He laughed harshly. 'Then why did I find them locked in a shameful embrace?'

'Oh, I did not think . . .'

'Obviously.' He glared at her before turning his baleful gaze on the younger man. 'Go away, sir, and stay away from my sister. If I ever catch you near her again, I shall thrash you. Do you understand me? Next time, I'll take a horse-whip to you.'

Charles went white. 'You don't understand, Mr Thorne. I know it may have been wrong of me to court your sister without your permission, but I love her and I want to marry her.'

'Oh, Charles!' Sarah's eyes lit up with an inner glow.

'Indeed? And do you imagine that makes the situation better?' Obadiah sneered at him. 'Do you think I would let Sarah marry a shipwrecked vagrant who doesn't even know who he is? How do you intend to support her? Perhaps you want your wife to live like one of these ignorant native women? Well, it might be good enough for you, but it won't do for me.'

The young man flinched as if he had been struck, his face blenching with the shock. It was cruel. Too cruel!

'Stop, Obadiah,' Jane cried. 'That is sufficient. You've said enough!' She looked at Charles urgently. 'I think you should leave. There is no sense in prolonging this.'

Charles was staring wretchedly at the girl he loved. 'Come with me now, Sarah,' he begged. 'We can live in the village until the next ship comes. Don't be afraid of him. The Queen will not let him harm you.'

'Oh, Charles,' Sarah whispered, tears running down her cheeks. 'I—I cannot. He is my brother. I have to obey him. I have to . . .'

'You only think you have to obey,' Charles said. He lingered uncertainly for a moment, seeing the pain and fear in her eyes. 'Stay if you must, but he won't part us for ever, I promise.' With that, he turned and walked across the sand in the direction of the village.

'I am relieved you have some sense left,' Obadiah said bitterly. He took two steps towards his sister, his eyes glittering coldly as he looked at her. He deliberately drew back his hand, slapping her hard on one side of her face and then on the other. 'This is my last warning, Sarah. Disobey me again, and I shall whip you.'

'You vile brute!' Jane cried wildly, hardly able to

believe what she was witnessing. 'How could you be so cruel?'

Obadiah's shoulders tensed, his whole body stiffening with anger. He turned very slowly to face her, and she thought that his eyes had never looked so cold. He was staring at her in a peculiar manner, almost as though he had never seen her before.

'Once I thought I saw the hand of God at work in you,' he muttered in a strangled voice. 'But now I realise that I was blinded by the Devil. It is your influence that has caused this disobedience in Sarah. She was always a meek, obedient girl until you began to contaminate her mind with your evil thoughts.'

'You call me evil?' Jane recoiled, feeling sick. 'I think you are the evil one, Obadiah. It is in your mind . . . You see wickedness in everything.'

'I see it in you, Jezebel!'

'Then you need suffer no more. I'm leaving you —tonight. Just as soon as I can pack.'

She turned and walked past him into the house. Her feelings of pity for him had evaporated, leaving her with nothing but disgust. She owed him nothing. He was a selfish, cruel monster, and she had been a fool to stay with him as long as she had. She began to pack a few personal items. She would ask Kumi to have her other belongings transferred to the village. She was free at last. There was nothing to keep her here now . . .

Hearing the swish of the grass curtain behind her, she swung round to face Obadiah, her hands suddenly stilled. The first spiral of fear curled through her as she saw the wild light in his eyes. And then she knew. She knew he was not going to let her go.

'What are you doing?'

'I'm taking what I can carry. I'll send for the rest.'

'You'll do nothing of the kind!' He snatched her bundle and tossed it aside. 'You're my wife, and you'll stay here, where you belong.'

'I don't belong to you. I never have!'

'You were the one who refused your duty, Jane.' His

nostrils flared. 'You made a mockery of your vows.'

'It was never meant to be a true marriage,' she whispered, her throat tight. 'You know that, Obadiah. You agreed.'

'You are trying to break our agreement.' He grasped her wrist, hurting her as his fingers scored the soft flesh. 'But I shall not allow you to shame me with him, Jane. Oh yes, I know why you want to go. Did you think I was a blind fool? I saw how you nestled in his arms that day. How long have you been lovers? Was it before or after you met him again on the island?'

She recoiled before the fury in his face. Something about the intensity of his manner was frightening. She had never seen him quite like this. 'We are not lovers. It is true that I love him. If I had known that he was still alive, I should not . . .'

'You would not have married me?' His grasp tightened. 'But you did marry me, Jane. And now I intend to take what you have denied me—what is mine by right!'

'No! Oh please, no!' Her head began to spin as she saw the glitter in his eyes and guessed his purpose. There was something about him now that set her body shuddering with disgust. This must not happen. 'You cannot . . . I won't let you! You have no rights over me . . .'

'You gave me the right months ago. I have been patient with you, but now I shall no longer be denied.' There was a kind of triumph mixed with the anger in his voice.

She tried to break from him, but he held on to her, twisting her wrist until she cried out in agony. Then his arms were round her, imprisoning her so that she was forced to accept his hateful kisses. The touch of his moist lips sent a surge of revulsion through her. She struggled violently, knowing even as she did so that it was useless. He was too strong. She could not prevent him from forcing himself on her. No matter what she did, he would prevail. It was hopeless, and fighting it would only make her ordeal worse.

She felt the bed behind her, cutting at the back of her knees, unbalancing her as he bore her backwards. As she fell on it with him on top of her, instinct told her to lie still. It would be easier if she just let him have his way. She must try to block it all from her mind, pretend it was not happening. For a moment she went limp beneath him, hoping he would relent and release her.

'Please, Obadiah, don't do this,' she begged.

She might as well have saved her breath. He was like a mad beast, tearing at her clothes in the urgency of his lust. It was then that the hatred was born in her and she began to fight him with all her strength. She fought wildly, bitterly . . . uselessly. But she fought him to the last. Then, when it was suddenly over and he left her, she closed her eyes, wanting to die. Oh, merciful heavens, why was she not dead? How could she live with the knowledge of what he had done? The sickness swirled in her, making her lunge across the bed and vomit on the floor.

Wiping her mouth, she lay back against the pillows and looked at him, the hatred burning in her eyes as she saw him calmly straightening his clothes. 'What you have done makes no difference,' she said bitterly. 'I shall leave you anyway. You cannot stop me.'

'Go to him, and I shall kill him.'

'You wouldn't dare!' She stared at him in horror. 'You could never commit such a terrible sin.'

'It would not be a sin to defend my wife's honour. No court would convict me of murder in the circumstances. It would be thought justifiable in the face of such provocation. Besides . . .' He leered at her. 'We are in the midst of savages. Who would know how your lover died? Sarah would lie for me. She will be taught to obey me once more—the hard way, if necessary.'

'You—You are sick,' Jane whispered. 'You don't know what you're saying . . .'

'If I am mad, you made me that way,' he snarled, coming to stand threateningly over the bed. 'You are a wanton Jezebel, a woman of Babylon!'

'Then why won't you let me go?'

'Because you are my wife.'

Jane closed her eyes as he went out, his words lingering in her mind long after he had gone. The despair washed over her in an icy wave. What was she going to do? She could not bear to go through another night like this one, but if she left Obadiah, he might carry out his threats against both Stuart and Sarah. The man she loved might be able to defend himself, but Sarah would suffer terribly. She would be punished for something that was not her fault. It was a fiendish web Obadiah had woven, making it almost impossible for her to escape. Yet there might be one way left open to her. If she were dead . . .

CHAPTER FIVE

IT WAS AN effort to get out of bed. An effort to wash. Jane had scrubbed her skin until it bled the previous night, but she could not wash away the stain of her humiliation. She had wanted to die in the dark hours before dawn, but this morning her mood had changed to one of bitter hatred. Why should she die and let the brute who had raped her live? He would never touch her again—on that, at least, she was decided. Next time he tried it, she would kill him.

Her fingers stroked the little knife she had concealed inside the sash round her waist. Obadiah deserved to suffer, and he would if he attempted to force himself on her again. An icy wall had built itself round her heart during the painful hours she had spent in restless thought. She had never been a vindictive woman, always giving more than she expected to receive, never hoping for happiness for herself. Last night she had let herself believe for a little while, but now her dreams had been destroyed. Even if Obadiah had been prepared to let her go, it was too late. How could she go now to the man she loved? She was unclean, contaminated by what had happened to her. If he knew the truth, Stuart would turn from her in disgust, and she could not bear to see the look in his eyes. No, he must never know. He must believe that she had changed her mind. It was better for both of them that way.

Despair beyond anything she had ever known swept through her then. She leant against her sea-chest, feeling the pain tear at her heart as her eyes closed. What use was there in living, now that all hope had gone? Why should she torture herself with a longing that must forever be denied? It was so unfair . . .

Calling upon reserves of strength she had not known

she possessed until this moment, Jane straightened up, her face hard. To take her own life and leave Sarah at the mercy of her cruel brother would be the action of a coward. No, that would be to let Obadiah win. Somehow she must find the courage to go on living with her shame, at least until she discovered a way to make Sarah safe. Her own dreams had been shattered, but it was not yet too late for the girl she loved as dearly as if they had been sisters.

There was no sign of Obadiah, but Sarah was waiting for her when she emerged from the house at last. For a long moment they looked at each other in silence, then moved instinctively to embrace one another. Jane saw the girl's tears as she clung to her.

'Oh, Jane, I'm so sorry,' she choked. 'I heard—the walls are so thin—I know what he did to you. It was all my fault. You were trying to protect me, that's why he . . .'

'Hush, my dearest.' Jane held her away, wiping the tears with trembling fingers. 'It was not just because of the quarrel over you, Sarah. Never believe that. This was something much deeper. I should never have made that foolish bargain with him. It was unnatural and doomed to failure.'

Sarah swallowed hard, reaching up to touch a bruise on Jane's neck and another on her cheek. 'What he did to you was barbaric. No man has a right to do that to a woman! Even if she is his wife.'

'He believed he had rights over me; perhaps he has, according to the law,' Jane said bitterly. 'I denied him, so he raped me—but it will never happen again.'

'Are you going to leave him?' Sarah stared at her with wide, dark eyes. 'Let's both go to the village and ask the Queen to protect us.'

'Is that what you really want, Sarah? Once you leave your brother, there will be no going back.'

Sarah gave a little sigh, her face clouding. 'I'm sure he cared for me once. I don't know what to do, Jane. I—I think I'm in love with Charles. I know he would marry me if I consented . . .'

'You must decide for yourself. Remember that I shall stand by you whatever you do. If you go to the village, I shall come with you—but you must make up your own mind.'

'I must talk to Charles.' Sarah clung to her arm emotionally. 'I'm torn between my duty to Obadiah and my love for Charles. It—It isn't easy to break away from my brother, Jane. I've relied on his guidance all my life.'

'I know that.' Jane smiled at her. 'Your happiness is all that I care for now, my dear.'

'You've done so much for me.' Sarah studied her face, still feeling uncertain. 'Will you tell Captain Smithson what happened last night?'

'No. And you must promise not to say anything. No one must guess what your brother did last night. I think Ma-Llalla might have him killed if she knew that he had hurt me.'

'Perhaps he deserves it. You must hate him, Jane?'

'Yes, I do.' Jane's eyes were bleak as she stared at a point somewhere beyond the girl's head. 'But that doesn't give me the right to take his life. Unless . . .' She shivered as the revulsion swept over her. 'I shall never let him use me like that again. I would rather die.'

'Oh, Jane!' Sarah gave a little sob. 'I hate him for what he has done to you.'

'No, you must not. You told me he was good to you when you were younger. Don't hate him because of what happened last night—that is something apart from you.'

'How can you be so understanding? I should want revenge, if it were me!'

'I told you, your happiness is all that matters now.' Jane blinked back the useless tears and took her arm. 'We must go. The Queen will wonder what has happened to us.'

Sarah stared at her, wondering how she could be so calm. It must be costing Jane dear to follow her usual routine as though nothing untoward had happened. She hugged her arm, wanting to show the warm affection she felt for the woman who was mother, sister and friend to her.

Not even Sarah could have guessed how much courage it took for Jane to behave naturally that morning. Far from wondering why they were late, the villagers were scarcely awake, most of them heavy-eyed from lack of sleep after the feasting the previous evening. The Queen apologised, explaining that she had meant to tell Jane not to come as it was traditionally a day when no work was done.

'Stay and talk to me if you wish,' she said. 'Shall I have food brought?'

'I—I am not hungry, Ma-Llalla. I think I'll walk on the beach for a while, since I'm not needed . . .' She flushed as she felt the Queen's gaze on her face and knew that those dark eyes had seen the purple bruises.

'Who hurt you?' the Queen asked. 'Tell me, and he will be punished. It was not Captain Smithy?'

'No. I tripped and hurt myself. It's nothing to worry about.'

The older woman's kindly face creased with concern. 'Why you not come to village? It is as I dreamed. Stay with me, Jane. You be safe here.'

'Sarah cannot leave her brother. He might . . . resent it if I left him.'

'Sarah come with you, yes?'

'No. I thank you for your concern, but it is impossible, Ma-Llalla.'

The Queen sighed. Jane was stubborn. She would not listen, and so must suffer as the dream had foretold. She stood up and embraced the girl, hugging her fiercely.

'Go then, if you wish, but remember that there is always a place for you here with us.'

Jane smiled sadly. 'I know. Thank you, my friend.'

Ma-Llalla shook her head as the girl walked away. From now on, she would be watched over constantly.

There was no sign of Sarah as Jane left the village, and

she realised that she had gone in search of Charles. It was a risk, but one that must be taken. Even if Sarah decided to end her friendship with the young man, she needed to speak to him alone. Matters could not be left as they were.

Jane's heart jerked as she saw the man waiting for her beneath the shade of a tree. She knew a deep, urgent longing to run to him and feel the comfort of his arms round her as she sobbed out her pain. She loved him so much, but how could she give up all her dreams? Yet she could not bear to tell him—could not bear to see the disgust in his eyes when he knew. And Obadiah had threatened his life. It was this last consideration that decided her. She must be strong enough to let him go for his own sake. If she told him the truth, he might try to kill Obadiah. She could not let him risk his life for her sake. He had to believe that she had changed her mind about leaving her husband. Walking slowly to meet him, she schooled her lips to a cool smile. What could she say that would convince him?

'Jane . . .' He moved towards her, smiling. 'I've been waiting for hours.'

His smile sent a surge of despair through her. How could she send him away? And yet she must. She must!

'Stuart, I . . .' She choked on the words. It was impossible to deny this need within her, but she had no choice. Confusion reigned in her mind, the calmness she had fought for so desperately deserting her as she looked into his face. 'I cannot. I've changed my mind. I have to go . . .' She tried to rush past him as the tide of emotion rose to swamp her. It was necessary to escape before she lost all control. 'Forgive me. I cannot . . .'

'You cannot what?' He grasped her arm, swinging her round to face him, his eyes going over her face searching. She turned aside in shame, unable to bear his scrutiny. This was not what she had planned. She had meant to be cool and calm, but she was not strong enough. This was weakness. Foolishness! She had to sacrifice herself for his sake. His fingers touched her cheek, compelling her to look at him. The tears rose in her throat, destroying her. 'What can't you do, Jane?'

'I—I cannot leave him.'

He frowned, stunned by the stark denial; then he saw the bruises on her throat, and his eyes narrowed in suspicion. It was unthinkable. No man could do that to a woman he was supposed to care for, and yet he knew instinctively what she had suffered.

'What did that brute do to you? My God! I'll kill him if . . . He's obviously beaten you. What else happened?'

'Don't look at me like that . . .' Jane closed her eyes as the tears squeezed beneath her lashes. Oh, why did she weaken whenever he looked at her? She had wanted so much to be strong for his sake. 'I—I never meant you to know.'

'Why?' His voice softened and his hand caressed her cheek. 'What is so terrible that you can't tell me?' Anger flared in him as he saw the shame in her eyes, and he understood. 'Damn him! I'll thrash the beast! Jane, my darling, I'm so sorry. Please forgive me . . .'

She gazed up at him then. He knew it all. There was no use in trying to deny it. 'It was not your fault. You could not have prevented it.'

'No?' His face twisted with self-inflicted pain. 'I should have insisted on coming with you. I should never have let you face him alone. Oh, Jane, what can I say? I would give my soul to undo what has been done.'

'You don't have to say anything. I know how you must feel.' She shivered as his fingers moved gently on her cheek. 'You can't want me now. I'm unclean, contaminated . . .'

'No!' He took her by the shoulders, holding her firmly as she tried to pull away. 'Look at me, Jane. Look at me!'

She was dominated by the force of his will, caught by his compelling gaze rather than by his physical strength. 'You must never say that again. You will not even think it. Do you hear me?'

She blinked, blinded by tears. 'It's the truth. You

don't know . . .' She choked as the sickness rose in her throat. 'I feel so dirty . . . so vile . . .'

'He is the vile one.' Stuart felt her pain stab his own heart. He held her close as she began to tremble, his lips brushing against her hair. 'You are as sweet and un-tainted as you ever were. You have to believe that, my darling. He abused your body . . . Don't let him crush your spirit.'

'Oh, Stuart.' She sobbed into his shoulder, overcome by the pain she had tried so hard to subjugate. 'I thought you would turn from me in disgust.'

'My love.' He held her tighter than before, wanting to absorb her hurt into himself. 'My disgust is all for the beast who calls himself a man—and a man of the cloth, at that! I am ashamed that any man could sink so low.'

'He said that he would kill you if I left him, and that Sarah would suffer for it, too.'

'So you meant to sacrifice yourself once more?' Stuart's face was grim as he looked down at her.

'I should never have let him touch me again. I would rather kill him—or myself.'

'I'll kill him myself and save you the trouble!'

'No!' She raised her gaze to his in urgent protest. 'Please don't murder him, Stuart. If it was ever dis-covered, you would hang for it. We must be careful until the next ship arrives; then we'll leave together.'

'I won't let you go back to him, Jane. What kind of a man do you think I am? I might as well cut my own throat now and have done with it. We should both be better off dead.'

Despite herself, she felt the relief wash through her. 'No, I can never go back to him now.'

Once she had admitted it, she knew it was true, and a sense of release flooded into her mind. Even if she were willing to take the risk, Stuart would never allow it. She had always known what his reaction would be. Now she accepted the inevitable. Her own weakness had betrayed them both. Their course was set.

'I shouldn't have told you.'

'Would you rather lie to me, Jane?'

'No . . .' She sighed, acknowledging her defeat. He was stronger than she—strong enough to carry her burdens as well as his own. She knew now that he would never have accepted her lies even if she had been able to carry them through. Yet there was still one worry on her mind, and she looked up at him anxiously. 'What about Sarah? Charles loves her, but he can't protect her from her brother.'

'They'll be safe enough in the village.' His lips thinned into a determined line. 'Go back there now, Jane. I'll join you when I've settled with Obadiah.'

She had known it must come to this, but her heart was heavy as she saw the anger in him. 'You—You won't do anything foolish?'

'I shall not kill him—this time—but he'll pay for what he's done to you!'

There was a cold vengeance in him that told her it was useless to argue. She was powerless to prevent the coming confrontation. All she could do was to wait and pray. Pray that neither man would kill the other . . .

'So she ran to you, after all?' Obadiah's face creased with spite as he stared at the man blocking his path. 'I might have known the bitch would betray me.'

Disgust made Stuart's stomach turn. The swine showed no sign of shame or remorse. He was a gentleman by birth, but he had behaved like an ignorant brute, abusing his wife in a way that would sicken any decent man.

'After what you did, I wonder you dare stand there and call her names! You're not fit to live!' Stuart's lip curled in scorn as he saw a muscle twitch in the missionary's cheek. 'I came here to kill you, but Jane was right. You're not worth the effort.'

His dart struck home as he had intended. Rage filled the other man's face as he made a sudden lunge at Stuart, flailing with his fists. Stuart laughed as he nimbly avoided the wild blows, parrying a succession of fierce hits with his forearms. He had learned to defend himself in a hundred dingy streets in every port in the world. He had faced broken bottles, knives and bare fists, surviving cowardly attacks in dark alleys and a score of grudge-fights with disgruntled sailors. He was more than a match for the missionary and he knew it, enjoying his superiority, and wanting to exact payment to the full.

Thorne was breathing hard, his frustration growing as he began to realise he was being soundly thrashed. He grunted, lunging recklessly as he tried to wipe the mockery from his tormentor's face, and succeeding only in wearing himself out. He was panting now, smarting from anger and humiliation.

'How does it feel?' Stuart asked. He saw an opening and took it, smashing an iron-hard fist into the other's mouth. A trickle of blood ran from his opponent's cut lip, and he smiled with satisfaction. 'Do you like being humiliated? Do you enjoy pain?' He landed several telling blows one after the other, causing the missionary to stumble and retreat.

Knocked to the ground by a final punch, Obadiah lay where he fell, panting for breath. His eyes were resentful as he looked up into the vengeful features of the man standing over him. He was beaten and he knew it, but the hatred spilled out of him in a torrent of spite.

'You'll pay for this! I'll sue you for enticement, and I'll divorce her. She'll be an outcast from her own class —and spat on by decent women.'

'You're a fool, Thorne!' Stuart looked at him with contempt. 'Do you imagine your threats frighten me? Where we're going, you will never find us.'

'You think you've won, but you'll be sorry. She's a child of the Devil!'

Stuart's laughter was chilling, silencing him at last. 'I'll take my chances with her. If she hadn't begged for your life, you would be dead. Remember that when you curse her, and be warned. Touch either her or Sarah again and I'll come after you. Next time I won't be so easy on you!'

Rising to his feet, Obadiah wiped the back of his hand

across his mouth. 'My sister is none of your concern. If you or that half-wit Charles Heatherton entice her away from my care, I'll see you go to prison for it.'

'I have no idea where your sister is, but if she has a grain of sense, she has gone to the village, where she will be safe.'

'Sarah is my ward. I have rights over her . . .'

'You sicken me.' Stuart's eyes narrowed. 'I ought to kill you now.'

Fear flickered momentarily in Obadiah's eyes. For a moment he met Stuart's hard gaze, then his own dropped as he realised his threats were useless. In England he might be able to cause a certain amount of unpleasantness for his rival, but here on the island he was powerless. Scowling, he turned and strode away without another word.

Stuart watched him go. While Thorne lived, Jane would never really be free. The man was vindictive, and he had no doubt that he would cause them all a great deal of trouble. It would certainly be easier for everyone if he were dead. Unfortunately, cold-blooded murder was not in his nature. In all his years before the mast he had never condemned a man to death without searching his conscience for any hint of self-interest; and though he had ordered many floggings, none of them had given him the slightest personal gratification.

Today, though, it had been very satisfactory to punish the swine who had hurt Jane. Feeling the slight soreness across his knuckles, Stuart smiled wryly. He could handle Mr Obadiah Thorne, no matter what. A surge of confidence went through him, and he realised he had not felt so good since *Sea-Sprite* had sunk. A look of dedication settled on his carved features. Somehow he would get Jane away from this island; he would make a decent life for them both, however long it took.

His smile faded as he remembered the shamed look in her eyes when she had told him what had happened. Anger flared in him again. He should have broken Thorne's neck! He recalled the moment when she had begun to awaken as a woman in his arms. She had been like a delicate rose, her petals unfolding one by one to the warmth of the sun. Now that sweet flower had been crushed beneath a swine's feet. Could he make it bloom again? Suddenly he knew that this was the most important of all. Jane was a sensitive woman, and he had gussed long ago that she had been badly hurt as a child. Despite this, she had emerged as a whole person, shy yet strong—and so full of love.

'I'll teach you to trust again, Jane.' He spoke the words aloud as if making a vow. 'God help me, I'll wait for ever if need be!'

Jane ran to meet Stuart as she saw him coming, her eyes searching his face anxiously for any sign of injury, and finding none. Relief flooded through her. He was unhurt, but what had he done?

He saw the expression in her eyes and smiled wryly, answering her unspoken question. 'He's still alive, Jane. I should have broken his damned neck, but I'm not a murderer—yet!'

She smiled, the anxiety leaving her eyes. 'I always knew that. You were a stern master of *Sea-Sprite*, but there was compassion in you. You would not otherwise have allowed Morna to nurse Jared after he was flogged.'

'That all seems a long, long time ago.'

'Yes. It was in another life.' She sighed, her face clouding. 'Has Obadiah agreed to let me go?'

'I doubt he will bother you again.' He reached out to touch her cheek, noticing the slight withdrawal in her. She conquered her fear almost at once, but it had been there. Damn Thorne to hell! He withdrew his hand and gave her an apologetic look. 'There was no sign of Sarah at the mission. Her brother seemed to imagine I had spirited her away. Do you know where she is?'

'Not exactly. She has gone with Charles, I know that much. Apparently he has found a secret place on the other side of the island. They mean to hide there until a ship comes.'

'They would have been safe enough in the village.'

'Sarah made the decision. I think she felt she might weaken if Obadiah came after her. She has been so much under his domination that she needs time to find herself.'

He nodded, his eyes thoughtful. 'And you, Jane —what do you need?'

She stared at him. 'I don't understand.'

'Don't you?' Had he misread that slight tremor when he touched her? 'Are you sure?' Reaching out, he drew her gently into his arms, his lips brushing hers in the lightest of kisses. Immediately she stiffened and he let her go, his eyes searching her face. 'You know I would never hurt you. I give my word that I shall never force you to do something that frightens you. Please believe me, Jane.'

'I know. I'm sorry.' She gazed up at him with a desperate appeal. 'I'm not afraid of you. It's just that . . .'

'You don't have to explain. I understand, my dearest, and I promise I shall be patient. You need time to forget. That's why I think it will be best if you take up the Queen's offer to occupy the hut she had built for you.' He saw the pain in her eyes and knew that he had guessed right.

'Perhaps. Just for a while.'

Jane turned her face aside, her emotions confused. Stuart was simply being considerate, so why should she feel so hurt? He had told her that what had happened would not change his feelings towards her, but how could she be sure? How could she be certain that his concern for her was not actually pity?

She gave him a tremulous smile, and began to walk away.

The islanders were fishing in the blue waters of the lagoon. Watching from the beach, Jane smiled at the way everyone joined in what seemed to be an occasion for fun rather than work. The large shoal of fish had been spotted only a short time earlier, and a summons from Kumi had brought the whole village pouring out on to the beach. Men, women and children were now in the water, driving the fish towards their nets. At first Jane had thought the noise of the swimmers would frighten the fish away, but then she realised that it was a clever method of securing a rich harvest from the sea. Her eyes dwelt for a while on the glistening, sun-bronzed back of the man she loved. Stuart had joined the men holding the nets, helping to drag their heavy load to the shore. It was obvious that he was enjoying himself, and she wished that she had the courage to join the women and children who were now amusing themselves in the shallows. Some of them were calling to her.

She hesitated for a moment longer, then kicked off her shoes, hitching her skirt to just below her knees as she gave in to temptation. The water was deliciously cool, and the wet sand squelched between her toes as she reached the happy group. She was immediately surrounded by the children. Now that she lived among them, they had lost all their shyness towards her. They had become accustomed to seeing her help with the daily chores of village life, and they saw no reason to differentiate between her and the other women. Laughing and giggling, they began to splash her, soaking her dress within seconds. Realising it was too late for anything else, Jane joined in the game, bending down to cup the water in her hands and chasing the youngsters, who squealed with delight and renewed their own efforts. Her hair was straggling wetly half-way down her back, and her dress felt heavy as it clung to her body. Laughing, she gave her young tormentors best and ran from the water, flopping down on the sand.

Still watching the children, she was unaware that she herself was being observed until the shadow fell across her. Glancing up, she found herself staring into a pair of smiling blue-grey eyes. Her heart jerked and then began to race wildly as Stuart threw himself down beside her.

She was very conscious of the muscular strength of him as his tanned skin glistened in the sun, little droplets of water trickling into the sand.

'You look as if you were having fun.'

'Yes, I was.' Her eyes met his and she felt a dizzy sensation, as if she were being drawn down into a whirlpool. 'They are such beautiful people.'

'You are beautiful, Jane.' She opened her eyes wide, her mouth trembling as he leant across to brush his lips gently over hers. 'Like a rose of early summer . . .'

'That sounds poetical, Stuart.' She smiled shyly up at him.

> 'Go, lovely Rose!
> Tell her, that wastes her time and me,
> That now she knows,
> When I resemble her to thee,
> How sweet and fair she seems to be.
>
> Tell her that's young
> And shuns to have her graces spied,
> That hadst thou sprung
> In deserts, where no men abide
> Thou must have uncommended died.
>
> Small is the worth
> Of beauty from the light retired:
> Bid her come forth,
> Suffer herself to be desired,
> And not blush so to be admired.
>
> Then die! that she
> The common fate of all things rare
> May read in thee:
> How small a part of time they share
> That are so wondrous sweet and fair!'

As he finished quoting the lines, Jane looked at him in wonder. 'I did not know you were a poet, Stuart.'

He laughed, and shook his head. 'Do not credit me with undeserved praise! Those words belong to a poet of the seventeenth century—Edmund Waller.'

'Yet you spoke them as though you knew them well.'

There was an odd, self-mocking light in his eyes. 'A man has to fill his time at sea somehow. I've read a great deal . . .'

'You are always surprising me,' Jane said, feeling the love flow out of her towards him. 'I like poetry, too. Do you know any of Colonel Lovelace's poems?'

> 'Tell me not, Sweet, I am unkind
> That from the nunnery
> Of thy chaste breast and quiet mind
> To war and arms I fly . . .'

She laughed in delight, joining in the last verse of the poem. It was odd to hear such romantic lines from the lips of a hardened seaman, yet it was also deeply touching. Looking at his strong, stern features, she realised that there was so much she still had to learn about this man. And she wanted to learn. She wanted to share everything with him. Her days—and her nights. She needed to put the nightmare of her unhappy marriage behind her.

'Stuart . . .' She reached out to touch his hand tentatively. 'I was thinking that I . . . that we might . . .'

'Yes, Jane?' he asked as she faltered over the words. His pulses quickened. What was she trying to say? Could it possibly be . . . The sudden, excited cries of the islanders distracted them both.

'Is it more fish?' Jane asked as she saw the men gazing seaward.

'No, I don't think so.' Stuart frowned as he followed the direction of the pointing fingers. For a moment he could not be sure what was causing the excitement, then he saw the ship on the horizon. At the moment she was still some distance away but seemed to be heading towards the island. 'It's a ship.'

'A ship! Where?'

Stuart got up, giving her his hand to pull her to her feet. They walked down to join the islanders who had gathered at the water's edge, watching as the sails loomed ever larger and the vessel bore down on them.

Jane glanced at her companion anxiously. 'It can't be the supply ship yet, can it?'

'No, I don't think it is the Commissioners' ship. She's more like a. . . .' He stiffened, his eyes straining seaward. 'It can't be . . .'

She sensed the tension in him, her eyes searching his face. 'What is it? What is wrong?'

'I'm not sure—but I don't like it.' He looked down at her, his manner suddenly authoritative. 'I want you to go to the other side of the island, Jane. Tell Charles and Sarah that a ship has arrived; they are to be prepared to leave, but they must not come unless I send for them. I want you to stay with them until I tell you it's safe to return.'

'I don't understand.' Jane stood unmoving, staring at him stubbornly. 'I can't just desert you—and these people. If there is danger, I want to . . .'

'What you want isn't important.' The harshness in his voice startled her. 'You will do as I tell you. Do you understand me?'

She had not seen that steely look in his eyes since the day he ordered Jared to be whipped on board *Sea-Sprite*. All at once he was in command, an entirely different man from the one who had quoted poetry to her a moment ago. For a few seconds more she gazed at him, wanting to refuse this peremptory order, then her eyes dropped. The man she loved was gentle and kind, but there was an iron will beneath the velvet mask. If she tried to disobey, he would drag her to the other side of the island himself. Besides, if there was danger, Charles and Sarah must be warned.

'Yes, I understand,' she whispered. 'I'll do as you say. But please take care.'

He laughed, his strong white teeth gleaming as they bared in a predator's grin. 'If my guess is right, it is not I who need to take care!'

Suddenly she knew why he was sending her away, and

she gasped. 'You think it's the mutineers who set you adrift, don't you?'

'Perhaps.' He moved towards her purposefully. 'Go now, Jane, or, so help me, I'll . . .'

She never knew what he meant to say. Whirling round, she began to run barefoot across the sand. If Stuart was right, it was terribly important that Sarah and Charles should remain hidden. Obadiah had threatened to thrash his sister's lover, but Jack Thorne would not stop at threats!

An odd hush had fallen over the islanders as the unfamiliar ship anchored in the lagoon. It was almost as if they sensed there was evil aboard her, Stuart thought. Some of the men had suggested taking their boats out to meet the newcomers, as was their custom, but Prince Kumi shook his head, his face grave as Stuart joined him.

'It is the ship from Ma-Llalla's dream,' he said. 'It is just as she described her to me. There are evil men on board.'

'If that vessel is still in the hands of the men who set Charles and me adrift, I fear you are right, Kumi.'

'These men are your enemies?' Kumi stared at him. 'What should we do, Captain Smithy? How can we stop these strangers coming to our island? Should we attack them at once and drive them into the sea?'

'Your weapons would be useless against their guns, Kumi. It may be that they come only to replenish their stores, and will leave again when they have what they want. To attack them might cause unnecessary bloodshed.'

Kumi nodded. 'You speak wisely, my friend. It may be as you say. We shall wait and see what happens. But what will you do if these men are your enemies?'

'I have sworn to kill their leader if our paths should cross again, but I cannot endanger your people. I shall do nothing that might cause trouble, Kumi.'

'You are our friend, Captain Smithy. I believe we may need your help against these strangers.'

'You must know that I would do anything to help you. I owe you my life.'

'It is so,' Kumi agreed. 'Then you and I will meet the strangers together. I shall send my people to hide until we learn their intentions.'

A flicker of a smile passed across Stuart's lips. 'You are a wise leader of your people.'

'Ma-Llalla is our Queen. Her word is law, but it is my duty to protect her and the others.'

He turned to give instructions to the villagers, who fled swiftly and silently into the trees; then he came to stand by Stuart's side as together they watched a small boat put out from the ship. They waited in silence as the craft beached and about ten men got out. The newcomers were all carrying long guns and seemed ill at ease, hesitating uncertainly and looking up and down the long, deserted beach as if they expected something to happen. They held an urgent conversation, then three of them detached themselves from the main group and began to walk up the beach towards Stuart and the Prince.

Stuart stiffened as he recognised their leader, and the memory of their last meeting caused a burning sensation in his guts. His hands clenched at his sides, and it was all that he could do to control the anger that flared in him. He had fought the agony and hardships of the days adrift on the open sea by promising himself revenge if ever he met Jack Thorne again, and only his duty to Kumi kept him silent as his enemy halted a few paces in front of him, smiling cockily.

'So you survived, Smithson? Well, I can't say I'm surprised. I thought at the time that I should have slit your throat and had done with it.'

'That might have proved harder than you expected,' Stuart replied in a deceptively mild voice. 'In case you're thinking of trying something similar now, I should warn you that you are being observed. Admittedly you could slaughter a few of the natives before they got to you, but there are far too many of them. My advice to you is to trade fairly with these people and go quietly.'

'I'm not a complete fool!' Jack Thorne said. 'Besides, we haven't come here to murder or plunder. I've heard there's a missionary here by the name of Obadiah Thorne. Is that true?'

'Yes. Where did you hear that?'

'We called at an island two days' sailing from here, where there's a planter by the name of Stretton. He says he travelled with the missionary.'

'If you come in peace, why did you bring the guns?'

'We weren't sure if the natives were friendly. We've had some nasty experiences on some of the islands in these waters, I can tell you! We didn't even know if this was the right one.'

'I'd have thought you would be living in luxury in Europe or the Americas by now.'

'With every British ship on the high seas searching for us?' Jack Thorne's mouth curved in a sneer. 'There's a price on our heads, Smithson. We've been playing hide and seek with the British navy for months. Somehow they seem to know more about us than they should.'

'So the gold is worthless to you. You should have thought of that before you incited the men to mutiny.'

'We'll use it to buy ourselves a pardon.'

Stuart's hands itched to fasten themselves around his throat. The cool impudence of the man was beyond belief. It was obvious that he had come here in the hope of persuading his brother to act as an intermediary for the mutineers. He believed he could rectify his foul crimes simply by offering to give back the stolen gold. Rage burned in Stuart's heart, and it took all his will-power to keep up the pretence of calmness.

As if sensing the tension in him, Kumi laid a restraining hand on his arm. Then he turned his black gaze on the stranger, his expression giving no hint of what was in his mind as he spoke.

'If you and your men come in peace, you are welcome to food and water. You may visit the missionary and stay at that end of the island, but you will not enter our village without permission.'

Jack Thorne stared at him, surprise in his face. Until Kumi spoke, he had not realised that the native understood English. A sarcastic comment rose to his lips and died as he met the Prince's steady gaze. Although he felt only contempt for the ignorant people of the islands and would not hesitate to turn his guns on them at the slightest provocation, there was something about this one that evoked a grudging respect. A shiver went through him; it was almost as though someone had walked on his grave, he thought, then dismissed the foolish notion with a wry smile. He had never feared death and he did not fear it now, yet there was something in those dark eyes. . . .

'I thank you for your welcome,' he said, forcing a smile to his lips. 'Who are you, sir?'

'I am Kumi, brother of Queen Ma-Llalla.' The Prince's fingers gripped Stuart's arm. 'This man is my friend. Walk in peace on our island, and none shall harm you. But destroy that peace, and you shall none of you leave here alive.'

Stuart sensed the conflict in his enemy, seeing the fear, anger and resentment battle in his eyes for supremacy. Jack Thorne did not take orders easily, especially from a man he would consider his inferior. For a moment he seemed to hesitate, as though his mind played with the idea of killing Kumi and found it pleasurable, then he shrugged and turned away, walking back to join his companions. They appeared to argue for a while, then half of them followed their leader down the beach towards the mission, while the others rowed their boat back to the ship.

'So far, so good,' Stuart murmured. 'If I were you, I should keep a close watch on them, Kumi.'

'We are as one in our thoughts, my friend.' Kumi's eyes were as black as the night. 'That one has no truth in him. He will bring evil to us. I feel it here.' He thumped his chest with his fist. 'Ma-Llalla was right to fear his coming, and it was the missionary who brought him here . . .'

Stuart opened his mouth to defend Obadiah, but the protest died unspoken. In his own way, the missionary was every bit as bad as his rogue of a brother. Perhaps Jack was the better of the two, Stuart thought. At least his evil deeds were done openly, not behind a cloak of respectability. He did not attempt to justify what he did by saying it was done in the name of justice. A grim smile touched Stuart's lips as he pictured the reunion between the brothers. There could be little love lost on either side. Perhaps Jack would realise that his cause was hopeless and take his ship and his crew elsewhere; it would be the best thing for everyone concerned.

'I must find Jane and tell her what has happened,' he said. 'It will be safer for her and the others to stay where they are for the moment. You should warn your women not to stray from the village alone while that ship is in the lagoon. These men are not to be trusted.'

'It will be difficult for them to understand,' Kumi replied sadly. 'They have known only freedom.'

'Perhaps it will only be for a short while.'

'Perhaps.' Kumi's expression did not lighten. 'Yet I fear that this is the beginning . . .'

'You are sure he is Obadiah's brother?' Jane looked at Stuart anxiously. 'Yes, he must be. Why else would he come here?'

'I think the mutineers have been running scared since they stole the gold and murdered the Captain. The British navy is hunting for them, and they're afraid to risk an encounter in the port of a civilised country, so they've been sailing round these seas, hiding on uninhabited islands. The gold is useless without the freedom to spend it, so now they hope to bargain for a pardon.'

'With Obadiah's help? He will never consent! You know how righteous he is. He'll tell them they must give themselves up.'

Stuart nodded, his expression grim. 'That was my first

thought. But supposing Jack convinces him that the men never meant to mutiny, that it was forced on them by harsh treatment? If he believed they were truly repentant, he might feel it his duty to try to help them.'

Jane considered the idea for a moment, then shook her head. 'I believe he would be more concerned with saving their souls.'

'You're probably right.' Stuart drew a deep breath. 'Which means that their last hope will be gone.'

'You think that will make them more dangerous?'

'I'm afraid it might. If they know there is nothing but a hangman's noose waiting for them, they have nothing to lose. Why should they simply sail away? It's months since any of them have been near a woman, and they must have seen the women on the beach before Kumi sent them to hide.'

Jane shuddered inwardly. Having experienced the horror of rape herself, she feared for the innocent girls who had been her friends. They thought of loving as a natural, spontaneous happening between individuals who cared for one another; the brutal lust of drunken sailors would terrify them. They would not be prepared for it, and they would not understand the minds of their tormentors.

Stuart saw the look on her face and cursed himself for a fool. How could he have forgotten, even for a moment. 'I'm sorry. I didn't think about what I was saying. I'm a careless idiot!'

She blinked in surprise, then realised that he thought she was afraid for herself. 'Don't be sorry, Stuart. I was thinking of those lovely, innocent girls, not myself. I—I have come to terms with what Obadiah . . . It doesn't hurt me so much now.'

'I'm glad.' Stuart reached out to touch her cheek gently. 'You know I have to go back, Jane. I promised Kumi my help, and you'll be safe enough here with Charles and Sarah. I could never have found this place if he hadn't shown me the entrance.'

'Yes, I understand. You must do what you can.' Jane

smiled at him shyly. 'Please take care of yourself. You know I love you . . .'

'My dearest girl.' He drew her into his arms, kissing her softly on the lips. He felt her tremble, but she did not draw away, even when his embrace tightened round her. 'I'll come back to you as soon as I'm able,' he whispered. 'Promise me you will stay here until it's safe?'

'Yes, of course. You have enough problems without worrying about me.' Jane looked up at him in concern. 'Do you think I should tell Sarah that her other brother is here? She seems to remember him with affection, but I'm afraid of what he might do to Charles.'

'The man she thinks she remembers no longer exists. He might still care for her a little, but what of Charles? He is slowly recovering his health—especially since he's had Sarah to care for—but the shock of seeing the man who condemned him to a living hell might be too much for him.'

Her instincts told her that he was right. It would be better for the young couple to remain in their hideaway for the moment. No good could come to either of them from a meeting with the mutineers, and Sarah would simply be ashamed to discover the depths to which her favourite brother had sunk. There was no point in giving her pain.

'Then I shall tell her nothing.' Jane caught Stuart's sleeve as he turned away. 'You will be careful?'

Laughter glowed in the blue-grey eyes. 'I'm a hard man to kill! The sea has tried many times, but I've fought her. I'll not die before my time, and I don't think it has come yet.'

She smiled despite her fears, watching as he left her. Her eyes followed him as he disappeared into the dense mass of trees that covered the lower slopes of the mountain, hiding the secret caves in which Sarah and Charles had taken refuge.

Sighing, she turned away at last. Why did Jack Thorne have to come to the island, she wondered. On the beach earlier, it had seemed that she and Stuart were at last beginning to find a way to reach each other, and just now his kiss had seemed to promise so much. Within her, Jane knew a feeling of peace. She had conquered the fear that Obadiah's savage attack had instilled in her. Now she was ready to begin a new relationship with the man she had loved for so long . . .

The pale light of the moon cast a silver shadow over the sea as Stuart paused to gaze down at the bay. It stirred him deeply, arousing a nostalgic longing to be the master of his own ship again. His love of the sea had been born in him. He had been brought up in Sussex, and the salty tang of the air seemed to have mingled with his mother's milk. It was in his blood, a part of him that would never die. The sea was a cruel mistress sometimes, but at others she filled his soul in a way that no mortal woman ever had . . . And yet there was a new hunger in him now. A hunger that grew every time he saw Jane. He had never believed that he could feel so strongly . . .

Stuart's thoughts were arrested as he heard the despairing cry from somewhere ahead of him. A nocturnal creature or a bird? It had sounded like a creature in pain. As a second and then a third cry rent the stillness, he realised that it was a woman's cry, or that of a young girl. He began to run towards it, his fear mounting as he heard other noises and realised that a struggle was going on. As he crashed through the trees, there came a scream so terrifying that it made his blood run cold. In another moment he understood what had caused it as he witnessed the bestial scene.

A young girl of barely fourteen was lying on the ground, her neck bent at an unnatural angle. Even before he was close enough to see her face, Stuart guessed that she was dead. Her pitiful body was naked, the shreds of her clothing scattered over a wide area as testament to the fight she had put up. It was quite obvious what had taken place before the final struggle that had killed her. Rage exploded in Stuart's head as the man turned to look at him, a drunken leer on his face. For a moment they stared at one another, and then Stuart sprang.

His first attack sent the sailor tumbling to the ground. For a brief second he seemed stunned, as if he hardly realised what was happening; then he gave a roar of anger and scrambled to his feet. A gleam of silver showed in his hand as he lunged at Stuart with the knife, only to find himself stabbing at air. He gawped stupidly at the empty space, his brain fogged by the wine he had imbibed. A second hammer-blow caught him on the chin and he staggered back, dropping the knife. Then he gave a shout of fury, shaping his fingers into claws as he went for Stuart's eyes.

'Damn you, Smithson,' he yelled. 'I'll kill you, you ba——!'

His curse was lost as Stuart's fist chopped across his throat, cutting off the flow of air. He choked, stumbling backwards, the beginning of fear in his eyes. Another blow sent him rocketing, his head jerking up as he reeled under the flurry of punishing hits. The blood poured from his nose and one eye closed beneath the painful blows, but still they came, hammering into him so that he could no longer think or see. Finally he fell, striking his head on the knob of a protruding tree root. He made a sighing sound, and then lay still.

Stuart stood over him, breathing hard as the anger raged on in him. Then, as the strange stillness registered in his heated brain, he bent over the sprawled body, turning the sailor's head to look at the back where it had split open. It was clear that he was dead. As his anger drained out, he cursed his own strength. He had not meant to kill the man, only to punish him for his crime. There would be trouble now, for sure. If the mutineers found his body, they would come looking for a fight. Swiftly removing the dead sailor's gun belt, he fastened it round his own waist; then he dragged the limp body into a clump of bushes, covering it as best he could. He would have to return later and make a proper job of it. Turning to the girl, he knelt beside her, feeling for any sign of a pulse, but, as he had feared, she was dead. She must have tried to escape after her ordeal and her attacker had broken her poor little neck. He was glad he had killed the brute! As he looked into the child's face, he suddenly recognised her.

'My God!' he exclaimed. 'It's the Queen's eldest daughter.'

There would be trouble now for certain, and not just because he had killed one of Jack Thorne's men. Kumi would be certain to exact payment for what had happened.

He lifted the girl's frail body in his arms, tears stinging his eyes as he gazed down at her. She was so young and innocent—and she had died at the hands of an evil beast. He knew that if he were Kumi he, too, would want revenge!

CHAPTER SIX

'I HAVE BROUGHT your daughter to you,' Stuart said, placing the girl's limp body in Kumi's arms. 'I am sorry—so very sorry. I heard her cry but I was too late to save her.'

Kumi's eyes were blacker than the night as he cradled the dead girl to his breast, crooning the distress he felt in a wail of grief and anger. Watching him, Stuart recognised the grief of a father for his child. It had vaguely shocked him when he first realised that Kumi was the father of Ma-Llalla's children, but gradually he had come to understand the islanders' culture, and now he saw no wrong in the relationship. It was their law that only royal blood should mingle with the Queen's, and had she had no brother, she must have taken her first cousin as her consort. It had always been so and would remain so—unless the missionaries succeeded in bringing change to the island. In any case, all the islanders were closely related, so that there had been no new blood for generations, something that Stuart believed must make them very vulnerable as a race. He had noticed that there was a high level of sterility among the women, and though there was little disease in the island, the slightest infection could quickly lead to death. He had wondered what might be the consequence if a contagious disease were ever to be brought to them from the outside world. It could wipe out the entire population within weeks. But Jack Thorne and his friends might accomplish that first . . .

Stuart saw that the Prince had passed his daughter Kalli to her mother, who was surrounded by several of her women. All of them were weeping bitterly as they carried the child away. Now Kumi's tears had dried and his face was set in lines of a cold, relentless anger. It was clear from his expression that he was determined on revenge.

'Where is the man who has killed Kalli, my child?'

'He is dead, Kumi. I hid his body under some bushes. I don't think his comrades will find it. They may believe he has just wandered off . . .' Stuart saw the bewilderment in Kumi's eyes and tried to explain. 'If you declare war on these men, it will mean much bloodshed.'

'You plead for them?'

'No. The man who killed Kalli deserved to die. It is for the sake of your own people that I ask you to stop and consider . . .'

'We are not warriors, Captain Smithy, but we shall fight to save those we love. If I allow one death to go unavenged, there will be others. If some of us must die to rid our island of evil, then so be it.' His eyes glittered in the moonlight, his face stamped with an ancient pride. 'You must choose. You stand with us or against us.'

'I have given my word that I will help you, and I shall keep it.'

'Good.' The Prince was thoughtful for a moment. 'I see that you have captured one of their weapons. If they did not have the fire-sticks, we would easily be able to defeat our enemies. I have a plan, but they must not suspect a trap. You did well to hide the body of the man you killed. Are you certain they cannot find it?'

'I shall return and make certain, Kumi.' Stuart stared at him. 'What do you plan to do?'

'Like you, I wish to prevent the shedding of innocent blood. We shall ask the strangers to a feast. The women will dance for them and we shall give them wine and food. When they grow careless, we shall take their weapons and . . .'

'If you disarm them, I can see that they are punished for their crimes, Kumi. They are all guilty of mutiny. In England they would face a trial for the murder of their Captain—and the punishment for that is death.'

'Yes . . .' Kumi nodded his agreement. 'They will be

tried and punished for what they have done. Your words are good, my friend. It shall be as you say.'

Stuart felt a surge of relief. 'Then we are agreed. I shall leave now and make sure that the corpse is well hidden.'

Leaving the village, Stuart wondered at the ease with which he gained the Prince's consent to take the mutineers back to England. He had expected Kumi to slaughter them without mercy once he had the advantage. He knew that there was nothing he could have done to prevent a massacre if the Prince had refused to listen. Except to warn Jack Thorne of the trap. That, however, was something he could not do. The islanders had saved his life; he owed them loyalty, though he disliked the idea of trickery.

It was an unsavoury business, but he felt easier about it now that Kumi had agreed to send the mutineers to England for trial. If Jack's men had attacked the islanders, he would not have hesitated to defend them, but a trap baited with wine and women left a sour taste in his mouth. Even swine like Jack Thorne deserved a fair trial. He would not be a party to murder.

He would need to be on his guard at this feast. Kumi meant him no harm personally, but he must be watchful all the same.

'Why do they keep beating those drums?' Sarah asked fretfully. 'I hate the sound of them; they frighten me.'

'They are having a feast, I expect,' Jane said, looking at her curiously. 'The drums have never upset you before. What's wrong? Why are you so worried tonight?'

'I don't know.' The girl shivered, hugging herself and staring moodily into the flames of their small fire. 'I just have a feeling that something terrible is going on. I wish Charles were here.'

'Yes . . .' Jane had to agree. 'I wish we at least knew where he was. You don't think he has gone to the other side of the island, do you?'

'He—He may have.' Sarah bit her lip. 'If he has, it's all my fault, Jane. Last night, after Stuart came to see you, I was curious about what was really going on. I wanted to know who these men are, and why they have come to the island. We've been waiting for a ship, so why has Stuart warned us to stay hidden?'

'He thought it was best, Sarah. You know that, don't you?'

Sarah nodded, looking guilty. 'I think Charles has gone to try and find out what he can, because I kept asking him about it.'

'Oh no!' Jane cried. 'We didn't tell you who they were, because it would only have frightened you. The men are the same ones who cast Stuart and Charles adrift in an open boat . . .'

'They can't be!' Sarah stared at her in fearful disbelief. 'Oh, why did I let him go? If they see Charles, they will kill him.'

'Why should they?'

'Because he was the only witness to the murder of their Captain. Stuart arrived a few seconds after he was dead. So without Charles's testimony, no one could be sure who actually did it.'

'But how can you know that? Charles can't remember anything. Did Stuart tell you?'

'No . . .' Sarah frowned. 'Charles has started to recall certain things. He can't remember everything yet, but he asked Stuart about it, and he told him the truth. It was the leader of the mutineers who murdered the Captain.' Sarah's eyes clouded with distress and she jumped to her feet. 'I'm going to look for Charles. He may be in danger.'

'No, you have to stay here. Charles will come back, my dear. Besides . . .' She paused awkwardly, not wanting to go on.

Sarah looked at her intently. 'What are you hiding from me, Jane? I've known there was something on your mind all day. What don't you want to tell me?'

Jane rose to stand beside her, taking her hand. 'I

didn't want to hurt you unnecessarily, my love. I thought it best you shouldn't know the truth, but if Charles has begun to recover his memory . . .'

Sarah gripped her hands, gazing into her face beseechingly. 'What should I know, Jane? Please tell me.'

Jane sighed. It was no use, she could not protect the girl any longer. She had to face the truth.

'The leader of the mutineers is called Jack, but I believe his real name is Saul. He came to the island to see Obadiah. He is your brother.'

'Saul is here?' Sarah's face was white with shock. She pressed her hand to her throat as she struggled to accept what Jane had just told her. 'He . . . Saul is the one who . . . Oh, I hate him for what he did to Charles. I hate both my brothers! They are both cruel and ruthless in their own way.'

'Hush, my love. You mustn't . . .'

Jane watched as the girl buried her face in her hands, her shoulders shaking as she began to cry. 'What am I going to do?' she choked. 'I feel so ashamed.'

'Don't cry, my love,' Jane said, stroking her hair. 'You are not to blame for what your brothers do.'

'But Charles will hate me for it when he realises who Jack Thorne is.' Sarah raised her tear-drenched eyes to Jane's. 'I love Charles so much, and—and I think I'm carrying his child.'

'Oh, Sarah . . .' Jane touched her cheek fondly. 'Charles will not stop loving you because of what your brother is. He cares for you deeply. Have you told him about the baby?'

'Not yet.' Sarah blushed. 'I can't really be sure, Jane, but I've stopped bleeding and I was sick this morning. When we were at home, I sometimes visited Obadiah's parishioners, and I used to hear the women complaining of sickness at such times. So I—I think perhaps I am with child.'

'Yes, I have wondered once or twice of late.' Jane looked at her anxiously. 'This is my fault. I have failed you, Sarah. You asked me for guidance and I failed to give it to you.'

'No—how could it be your fault?' Sarah laughed. 'I am not a child. I have never been so happy in my life as I have since I ran away with Charles. If Obadiah had been willing to listen, we might have married weeks ago. If I am a sinner, it is because he has forced me to it.'

'Do not talk of sin. How can it be a sin to love someone?' Jane smiled at her. 'Are you really happy?'

'Yes. Charles is so kind and gentle.' The radiance suddenly left her face. 'I couldn't bear it if anything happened to him. That's why I'm going to look for him and warn him.'

'Then I shall come with you,' Jane said, throwing water on the fire to douse the flames. 'But we must be very careful.'

Stuart stood with his back against a tree, watching the mutineers enjoy themselves. They had been drinking steadily for most of the evening, seeming to have no suspicions about the villagers' sudden change of attitude. Although they had come to the feast heavily armed with long-guns and pistols, most of their weapons lay carelessly abandoned on the ground as they cheered and shouted encouragement to the women dancing in the firelight. Some of them lost all caution as they joined the nubile dancers, laughing and capering wildly as they tried to follow the graceful movements of the lovely island girls. Several were already well on the way to becoming hopelessly drunk. Kumi's plan was working even better than he had hoped, Stuart thought as his eyes strayed to Jack Thorne. He alone had partaken sparingly of both food and wine, and his eyes were alert as he followed the antics of his men.

Could it be that he was suspicious? He was certainly an educated man, very different in background and inclination from the men he led. He must find his situation very frustrating, Stuart thought, wondering whether he had yet broached the subject of a pardon with his brother. The missionary had been invited to the feast, but had declined, as Kumi had expected. Since his parting from Jane, Obadiah had come to the village only when the Queen sent for him. His church was built, and a small congregation gathered there once a week at Ma-Llalla's insistence. Apparently he found the situation satisfactory. At all events, he had not tried to change it. Nor had he gone out of his way to speak to Jane. Perhaps he had at last realised that he was here on sufferance . . .

Stuart stiffened, his mind suddenly alerted as he saw a man step into the golden circle of the firelight. What on earth was Charles doing here tonight? He had expressly forbidden it. The young idiot's presence could ruin everything! If Jack recognised him, it could mean trouble.

Even as the thought entered his head, Stuart realised that his young friend was behaving very strangely. He was standing in the space before the fire, staring at the leader of the mutineers with a dawning horror in his eyes. It was as though he was frozen to the ground—as if he knew who the man was and what he had done.

'No, Charles, don't do it!' Stuart yelled, but his warning came too late.

With an agonised scream, Charles launched himself on the man he had just recognised as a murderer. His mind was hazy, still reeling from the shock of his discovery. Not really conscious of what he did, he remembered only the suffering of those hellish days and nights adrift on the sea when he had prayed to die—and he wanted to kill the man who had sentenced him to such an ordeal. His attack took the older man by surprise, and he went sprawling on his back in the dust as Charles hit out unmercifully. His advantage was short lived, however, and the two rolled over and over on the ground in a fierce fight.

Jack Thorne's shouts alarmed the other mutineers, sending a ripple through their ranks. They were not sure what was happening, but immediately suspected a trap. Cries went up from several throats, and one man grabbed for his gun. He began to shoot wildly, firing at anyone who moved, and wounding one of the girls he had been dancing with only a few seconds before. All at once everything went mad. The girls fled screaming as other mutineers began to fire indiscriminately, and several villagers were hit.

A spear thudded into the chest of the man who had fired first. His screams as he lay on the ground writhing in pain incited those mutineers who had not yet gone for their weapons. Now they found that the guns they had carelessly left lying around had somehow disappeared. Those with pistols pushed through their belts fired in panic as the menacing villagers closed in on them. Screams and shouts mingled with the thud of well-aimed spears. Men fell dying on either side as the short, fierce battle was fought to the bitter end. Perhaps a dozen of the villagers were killed or wounded, but they had been prepared for trouble and the mutineers had not. Outnumbered, drunk and confused, they threw away their empty pistols and fought hand to hand with the islanders.

Stuart's action in stopping the fight between Charles and Jack Thorne went unnoticed in the general confusion. He pulled Charles to his feet, holding him firmly as he struggled and begged to renew his efforts.

'Let me get at him . . . I'll kill the devil!'

'Be still, you young fool! You've done enough damage as it is.'

'I'll kill him! He deserves to die!'

'Don't be an idiot, Charles.' Stuart hauled him back as he tried to throw himself at the mutineer again. 'Let the law deal with him. Kumi has promised I shall be allowed to take him back to England for trial.'

Jack Thorne had been recovering his breath, eyeing them both with a kind of muted hatred. Now he wiped the blood from his mouth and got to his feet, staring at Stuart.

'Keep that fool away from me or I'll break his neck

next time!' He spat on the ground. 'So you were behind this little plot, Smithson? I ought to blow your brains out.'

'I wouldn't try it, if I were you,' Stuart warned. 'Take a look at what's happening around you. Kumi's people are in the mood for revenge. One of your men killed the Queen's eldest child. You were warned at the start, and you should have kept them under better control.'

'So that's what happened to Bracknell. I wondered where he had got to.'

'He's dead,' Stuart said calmly. 'I killed him when I found him attacking the girl. If you value your life, you had better give me your pistol.'

'Do you take me for a fool?'

'You're a fool if you resist! Kumi gave me his word that you would be granted a fair hearing.'

'The word of a savage!' Jack's lip curled. 'I'd as soon take my chance with a cobra.'

He reached for the pistol in his belt, but as he did so, Stuart lunged at him, knocking him backwards. They fell to the ground, Jack struggling and swearing wildly as they tussled for the pistol; then his head snapped back as Stuart's punch struck him on the chin, and he lay still, stunned. Stuart bent over him, removing the pistol and handing it to Charles.

'Shoot him if he tries anything, but only if he refuses to be sensible. There's been enough killing.' He clutched Charles's shoulder. 'We'll see him stand trial. It's the best way, lad.'

'Yes. I'm sorry I lost my head.' Charles looked around at the scene of devastation. Bodies lay everywhere, and the remaining mutineers were being herded into a small group. 'I never meant this to happen.'

'It might have happened anyway. Kumi was determined on revenge for his daughter's death. I only hope he will remember his promise to let me take the prisoners back to England. I must speak to him before he slaughters them all. Keep an eye on Jack! Don't let him escape.'

'Trust me!' Charles nodded grimly. 'I'll shoot him in the legs if I have to.'

'Good man.'

Stuart smiled briefly, than walked towards Kumi. The islanders had succeeded in rounding up half a dozen or so of the mutineers, all that were left out of a party of fifteen who had attended the feast. It was as he had feared: the Prince had wreaked a terrible revenge on his enemies, and there might be yet more bloodshed.

'We have vanquished the white demons!' Kumi cried as Stuart reached him. 'See! They are all taken.'

'You promised to capture them without bloodshed.'

Kumi's eyes were as black and cold as granite. 'It was not my people who began the fighting. We had to defend ourselves.'

'Yes, I know it was Charles who started it. Yet I have come to ask you to keep your word, Kumi. These men are criminals, and they must be tried in their own land.'

'They will be put to the test by the Wise One. If they are found guilty, they will be executed.'

The Wise One was a kind of witch doctor. He lived near the top of the mountain in a little cave, and Stuart knew that most of the islanders were afraid of him. He was called upon only in times of dire need. There was little doubt that he would find the mutineers guilty and condemn them to a cruel death.

'That's barbaric!' Stuart exclaimed without thinking. 'You can't do it, Kumi. You gave me your word.'

'I promised a fair trial.' Kumi's expression was unreadable. 'They will be tried and punished for the evil they have brought upon us.'

'But only one man attacked your child. You can't kill all of them because of that.'

'Seven of my people are dead; many more will die of their wounds. If I let these evil ones live, others like them will come and destroy us. This will be a warning to all who visit our island. I must defend my people.'

'I understand your anger, but they will be punished if you let me take them back to England. Many more people will hear of your brave deeds, and all will know that it is foolish to invade your island.' Stuart met his glittering gaze. 'I killed the man who murdered your daughter, Kumi. You owe me this much.'

'My people saved you from the sea. There is no debt between us.' Kumi made an impatient gesture, and three of his men came to stand at either side of Stuart. 'Go to your own hut, my friend. You will not be harmed, but do not try to interfere in what does not concern you.'

Recognising defeat, Stuart shrugged his shoulders and turned away. He was met by Charles, who was looking white and shaken.

'They dragged Jack off to one of the huts and locked him in with the others.' He shuddered. 'I daren't try to stop them. I would never have believed these people capable of such savagery; they've always seemed so gentle.'

'The sleeping demon lives in us all, Charles. Civilised men manage to control it most of the time, but it's there just the same. Kumi thinks he's saving his people from some unknown evil, but I believe they are doomed anyway.'

'Why?' Charles stared at him as they walked from the village together.

'It's just a feeling I have. Ma-Llalla feels it, too. That's why her dreams frighten her.' Stuart put his arm across the younger man's shoulders. 'So you've recovered your memory?'

'Yes. It all came back in a rush when I saw Jack's face. I couldn't think of anything else: I just knew I wanted to kill him.' He smiled oddly. 'It seems I have my own private demon.'

'Perhaps you have more reason than most.' Stuart's frown lightened. 'But I'm not sure that you would have killed him.'

'He would more likely have killed me if you hadn't stopped the fight.' Charles grinned self-consciously. 'You saved my life during the mutiny and kept me alive while we were adrift. I hadn't realised how much I owe you. I'll repay you when we get back to England.'

'What do you mean?'

'I've remembered who I am . . . and why I ran away to sea.' Charles gave a sheepish laugh. 'I'm afraid I was a spoiled brat. My father died when I was twelve, and my mother wanted to keep me tied to her apron-strings. So I ran off to be a sailor. My uncle is Lord Redbridge, and I'm his heir.'

'I see.' Stuart frowned. 'I'm glad for you, Charles. It means you have something to go back for, but you owe me nothing. I only did what any man would do for a friend.'

'Don't spurn me. I want to help you—and Jane.'

'Then don't offer me money, Charles. Not if you want us to remain friends. I may have lost everything else, but I still have my pride.' Stuart stiffened as he heard a slight rustling sound, placing a warning finger against his lips. 'Be quiet now; I heard something. Jack is not a fool, and will have left lookouts on board. Give me your gun. It may be they . . .'

Charles pulled the pistol from his belt, hardly daring to breathe as he handed it to him. 'It came from over there,' he whispered as he too heard the sound. 'What shall we do?'

'Follow me.' Stuart laid a hand on his arm. 'As softly as you can.'

He began to move stealthily towards the source of the sound, his finger resting lightly on the trigger of his pistol. Then, as he approached the clump of bushes from which the suspicious noise had come, a figure darted out and called to him.

'Stuart? Thank heavens! We were so frightened when we heard the shooting. What has happeneed?'

'Jane?' Stuart released the trigger, handing the pistol back to Charles as he moved to catch her in his arms. 'What are you doing here? I could have shot you! We thought you were a lookout from the ship.'

'I'm sorry, but we were anxious about Charles.'

'He's here with me,' Stuart growled. 'I suppose this

was Sarah's idea. They're a pair of young idiots, the both of them!'

Sarah had now emerged from the shadows, to be caught up in her lover's embrace. She glanced towards them, her manner obviously subdued. Jane saw her, then gazed up at Stuart with an appealing smile.

'They are in love,' she said. 'Sarah was determined to come, so I had to accompany her. I couldn't let her wander about on her own, could I?'

'No, I suppose you couldn't, you being you.' He laughed wryly. 'Oh, Jane, Jane . . . What am I going to do with you?'

'I've no idea.' She squeezed his arm. 'Please tell me what has been happening? We heard screaming and gun-shots. Did the mutineers turn on the villagers?'

'Charles precipitated the fight by attacking Jack. He recognised him and lost his head—but it might have ended the same way in any case.' He sighed deeply, knowing that she would be shocked and sickened by what he must tell her. 'Last night, after I left you, I stumbled on one of Ma-Llalla's daughters being abused. I was too late to save her, and I brought her body back to the village. Kumi wanted revenge. He led the mutineers into a trap . . .'

'Oh, Stuart, no! Couldn't you have stopped it somehow?'

Her look was almost accusing, and it pricked his conscience. He knew he ought to have done something —but what?

'Kumi promised to let them stand a fair trial—but it seems he meant his justice, not mine.'

'Surely he won't kill all of them?'

'I think it likely. He intends to try the prisoners and punish them himself. At least, they'll be judged by the witch doctor . . .'

'The witch doctor!' Jane cried in dismay. 'I didn't know they had one. I've never seen him in the village, have I?'

'No. They call him the Wise One, and he lives in a cave

near the crater. Most of the villagers are afraid of him.'

'The Wise One . . .' Jane shivered. 'Ma-Llalla called me that once. Do you think she imagines that I have some magic power? Is that why she wanted me to live in the village?'

'It's possible. You did save one of her children from choking the day you arrived.' Stuart put his arm about her waist. 'Who can know what these people really believe?'

'They seemed so innocent . . .' Turning to lay her head against his shoulder, she felt suddenly faint. 'It's horrible. Please, can we go back to the other side of the island? I don't think I can bear to be near the village while something so barbaric is going on.'

'Yes, of course. Come, I'll take you there.'

He smiled down at her, feeling surprised at the depth of the feeling she aroused in him. There was something about this woman that made him want to protect and care for her. He believed she needed him, and that was good. It warmed him inside. He had often felt the emptiness of his life during his years at sea, and now he knew what had been missing.

Taking Jane's hand, he led her away from the village as the drums began. Tonight there was something savage about the rhythmic beat that pulsated through the darkness, following them as they made their way to the far side of the island. Sensing the horror in the woman at his side, Stuart's arm was warm and comforting about her. He knew that her gentle nature had been shocked by what had happened earlier, and he could feel her trembling. He had intended to see her safely away from it all and then do what he could to secure the ship. If he could manage to persuade the remaining sailors that their best hope lay in a fair hearing in England, he might be able to rescue the situation even yet.

Now, however, he abandoned the idea of swimming out to the ship tonight. He could not desert Jane when she was so obviously distressed. She stumbled in the darkness, and he caught her against him. As her body pressed close to his, the heat flowed through his veins, becoming a flame—a flame of desire. He struggled to suppress it, telling himself that now was not the time to think of making love. Yet even as he tried to deny his own hunger, he felt an answering need in Jane herself.

'Oh, my dear one,' he whispered as she clung to him, her arms sliding up about his neck. 'I want you so much . . .'

'Help me,' Jane said, lifting her face to gaze up at him entreatingly. 'I've always been afraid of—of loving, and Obadiah made me feel so ashamed. But in your arms I think I might learn the true joy of being a woman. I want to be yours, Stuart.'

'My darling . . .' He traced the line of her cheek with fingers that throbbed with emotion, stroking gently down the slender arch of her throat and back to the nape of her neck. 'Are you quite sure?'

'Yes.' Jane's smile was fearless as she answered. 'I want to be with you now. Tonight . . .'

His lips moved softly over hers, demanding nothing yet, but promising much. 'Come,' he murmured. 'There is a secret cove where we can be quite alone.'

His smile sent her heart fluttering as their fingers entwined. Eager now, he pulled her in a new direction, encouraging her to run. Soon they were breathless, laughing as they dipped and weaved to avoid the over-hanging branches of the lush greenery. The ground veered away suddenly, and he urged caution, helping her as they scrambled down the rocky incline. The entrance was thickly covered with trailing plants, and they had to force their passage, but then the sandy floor of the cove was beneath them, the encircling arms of cliff on either side enfolding them in a silent, secret world of their own. Silent save for the gentle swish of the water as it lapped and sighed about the rocks.

'It's beautiful here,' Jane cried in delight. 'The water looks so clear.'

'And shallow in that pool by the rocks.' A gleam of mischief showed in his eyes as he reached to pull the combs from her hair, watching it tumble about her shoulders like a silken mantle. I've always wanted to see it like that, Jane.'

'It's too straight,' she protested shyly.

'No, it's like spun silk.' He slid his hands beneath it, letting the strands run through his fingers. 'Beautiful . . . like you. Now I want to see the rest of you, Jane.'

She trembled as his fingers began to unfasten the tiny buttons at the front of her bodice, but it was not from fear. Her heart was beating wildly as she stood unmoving, allowing him to undress her. He did so with a calm efficiency, as if his very deliberateness was meant to reassure her. She felt that she could have stopped him at any moment, but she did not want him to stop.

He pushed her shift down over one shoulder, kissing the satin skin, his lips trailing fire to the soft mounds of her breasts. Beneath the teasing of his flickering tongue, her nipples hardened, becoming erect as she felt the first stirring of desire. A tiny moan escaped her, and she swayed towards him.

'Not yet, my darling,' he laughed. 'We must learn to know each other's body first. We have all night for discovering what pleases us.'

With a little help from his strong hands, the last of her clothing slid to lie unheeded on the sand. For a moment he stood without touching her, drinking in the beauty of her body. Without the encumbrance of her clothing, she was even more slender than he had imagined, her breasts small but perfectly in proportion with the tiny waist and narrow hips. In the pale moonlight she looked like a marble statue, he thought, catching his breath. Then she made a hesitant move towards him, and he knew that she was human after all. A very vulnerable, desirable woman. She gazed at him uncertainly, her eyed seeming to ask for reassurance.

'Do—Do I please you?' she whispered. 'I—I know I am not beautiful, but . . .'

'You are lovely, and you please me very much!' He stopped her protests with a kiss. 'Come, I know you've always wanted to bathe naked in the sea.' He laughed as she looked startled. 'Don't deny it, Jane. I've seen you look at the native girls with such envy.'

'How well you know me! It always looks so wonderful, though I know it's quite immoral of me to think like that.'

He let her go briefly while he stripped off his own clothes, then he took her hand, pulling her towards the shallow pool. 'Forget all you've been taught, Jane. There's no shame in being like this together.'

'No, not with you,' she said, suddenly feeling gloriously free. She had never felt like this in her life. Never!

Breaking free of his grasp, she entered the pool first and shrieked as the cool water touched her skin. The water was so shallow that she could safely sit on the sandy floor. Stuart was laughing as he joined her, reaching out to catch her to him. She was unprepared for the shock as their flesh met briefly, sending little ripples of desire through her. Gasping, she moved away, splashing him to cover the intensity of her feelings. This longing to be one with him was so strong that it frightened her. His kisses were so sweet—but would it end in the same, hateful way as when her husband had raped her? If it did, she could not bear it. She loved this man so much, but what if he were as unfeeling and selfish as Obadiah?

Yet as he lay back in the water, pulling her down to kiss her once more, she knew that he could never be insensitive. If he cared only for his own pleasure, he could have taken her at once. This game he was playing was for her sake. Already his own desire was evident in the throbbing maleness that moved urgently beneath her. Yet he made no attempt to bring their loving to a hasty conclusion, his hands moving slowly but firmly over her back to arouse and tantalise her. Together they explored the secret places that had been forbidden to each, taking time to give and receive pleasure, savouring the moment of fulfilment to come.

Before Stuart lifted her in his arms to carry her up the

beach to the bed he had made of their clothes, Jane had already discovered the true meaning of physical love. She began to learn also that there were many ways in which a man and a woman can pleasure each other. Their coming together in the ultimate union was something to be anticipated, delayed until the last possible moment.

When that moment finally arrived, it swept her away on a tide of such intense joy that she cried out wildly, digging her nails into the flesh of his shoulders as she jerked and moaned beneath him. How could she ever have believed herself cold? But she had never understood herself until now. It was like being awakened from a long sleep. She was truly a woman at last. This was the glory of love. This was what the poets wrote of—the true meaning of life itself. It was not something dirty to be hidden behind closed doors, as so many women of her class seemed to imagine—as her own mother had clearly felt! The brutal act of Obadiah's lust had taken her to the depths of despair, but Stuart's love had lifted her to the heights. Love had triumphed over lust.

It was for love that she wept softly into the satin hardness if his shoulder. 'It—It was so beautiful,' she whispered. 'How can I ever thank you? I didn't know . . . I didn't know . . .'

'You made it beautiful for me,' he said huskily, stroking her hair. 'As a young man I knew my share of women, but I soon tired of sporting in the arm of a whore. There is physical pleasure, yes, but afterwards a great emptiness.' He laughed self-consciously. 'I have sometimes wondered at my celibate nature. Perhaps I should have been a monk?'

Jane lifted herself to lean on one elbow, her hair brushing his cheek as she looked down at him. 'I'm glad you aren't.'

He saw the teasing look in her eyes and marvelled at the change in her. She seemed to glow with an inner radiance that had not previously been there. He pulled her back down to him so that their bodies were pressed close again, his lips whispering about her neck as he tasted the salt of her sweat. 'So am I,' he murmured throatily. 'The thing about fasting is that, once you start to eat, you suddenly discover how hungry you are . . .'

All at once, he rolled her beneath him in the sand, their fingers entwining as he began to kiss her lips. She had not thought it possible to feel desire again so soon after it had been slaked, but her pulses raced and her breath came faster as she arched to meet his new demands.

She could hear only the rasp of his breathing, feel only the touch of his hands. She was not even aware that far away, on the other side of the island, the drums had stopped beating . . .

Ma-Llalla was angry. Kumi could see it in her eyes as she stared at him, and he felt her displeasure weigh on him heavily. He had served her faithfully all his life, obeying her orders without question. Even his vengeance on the strangers had been undertaken for her sake, so that she might rest easily at night, but now she was angry with him. He sank to his knees before her, finding no shame in his submission to his Queen. Her will was the law.

'What you have done tonight is bad, Kumi,' she said, her face stern. 'I fear it will bring a terrible evil to our people.'

He gazed up at her. It was as if she had stabbed him to the heart. 'But your dreams told of the pain these men would bring. It was they who attacked us. I have destroyed them so that you may be at peace.'

'You broke your word to deliver these strangers to justice—their justice, not ours. That was wrong, Kumi.'

'They were condemned by the Wise One. He saw their guilt written in the fire. This has always been our way.'

'It was the old way,' the Queen said. 'We must learn to change if we are to survive. Because of what you have done, Jane will leave us. I have seen into her heart, and I know she will be sickened by so much death. If she goes, we are doomed. I have seen this in my dreams.'

'Then I shall make certain that she cannot leave.'

Ma-Llalla's face was troubled. 'This will mean more killing. Yet I fear it must be done. Jane must not leave us.'

Kumi bowed his head, bending to kiss her feet. 'What must be done, will be done. I give you my word.'

'Then let it be done swiftly.'

'Your word is my law, O Gracious One.'

Kumi got to his feet, making a signal to his men. The Queen must be obeyed. There was but one way to be certain that no one could leave the island.

Jane was still sleeping, her head resting against his shoulder as trustingly as a child's. Looking down at her, Stuart felt a deep tenderness. She had wept in his arms before she slept, tears of happiness, and she had opened her heart to him, telling him things that he was sure no one else had ever heard from her. He had felt her pain as she recounted her memories of childhood, understanding at last the true nature of this woman. He wondered at the strength that had brought her through the lonely years. She had so much love within her: love that the years of repression had failed to extinguish. Now she was offering that love to him, and he felt humbled and a little afraid. How could he deserve a love like that? It was a great responsibility, and it would kill him to fail her . . .

For a moment he could not place the reason for the red glow in the sky. The sun would not rise for another hour or so. Besides, there was something odd about that ruddy sky—Damnation! The certainty was in him as he gently dislodged Jane's head from his shoulder, placing a pillow made out of his shirt beneath it so that she should not wake. His heart was drumming a wild beat as he ran across the beach, scrambling up the rocky incline to find a vantage-point that would give him a view of the lagoon.

It must be the ship. It had to be. He knew it even as he prayed that he was wrong. What a stupid fool he had been not to realise what Kumi would do, but it had not occurred to him that the Prince would set fire to the ship. It should have done. He ought to have secured the vessel at once . . . At the top of the cliff, he saw the fierce red glow above the lagoon. It was not possible to see the fire from this distance, but there was no mistaking that ball of flame and smoke. He could smell the stench of tar, wood and canvas on the air. The waste of it all made him groan aloud.

'Damn you, Kumi! Why did you have to do it?'

They were trapped on the island, and it was his fault! His own stupidity made him feel sick and angry. There was no excusing it. Jane would have understood why he had to leave her if he had explained. It would not have been easy to hold the ship against Kumi, but if he had been on board, he might have been able to persuade him against destroying it. Now they would be forced to remain on the island until the Commissioners' ship came—if they all survived until then. There was no telling what Kumi might do now he had tasted an easy victory. Besides, Obadiah might decide to return to England with them, and that would make it an uncomfortable journey for them all.

He really was a fool! It had not entered his mind until this moment that the missionary could be in danger. If Obadiah guessed what had been going on, he would be terribly angry and would try to remonstrate with the islanders. He might even do worse. In his present mood, Kumi was quite capable of killing him. He had never liked the missionary, and would consider himself justified if he discovered that the mutineers' leader had been Obadiah's brother.

Stuart could not stand by while yet another murder took place. Despite his differences with Obadiah, he had to warn him. Hurrying back down to the beach, he shook Jane's shoulder to wake her. 'I must go to the mission,' he explained as she looked at him in alarm. 'I'm sorry, Jane. It hadn't struck me that Obadiah's life might be in danger.'

She got to her feet, brushing the sand from her clothes. 'I'm coming with you. No, Stuart, you can't stop me. I owe him this much. If I am there, Kumi won't harm him.'

She was right. He acknowledged it with a nod. Jane's influence with the Queen was far greater than his own. 'Come then, I only hope we aren't too late.' He saw that she had noticed the strange glow in the sky, and he answered the question in her eyes. 'Kumi must have fired the ship. It's my fault. I should have secured it when we left the village.'

'Then it was just as much my fault,' Jane said. 'I asked you to take me away. I kept you with me.'

'I wanted to stay.' He pressed her to him briefly. 'Whatever happens, I shall never forget this night.'

'Nor I . . .' She smiled as he took her hand, helping her to climb the steep cliff. Then the smile died from her eyes as the stench of the burning ship reached her nostrils, reminding her of all the horrors that had taken place. The sun was beginning to lighten the sky as they reached the top of the incline, leaving their secret cove behind. Jane shivered as she looked at her lover, feeling a stab of guilt. What if Obadiah had been murdered as they lay in each other's arms? 'We must hurry!' she cried. 'Pray God he is still alive . . .'

The mission house was strangely silent as they approached, but there was no sign that the islanders had been there. Jane noticed a pile of dirty dishes by the wash-tub, and scraps of rotting food that had not been cleared away. She grimaced as she saw dirty clothing strewn over the furniture in the minister's study. It was not all his, and she realised that it probably belonged to his brother. Obadiah had always been a tidy man—this was not like him.

'It is unusual for Obadiah to lie abed once the sun is up.' She looked at Stuart apprehensively. 'Do you think . . .'

'No, I'm sure they have not been here yet,' he

reassured her. 'Perhaps he overslept. Shall I look in his bedroom?'

'Please. It might be best.'

As he went to investigate, she glanced around, vaguely disturbed by the signs of neglect. It was against Obadiah's fastidious nature to live like this. One of the things she had liked about him was his cleanliness. Was this her fault for leaving him? Yet surely he was capable of looking after himself.

'Jane!' Stuart's call startled her. 'You had better come. He's ill.'

He was standing in the doorway of Obadiah's room, and she hurried towards him. Pausing for a moment to gaze up into his face, she saw that it was serious, and moving past him to the bed, she gasped, distressed by the sight that met her eyes. Obadiah was lying on a bed that was stained with vomit and urine. His eyes were closed and he was obviously in a state of unconsciousness, a fine film of sweat covering his naked chest.

'It's a fever. I've seen it before,' Stuart said. 'I don't think it's highly contagious. All we can do for him at the moment is to clean him up and see what happens.'

'I'll get linen and water.' Jane puckered her brow. 'You know I have to stay with him, don't you? At least until he's well enough to get up and see to himself.'

'Couldn't Sarah nurse him?' There was resentment in his eyes. 'After what he did to you, you owe him nothing.'

'It isn't a case of owing him anything,' she said, looking at him entreatingly. 'If I left him to die like this, it would haunt me. I would do the same for anyone who needed help.'

I need you, he wanted to cry, but the words died unspoken. She was right, and he respected her for her courage even though the resentment bit deep into his guts. Thorne was a brute and he did not deserve her consideration, but there was no one else. Sarah was too frightened of her brother, and the islanders would probably make certain the missionary never recovered from the fever.

'I'll help you to make him comfortable,' he said, giving her a rueful smile. 'I understand, Jane. I know there's no choice.'

'Thank you.' She smiled at him gratefully, then hurried away to collect linen, water and salves.

It was as she was starting to draw water from the barrel that she heard an odd rumbling sound. It seemed to come from deep within the mountain, and she tensed, half expecting to be flung to the ground. However, the Sleeping Demon had merely moaned in his slumber, reminding everyone of his presence before settling down again.

Jane filled her bucket with water and went inside the house.

CHAPTER SEVEN

JANE WRUNG OUT a cloth in cold water, pressing it to the sick man's brow. She had nursed him for several days now, watching as his illness took its course. There was very little she could do for him, except to keep him clean and comfortable. Queen Ma-Llalla had sent a potion of her own for the fever, but it smelt foul, and Jane could not be sure that it came from the Queen herself, so she poured it away. She had used her own simple remedies to ease his pain, believing that the fever would eventually abate of its own accord.

Sometimes Obadiah was almost lucid, and seemed to know her. At other times he lay in a state of delirium, and then she feared for his life. Many women in her situation would have prayed for such an eventuality, knowing that it would set them free, but Jane could not. She felt no tenderness for him in her heart, but a sad pity. He had something within that tortured him, a secret that had made him into the bitter man he was. She had hated him for a time, but now she was calmer. Obadiah meant nothing to her, but she would save his life if she could.

Getting to her feet, she went outside to fetch fresh water. Stuart had filled the barrel from the spring earlier that morning before he left. He came several times a day to see that she had all she needed, but would not stay at the mission. She knew that he did not like her being Obadiah's nurse, though he realised there was no alternative. If she left the mission, her husband would die: it was as simple as that. Surely Stuart must know it! Yet she felt that he had drawn away from her these past few days. Could he imagine that she felt anything but pity for Obadiah? If so, he was totally wrong. Any attraction she had felt for her husband had faded when she discovered his true nature. Immersed in her own thoughts, Jane was not immediately aware of the bright blue eyes watching her as she moved about the bedroom, tidying it. So Obadiah's first words startled her.

'Am I dreaming—or is it really you?'

She turned, and saw that he was staring at her. Moving towards the bed, she smiled: the cool, calm smile she would give to a stranger.'

'So the fever has broken at last,' she said. 'Would you like something to drink?'

'Yes, please.'

He watched as she poured water into a cup, trying to sit up as she brought it to him. He failed, and was forced to submit tamely as she slid an arm behind his neck, helping him to swallow. Afterwards he fell back against the pillows, looking exhausted.

'Why didn't you let me die?'

The question made her brows rise. 'Should I have let you die?'

'Most women in your place would have thought about it.'

Jane laughed wryly. 'I suspect that, like me, they would have done their duty even so.'

'So you did think about it?'

'What else could you expect? I never pretended to love you.'

'No, but you promised to be a faithful wife, and you broke your word.'

'I could not stay here after you raped me.'

She saw him blench, and turned away. As she had always known, there was a mixture of good and evil in him. He struggled to do what he believed was right, and it was because of this that she had married him.

'I—I am sorry if I hurt you that night.'

Her eyes blazed with sudden fury. How dared he imagine that an apology would put things right? 'It's too late to beg my pardon now! Do not imagine that I am here because I care about you. I despise you—but there was no one else to nurse you. As soon as you are well again, I shall go.'

He flinched at the fierce anger in her. 'Jane, I . . .'

What he meant to say was forever lost. A loud roaring issued from deep inside the mountain, and a tremor shook the ground. Jane was thrown forward across the bed, the shock of it driving the breath from her body. For a moment she lay where she fell, scarcely daring to breathe, then she realised that she was lying across Obadiah's chest and tried to withdraw. As she did so, his fingers gripped her wrist, holding her more firmly than she would have supposed possible in his weakened state. She pulled away from him, a surge of revulsion running through her.

'Don't leave me, Jane. I need you!'

The anger rose in her like a great tide. She had given him every chance in the early days of their marriage and he had returned her kindness with cold words. He had raped her brutally—now he was asking for forgiveness. She felt the sickness in her throat, choking her. 'Don't you dare to touch me!' she snarled, her face mirroring her disgust. 'I would rather die than stay with you.'

His fingers slipped away, and she regained her balance, glancing round the room. The tremor had dislodged books, furniture and ornaments, spilling her jug of water on the floor.

'Then why did you save my life?' he cried. 'Why didn't you just let me die?'

'Do not imagine it was for love of you!' she replied bitterly. 'I am a Christian woman, Obadiah, and I would not let any man die without at least trying to save him. I did what needed to be done not because I wanted to, but because no one else on this island cares whether you live or die.'

'If you intend to leave, go now,' he muttered, his face resentful.

She had begun to move about, restoring order, but the spitefulness of his tone made her stop. Why should she bother with him? He did not deserve anything more from her. She picked up his Bible and placed it on the table beside him, scorn in her eyes as she looked at him. There was too much bitterness in him: he was, and always had been, beyond her reach.

'I shall stay until you can look after yourself,' she said, then turned and walked out.

'The Sleeping One is angry because we have abandoned him,' Kumi said, meeting the Queen's anxious gaze. 'He warns us of his displeasure.'

Ma-Llalla glanced up at the mountain. A tiny cloud of smoke had hung over it for several days, ever since the morning after the massacre of the strangers.

'Jane says that there is no demon in the mountain. She says it is the forces of nature at work, and only the true God can protect us.'

'Jane no longer comes to the village. Your trust in her is misplaced, O Gracious One. You must abandon the new ways and return to the customs of our ancestors.'

'No, you are wrong, Kumi.' The Queen sighed, troubled by the fear that lay in the darkened corners of her mind. Her dreams had foretold the evil that would fall on them with the coming of the strangers, but they were dead and no longer a threat. Now she felt threatened by the stubborn look on her brother's face. She felt her power to dominate him slipping away, and she feared for the future. 'I must talk with Jane. Send to her again. She will come, now that the missionary grows stronger.'

'Listen to me, Ma-Llalla,' he urged. 'We must make a sacrifice to the Sleeping One. Send Jane and her friends away.'

Anger glittered in the Queen's eyes. Kumi's tone was too strong, too demanding. He had forgotten his place. His victory over the strangers had changed him.

'No, I shall not listen to you, Kumi. If the Sleeping One is angry, it is because of what you have done.'

'What I have done was done for our people.'

'You do not rule here yet.' The Queen's eyes were as dark as the smoke above the mountain. 'You speak of the old ways, yet you forget your duty. Tell Jane that I wish to see her. If she will not come to the village, I shall meet her on the beach.'

'You will go to her?' Kumi stared disbelievingly. 'You would honour her too much!'

'If need be, I shall plead with her.' There was sadness in Ma-Llalla, and her body trembled with emotion. 'I have a terrible fear, Kumi. I see all our people wailing in grief and I feel their pain even as I lie in my grave. Do not turn your face from me. I need your devotion for the time that is left to me. Soon I shall be gone from you . . .'

'No!' Kumi cried, throwing himself at her feet as the tears spurted. 'Kill me if I have displeased you, but do not talk of dying!'

She knelt beside him in the dust, enfolding him in her arms like a child. 'It must be, my dear one,' she said. 'I have seen it, but I have no fear for myself. It is for our children and theirs that I weep. They must learn the new ways or they will all die, and their deaths will haunt my sleep. I shall be doomed to an endless wandering . . .'

Kumi stood up, helping her to rise. 'Then I must do as you ask, Ma-Llalla, for I would not have you condemned to an eternity of pain.'

'Go then,' she said, smiling now. 'Ask Jane if she will speak with me.'

He nodded and turned away, his heart heavy with the sadness of the parting that was soon to come. There was no doubt in his mind that it would be as Ma-Llalla had foretold; he could not prevent her death, but he would pray to the old gods and make the sacrifices necessary to ensure that her spirit would find peace.

'That was Kumi's voice,' Obadiah said. 'What did he want?'

He was sitting at his desk, a pen in his hand. Three days had passed since the fever waned, and he had insisted on rising from his bed, though he was still weak. Jane had not argued, knowing that it would be useless. As his strength returned, so the bitterness in him increased. She was not sure how much longer she could endure her self-imposed task of caring for him.

'The Queen wants to talk to me,' she replied. 'I have told Kumi that I shall see her tomorrow.'

'And then you will leave me,' he grunted, scowling as she made a silent protest. 'Oh, don't trouble to deny it! I am well enough now. Already you are impatient to return to him.'

'I shall not lie to you. I love Stuart.' Jane met his angry gaze. 'Why bring this up again, Obadiah? Our marriage is over.'

'Only because you refused to be a wife.' He held up his hand as she would have argued. 'Do not subject me to more of your excuses, Jane. You have chosen your path, and there is nothing to be gained from discussing it. When you go, will you kindly ask Saul to come and see me. He was here before I was ill. I think he must be at the village.'

A cold chill ran down her back. She had dreaded this moment, hoping that he would not ask her where his brother was. What could she tell him? How could she explain something she did not understand herself? Obadiah would have to know the truth, of course, but perhaps not yet. Not until he was stronger.

'Saul is not here,' she said. 'He has gone.'

'Gone?' Obadiah stared at her hard, and she tensed, expecting him to demand an explanation, but then he shrugged. 'Perhaps it is as well. I could never have done as he asked. He has shamed me—as Sarah has shamed me. I knew the bad blood was in them, but I had hoped they would learn to subdue it, as I have.'

'What do you mean?' He had hinted at something like this once before. Now she intended to know what was behind his mysterious words. 'Why do you say that Sarah has bad blood in her? I demand an answer!'

He glared at her then, his eyes blazing. 'You thought me cruel to forbid her pretty clothes, didn't you? You thought I kept her too strictly—but now see what has become of her! She is a shameless hussy, like her mother. Her mother was a wanton. She found life in a country rectory too dull, so she ran away with her rich lover, leaving three small children to the care of a sickly father. When he died, I was still only a boy. I had to work late at night to pay my way through school.'

'I'm sorry, Obadiah. I didn't know.' Jane frowned. 'But that still doesn't mean that Sarah . . .'

'What do you know of my sister?' Obadiah was shaking, his face white and strained. 'She is like our mother. When I look at her face I can see that whore . . .' He got to his feet and walked towards Jane, his eyes glittering strangely. 'When I was twenty, I received a letter from a woman who knew my mother. She begged me to come.' He paused, breathing hard as if he found it difficult to speak. 'She was lying in a bed. I could hardly see because the room was so dark—but I could smell the stench. It was the stink of decay. I lit a candle and bent over her, and then I saw . . . She had the whores' disease. It had begun to eat at her flesh.'

'So that's why . . .' Jane gasped in horror. 'You should have told me before.'

'Would it have made a difference?' He gripped her wrist as she tried to turn away. 'No, I do not think so. You would still have thought me harsh to deny her. Perhaps I was, but I had to protect Sarah. I could not see her end like our mother, rotting in both mind and body.'

She could see the horror of the memory in his eyes, and realised how much it had soured his life. She felt sympathy for him, but also a kind of distaste. He should have pitied his mother, not hated her.

'Sarah won't end like that!' She jerked away from his grasp, angry again. 'I'm sorry about your mother, Obadiah, but I don't believe Sarah is like her. She loves Charles and he loves her.'

'Don't speak to me of them!' Obadiah raised his hand as if he would strike her, but the look in her eyes made him hold back.

'Touch me, and I'll kill you!' Her hand went to the knife at her waist. 'I'm warning you, Obadiah.'

'Jezebel!' His face contorted with fury. 'Get out of my house, woman! You were sent by the Devil to torment me.'

He was shaking badly. As Jane stood staring at him defiantly, he staggered back, half falling into his chair. The fear left her as she saw how weak he still was.

'Go back to bed, Obadiah,' she said coldly. 'I'm going now. I'll come back in the morning to see how you are.'

'I've missed you.' Jane shivered with delight as Stuart's lips moved against her hair. 'You can't imagine how I've felt, knowing that you were there in that house with him, touching him . . .'

She looked up into his eyes. 'He was ill, Stuart. You must know that I had no choice.'

'Yes, I do know. Sarah would have let him die. She refused to go near him at all.'

'She shouldn't hate him so much. It is not good for her. I know he was harsh with her, but perhaps he had his reasons.'

'You sound as if you sympathise with him.'

'I do, a little.' She sighed as he frowned. 'Oh, don't look like that. I could never live with him again, but I do feel some pity for him. Perhaps there are reasons to account for the way he is.'

'You've said that twice.' His eyes proved her. 'Why don't you tell me what you mean?'

'He blames me for Sarah's defiance, and I may have been at fault to encourage her to disobey him. If he had told me at the start . . . But I still cannot believe it was right to make her almost a prisoner because of what her mother did. Oh, Stuart, I don't know what to do!'

'Tell me what's worrying you,' he said with a smile. 'I might be able to help. At least I can listen.'

'Yes.' Jane took the hand he offered, feeling his strength flow into her. It was so good to be with him again, away from the oppression she had felt at the mission. 'Let's walk for a while. You see, I'm not sure if I ought to tell her.'

*   *   *

Jane reached up to kiss her lover's lips, smiling as he bent over to stroke the damp strands of hair from her forehead. While she was nursing Obadiah, Stuart had seemed to withdraw from her, and she had thought he was angry because she had defied him, but his love-making had been as tender as the first time.

'It seemed like forever when I was at the mission,' she whispered, looking at him shyly.

'You were a fool to do it,' he said, a grating harshness in his voice, 'but I admired you for your courage. Not many would have done what you did.'

'You are not angry because of it?'

'No. Why do you ask?' He looked down at her enquiringly.

'You seemed—a little distant.' She wrinkled her brow. 'Perhaps I imagined it?'

'Did I?' He smiled and bent to trail his lips down the arch of her white throat. Why did he not tell her of the doubts that still possessed him and have done with it? It was not that he had been jealous or angry because she had insisted on doing what was right. Yet why trouble her with the problems that he had vowed to overcome. He touched his lips to hers, kissing her so sweetly that she forgot everything but the white-hot desire surging through her body.

'Oh, Stuart,' she whispered, winding her arms about his neck. 'I never knew I could feel like this . . .'

'You are so lovely,' he muttered, catching her to him as the doubts fled to a tiny corner of his mind.

'I always wondered why Obadiah changed so suddenly,' Sarah said, her eyes clouding. 'It must have been terrible for him to see our mother like that!'

'Yes, it must have been dreadful.' Jane took her hand, holding it gently. 'It makes it easier to understand why he was always so strict with you, doesn't it?'

'If only he had told me!' Sarah cried. 'If he had tried to understand me. I am not like my mother, Jane. I love Charles and he loves me. We shall be married as soon as possible. If only Obadiah would marry us now, before my child is born.'

'I think that is unlikely. He will not let me even mention Charles.'

'That is because he thinks of him as worthless sailor, but it might be different if he knew the truth.' Sarah's eyes glowed suddenly. 'If Obadiah knew that Charles is Lord Redbridge's heir, it might change his attitude.'

'I'm not sure that it would,' Jane warned cautiously. 'He cannot forgive you for running away.'

'Oh, but he must relent when I tell him how happy I am,' Sarah insisted. 'If he cares for me at all, he will want to see me wed to a respectable man. I shall go to see him. I am sure he will listen to me now.'

'I don't think that's wise . . .'

'Please, Jane, come with me,' Sarah begged. 'Think how wonderful it would be if he agreed to marry us.'

Jane stared at her doubtfully. She did not believe that Obadiah would relent simply because Charles happened to be the nephew of a rich man, but perhaps she was wrong. In any case, she could not refuse to go with Sarah.

'I dare not encourage you to hope for anything,' she said, slipping an arm about the girl's waist. 'But if you want to see your brother, I shall come with you.'

'Thank you, my dearest Jane.' Sarah kissed her cheek. 'You are always so good to me.'

'We shall call on Obadiah first. Then I must keep my appointment with the Queen. She wishes to talk with me, and I believe it is important.'

'Of course. Wait only a moment while I explain to Charles.'

Jane smiled as the girl ran off. She used the time to fill a basket with fruit for Obadiah. This was the last visit she intended to make, and the food would be sufficient for several days.

Sarah rejoined her after a few minutes, and they began the descent down the mountain to the mission. It was still early in the morning, the sun only now beginning to filter through the trees. They walked together in a companionable silence, content to listen to the sound of birdsong and the whisper of the sea against the shore. It was so peaceful. Although a cloud of smoke still hung over the mountain, there had been no more rumblings from the demon within.

When the mission house was in sight, Jane paused for a moment, her feeling of peace vanishing as she saw the tall, black-gowned figure outside. He had been to fetch water, and was obviously intending to start a cooking-fire. He straightened up, frowning, as he became aware of their approach.

'Are you sure this what you want, Sarah?' Jane asked.

'Yes.' The girl smiled slightly. 'I can't run away now, can I?'

'No.' Jane looked at her with affection. The healthy, glowing girl beside her was so changed from the pale, timid creature she had been when they first met that anyone who cared for her must see how happy she was. 'Perhaps your brother will listen this time.'

He was waiting for them when they reached him, his face hard and unwelcoming. Sarah squeezed Jane's arm nervously, then determinedly let go and stepped forward alone.

'I've come to visit you, Obadiah,' she said, lifting her eyes to look at him proudly. 'How are you?'

'Well enough,' he muttered. 'What do you want, Sarah? You have not come to enquire after my health. If that rogue has thrown you out, you need not look to me for help. I washed my hands of you the day you ran away with him.'

A dull flush crept into her cheeks, but she held her ground, refusing to be intimidated. 'Charles hasn't thrown me out, Obadiah. He loves me, and he wants to marry me.'

'And how will you live?' The thin lips curved in a sneer.

'Charles is Lord Redbridge's heir. He will inherit the title and his uncle's money one day.'

'So he has conveniently remembered a wealthy relative—and you believe him? You are a fool, Sarah! Either he's lying, or he will abandon you once he returns to England.' His brows met. 'Besides, it makes no difference. You have disgraced me, and I have finished with you.'

'Then you will not marry us?' Sarah's mouth quivered with disappointment. 'Not even to save my child from the stain of illegitimacy? Oh . . .' She gave a cry as her brother's arm went back. 'No! Please don't!'

Obadiah ignored her entreaties, hitting her across the face so hard that she staggered and almost fell. His eyes glittered dangerously as she screamed and backed away from him.

'You are a slut,' he yelled, his face contorting with rage. 'A shameful, wanton hussy! God forgive me, I should have beaten some sense into you weeks ago.' He raised his hand to strike her again.

'No, Obadiah!' Jane darted forward, thrusting the girl behind her. 'Go, Sarah! Run away now!'

She gave a little scream as Obadiah's fist contacted the side of her head, half stunning her. Recoiling in horror before his furious attack, she stumbled as he hit her several times, putting up her arms to try and fend off the worst of it. He seemed to have lost all control, continuing to strike her when she fell to her knees, and covered her head. His foot stabbed into her side, sending her sprawling on the ground. She knew there was no way of reasoning with him, he was beyond all rational thought. There was no chance of escape for her. She was almost fainting from the pain in her side, unable to stand or even crawl out of his reach. Dimly, she realised that he wanted to kill her. He was wreaking revenge on her for his mother and Sarah as well as for her own betrayal. Her lips moved as if in entreaty, but no sound came out.

She was not really aware of what happened next, lying motionless on the ground even after Obadiah's attack ceased. Dazed, slipping slowly into unconsciousness, she neither heard nor saw the desperate fight between her lover and her husband. Nor did she know that it was ended by Kumi and his warriors. She did not hear the struggle that took place, neither did she see Obadiah dragged away by three islanders. Even when Stuart knelt by her side and bent to lift her gently in his arms, she remained in that place of darkness from which not even her lover's pleas could rouse her.

The Sleeping Demon was angry. For three days and nights the rumblings had issued constantly from deep inside the mountain, and a cloud of thick smoke hung over the crater. Kumi knew that the god was demanding a sacrifice, and it had to be the right one. Only the death of the missionary could satisfy the Sleeping One's demands. They must abandon the new religion and return to the old ways, or the island was doomed. Yet even now he could not persuade Ma-Llalla that she was wrong.

'Why will you not let me sacrifice the evil one?' he asked. 'Has he not proved his wickedness by turning his hand against her that you love?'

'You speak the truth, Kumi,' Ma-Llalla said sadly. 'Jane is very ill. You will keep Missionary Thorne a prisoner until I have had time to consider. If Jane dies, surely he will die also.'

'He must be sacrificed now!'

'No, Kumi, I forbid it. If Jane lives, I shall ask her what she would have us do.' The Queen sighed as she saw her brother's angry face. 'Listen to me well, Kumi. You cannot kill every stranger who comes to the island. Jane has told me of huge cities where there are more people than you have ever imagined. If you do this thing, you may bring the evil we fear on us. The Sleeping One has grumbled before. Wait and see if Jane dies . . .'

She was aware of the pain now, though her mind was clouded by a strange grey mist. Everything seemed so far away. She wanted to tear the veil from her eyes, but her limbs were too heavy. It was impossible to move or even to think. Sometimes there were people around her bed, people who seemed to care for her. Once she thought she saw her cousin Morna Hamilton's face and tried to speak her name, but the words struck on her dry lips. She felt cool hands on her heated flesh, but she could not respond to their touch. Voices called to her, begging her to do something, but she was too weak to obey. Why must she struggle to hold on when it was so much easier to let go? One way lay pain and suffering, the other way led only to peace and forgetfulness. Her mother's pale face swam before her eyes, seeming to beckon her. She could see a long, dark tunnel ahead, and at the end there was a wonderful brightness. It was like the sun, except that it was cooler and seemed somehow to refresh her. All around was the sound of music, music so sweet that it filled her with joy. She ran towards the light, her arms outstretched, wanting to embrace the peace and love that waited for her there. Then, all at once, she was sliding away from that glorious light, back down the tunnel to pain. She gave a deep, agonised sob, and opened her eyes as she felt the cool cloth on her brow. A man was bending over her, and his cheeks were wet with tears.

'Why are you crying?' she whispered, suddenly aware of her cracked lips. 'I ache so dreadfully. May I have some water, please?'

'Of course.' Stuart touched her cheek gently, lifting her up so that she could drink. 'Not too much at first. Just rest now, my dearest.'

'Have I been very ill?'

'Yes. We've all been looking after you. Sarah, Charles, and I. We were all very worried. The Queen herself has been here to ask after you.'

'I must have been very ill.' Jane smiled weakly. 'Was it a fever? I cannot remember what happened. Where am I?' She glanced round the room, puzzled. 'Why am I at the mission?'

'Don't worry about it yet. You are quite safe now. He isn't here.'

'Obadiah . . .' A little gasp escaped her as the mists

cleared and she began to remember. 'I came with Sarah. He was hitting her, and . . .'

'Sarah is not hurt. You pushed her away and she ran for help. She found me with Kumi on the beach.' He shook his head, a grim smile on his lips. 'Why do you always have to risk your own safety for others? He did his best to kill you.'

'He hates me. He blames me for what has happened to Sarah.'

'He is a madman.'

'W—Where is he?'

'The Queen is holding him prisoner. Kumi wants to sacrifice him to their old gods, but Ma-Llalla has refused to allow it, so far. She says his life depends on you.'

'You must not let Kumi kill him.'

'Why?' Stuart's face was hard. 'I would have killed him myself if Kumi hadn't dragged me away.'

'No, you must not.' Jane's cry of distress moved him. 'Please promise me you will play no part in his murder?'

'Don't be anxious, my dearest,' he said, catching her restless hands in his own. 'I would have killed him in the heat of the moment, but I am no murderer. He deserves to be punished, but he is not worth ruining our lives for. Though why you should care what happens to him after . . .'

'I don't,' Jane said quickly. 'I care about you—about us. If we allow him to die, his death will always be between us. Don't you see that?''

'I see that you would suffer because of it.'

'Then go to the Queen, Stuart. Tell her that I beg her to spare his life. Make her understand that he must not die because of me.'

'As you wish.' He touched his lips to her damp forehead. 'But you must promise me that you will rest while I am gone. Sarah is here. She will sit with you now.'

'Thank you.' Jane smiled. 'Don't be anxious for me. I shall not die now. It was not time for me to die, you see. That's why I came back.'

He did not understand. She knew that he would not believe her if she tried to explain what had happened. No one could believe unless they themselves had been to the gates of Paradise. So she closed her eyes, letting herself drift into sleep. The healing sleep that her body so sorely needed . . .

'Jane will live,' Ma-Llalla said. 'She begs for the life of Missionary Thorne, and I must grant her wish.'

'Do you not hear the Sleeping Demon?' Kumi cried, raising his arm to point towards the mountain. 'Only the death of his enemy will appease him.'

'You speak truly,' the Queen said. 'It is many years since the Sleeping One growled so loudly. Yet I am torn between Jane's god and yours. My dreams tell me that I must keep Jane here with us. If I consent to what you ask, I know that she will leave us.'

'She has no magic,' Kumi said scornfully. 'Let her go. We do not need her or her god. Our ancestors knew the true ways. We have kept them faithfully for many centuries and the Sleeping One rested in peace. I beg you on my knees, Ma-Llalla. Let me do what must be done!'

'Give me a little more time, brother. I must be sure that your way is the right one.'

'Tomorrow night is the night of the moon's waning. If it is to be done, it must be then. You know this.'

'You shall have my answer before sunset tomorrow.'

Kumi nodded, his face grave. 'Think wisely, O Gracious One. Let your dreams show the way. And let it be the way of our ancestors.'

'Tomorrow, Kumi.' The Queen turned to go into her hut alone. 'The missionary's fate shall be decided tomorrow.'

'You should not try to get up yet,' Sarah said, setting a tray beside the bed. 'You are not well enough. Let me make your pillows more comfortable. I've brought you a jug of fresh fruit juice.'

'That sounds good.' Jane smiled at her, sighing faintly. 'I've been so much trouble to everyone.'

'Nonsense!' Sarah laughed and sat on the edge of the bed. 'For once you must be content to rest and let us look after you.'

'Yes, I suppose I must.'

'Oh, Jane!' Sarah caught her hand, holding it tightly. 'You were so brave. If it hadn't been for you . . .'

'I could not let him attack you! You might have lost your baby.'

'You almost died. Oh, how I hate my brother! I wish Kumi would kill him as he did Saul.'

'Don't say that, Sarah. Please don't let bitterness ruin your life. If you keep hatred in your heart it will destroy you—as it has Obadiah.'

'How can you be so forgiving?'

'God teaches us to forgive, Sarah. I suppose I have always believed that we should try to follow Our Lord's example.' She sighed deeply. 'Sometimes it is very difficult not to be bitter. I hated Obadiah for a while, but now I pity him. He let his bitterness sour his life. You have so much to be thankful for, Sarah. Accept what you have and forget the rest.'

'Yes. I know you are right. I have Charles—and soon I shall have my child.' Sarah poured the juice into a glass. 'Drink this, Jane. You have to get strong so that we can all leave the island together.'

'Leave the island?' Jane stared at her in surprise. 'The supply ship is not due for a couple of months yet.'

'Charles and Stuart are talking of leaving before that. They still have the boat that brought them here. With sufficient provisions, we could reach New South Wales.'

'Would Charles consider such a journey—after the suffering he endured the last time?'

'We may have to leave, Jane.'

'What do you mean?'

'Stuart believes the volcano may erupt at any day now.'

'Surely not?' Jane stared at her in dismay. 'I know it

has been rumbling for some time, but . . .'

'There were several strong tremors while you were ill. They seem to be getting worse each time.'

'What will happen to Ma-Llalla and her people if the volcano erupts?'

'Stuart says they will simply take to their boats and go to another island. They must have done it in the past. You are not to worry about them, Jane.' Sarah's face tightened. 'They are savages. Look what they did to Saul and the others!'

'They were frightened.' Jane understood Sarah's feelings. Even though she claimed to hate her brothers, she could not help but be upset at what had happened. 'I know what they did was very wrong, and I'm not excusing that. I know you must feel sickened by what they did, but they believed they were protecting themselves. One of Saul's men did kill Ma-Llalla's eldest daughter.'

'That was terrible,' Sarah said slowly. 'I don't hate all of them, Jane. Some of the women and children are my friends. Saul was a murderer, and he deserved to hang, but they are still ignorant savages. Charles thinks they may decide to kill all of us in the end.'

'Not if we don't upset them. Kumi thinks it would be better if we all left the island; I have known that for a while now, but the Queen wants . . .'

'She wants *you* to stay here.' Stuart stood in the doorway, his face grim. 'I think we may find it difficult to get away if our plans are discovered.'

'They wouldn't try to stop us?' Jane started up anxiously.

'I overheard them talking,' Stuart said. 'Kumi was trying to persude her to let him sacrifice Obadiah to his god. It seems that she is on the verge of giving in to him. She has promised that he shall have his answer tomorrow before sunset.'

'That's barbaric! Can't we take Obadiah with us?'

'There isn't room for us all, Jane. We need every bit of space for provisions if we ourselves are to succeed.'

Jane threw back the bedcovers, swinging her legs to

the floor. 'Then I must speak to the Queen and warn her to leave the island before it's too late. Perhaps she will listen to me.'

'No, Jane.' Stuart's tone was firm. 'I cannot let you do that. Our only hope of escape is to leave secretly. Queen Llalla seems to imagine that you are some kind of talisman. She will never let you leave.'

'But they'll murder Obadiah.' Jane raised clear eyes to his. 'I know you think I should hate him, but I don't. I feel partly to blame. Please, Stuart, let me speak to the Queen.'

He cursed softly. She did not realise it, but she was forcing him to risk his own life for that of a man he despised. He could not let her go to the Queen because it would mean certain captivity—and he could not stand by and see her husband murdered in cold blood. He wanted to yell at her, to take her by the shoulders and shake some sense into her. Obadiah had forfeited all right to their consideration. He ought to tell Jane once and for all that they were leaving without her husband. Her husband!

Damn it! She was right. They could not desert the man. *He* could not desert the man, no matter what he had done. His own conscience would not allow it. He had taken Jane from Obadiah, and he knew that his death would always be a barrier between them. If Jane had the strength to forgive her husbnd, he could do no less. Besides, he would not condemn any man to the cruel death Kumi was planning for the missionary.

'Yes, Jane.' He acknowledged her unspoken question with a wry smile. 'I know you're right. I have at least to try to save that wretched man's life.'

'Thank you. I'm sorry, Stuart. I know I'm asking too much of you.' She held out her hand and he took it, turning it up to kiss the palm.'

'Don't be sorry, Jane. I've always wanted to be a hero.'

'Let me go to the Queen, please?'

'No, I dare not risk it. I'll find a way of rescuing your

precious husband, don't worry.' He let go of her hand and walked to the door, turning to grin at her. 'Even if it's the last thing I ever do.'

'Stuart!' she cried, shocked as she heard the serious note beneath the mockery. She had only meant him to speak to the Queen, but suddenly she realised that she was placing his life in jeopardy. 'Stuart, come back!'

She jumped from the bed, running to the door. He was already striding purposefully away from the mission, but there was still time to call him back. Still time to tell him that his life was more important to her than her conscience, more important than saving Obadiah.

'Stuart,' she cried. 'Come . . . back . . .'

He turned and waved to her, smiling oddly. Then he walked on. He had heard her. She knew that he had heard her, but he would not change his mind now that it was made up. A terrible pain caught at her heart as she realised that she could have sent him to his death. How could she have been such a fool? Why, oh why, had she fought so hard for the life of a man who meant nothing to her? If Stuart was killed, she would never forgive herself.

'They are planning to leave the island—all of them. They have begun to hide food.' Kumi's eyes were blacker than hell as he looked at the Queen. 'Jane will go with them.'

'She must not leave. You must stop them, Kumi. I have seen it. When Jane goes it will be the end for me—perhaps for all of us.'

'Then she will never leave us.' He knelt to kiss her feet. 'Give me your permission to do what you know I must do, Ma-Llalla. Please, I beg you. For the sake of our people . . .'

He was too stubborn for her and she was so tired. The dreams had taken her strength and she was no longer young. Soon she would be called to the home of her

ancestors, and then Kumi would rule in her place. Her
eldest daughter was dead, and Oona was too young to
know what was right, too foolish to be Queen. She,
Ma-Llalla, had tried so hard to protect her people, but
she was no longer sure what was best for them. Her mind
was filled with confusion. She was ill . . . She was dying.
Perhaps Kumi was right, after all. Perhaps she had not
understood those terrible dreams, but they had been so
vivid night after night. The ship had sailed away,
carrying those who could have helped them far beyond
the horizon, and her people cried out in agony. What did
it mean? Was it only the foolishness of an old woman?
Perhaps . . .

'I am tired,' she said, closing her eyes as the weakness
swept over her. 'Do as you think best. Soon you will
have to guide our people. Oona is too young, and I shall
leave you very soon now.'

Tears stung his eyes but he held them back. He had
prepared for her death. She would not be condemned to
an eternity of wandering. Only one last ritual remained
to be performed. He must appease the Sleeping
One.

'Rest now, Ma-Llalla,' he said softly. 'And let your
dreams be of the sunrise . . .'

Stuart paused, looking at the hut in which the missionary
was being held prisoner. There did not appear to be any
guards, but it was near to the centre of the village. It
would be easy enough to release Obadiah, but getting
him out of there in one piece was another matter. Before
they had gone more than a few yards, the islanders
would be aware of what was going on, and he had no
illusions about their fate then. No, his only chance was to
wait for dusk, and hope to sneak past them in the gloom.
Meanwhile, he must watch and wait. It was less than an
hour until sunset.

Settling down beneath the shade of a tree, he half
closed his eyes. It was his custom to laze in the late
afternoon sun, and if the villagers noticed him, he hoped

they would think he was making the most of the warm evening, dozing until the sun finally vanished into the sea. In reality, he was taking mental note of the layout of the village. The prison hut had one thing in its favour, he realised, in that it was close to the stream. If they slipped into the water under cover of darkness, they could make their way towards a clump of large boulders near the small waterfall. The water, deeper there, might help to cover their escape.

His thoughts were abruptly interrupted as he saw Kumi and two of his warriors striding through the village. Something unusual was going on! He cursed softly as Kumi stopped and pointed towards the hut. Damn! He had miscalculated. He had thought the Queen would hold out against her brother, but it seemed that she had given way to pressure. He should have risked a daylight rescue, after all. If he was not mistaken, the missionary was about to be sacrificed to the pagan god of the island. Now what, he wondered, furious with himself. Why had he not realised that this could happen? Should he rush in now and try to drag Obadiah away from them?

As he watched in frustration, the missionary emerged from the hut, struggling with his captors. His words reached Stuart as he shouted and yelled furiously.

'I demand to see the Queen! What do you think you are doing? I shall demand an apology for this!'

'Be quiet, evil one,' Kumi commanded. 'Like the other strangers who came to our island you have broken the laws of our people, and you must pay with your life, as they did. The Sleeping One cries out for justice. Only when he has drunk your blood will he be satisfied.'

Obadiah stared at him, not really understanding what he was saying. 'I have broken no laws, sir. You are savages—heathen savages!—and you will pay for your crimes in hell.'

'You brought the evil on us—the strangers came to see *you*.' Kumi's eyes glittered. 'You attacked her who is beloved of the Gracious One. To harm a woman is a crime under our laws. Any man who strikes a woman must forfeit his life. It is our way.'

'You can't do this! The Commissioners will see that you are punished . . .'

'Take him!' Kumi pointed towards the clearing in the centre of the village. 'Bind him well so that he cannot escape.'

Following the direction of Kumi's outstretched arm, Stuart saw that a stake had been erected just beyond a newly-lit fire. Good Lord! Were they going to torture the missionary as well? For a moment it seemed as if they were, as the wretched prisoner was surrounded by jeering, threatening warriors, brandishing spears in his face. Fortunately all they did was to bind him tightly to the stake. Stuart realised that they were about to begin a pagan ceremony before sacrificing their victim. He saw that a feast had been prepared, and his hopes began to revive. If this feast followed the pattern of all the others he had witnessed, it would be some time before they killed the missionary. Surely there would come a moment when he might stand a chance of snatching Obadiah from under their noses? He would wait until the last possible moment, and then if there was nothing else for it, he would have to rush in and do his best.

Dusk was falling fast now, and the flames of the fire cast weird shapes on the ground. When the dancing began, Stuart sensed that this was a vastly different ceremony from any that he had seen previously. No women were present, and there was something so sinister in the slow, deliberate movements of the warriors that their meaning was quite obvious. They were entreating the god of the mountain to accept their sacrifice, and demonstrating how they meant to kill their victim.

As Stuart had hoped, the dancers became more and more abandoned, absorbed in their rituals and working themselves up into a mindless frenzy. At last he judged that the moment to attempt a rescue had come. It was now or never! Dropping to the ground, he crawled on his stomach towards the prisoner. Fortunately, the flames of the fire had begun to abate, and he was hidden by shadow for most of the time. Reaching Obadiah, he took a knife from his belt and began to work at the ropes, using the missionary's body to shield his actions from the natives.

'Keep still,' he warned in a harsh whisper as Obadiah half turned his head. 'Say nothing, and do exactly as I tell you. Wait until I tell you to move, then run for the shadows.'

For once in his life, Obadiah obeyed instinctively, perhaps because he was too frightened to think of arguing. Even when he felt the frayed ropes give way, he stood unmoving, waiting for Stuart's signal.

Kumi alone had remained calm throughout the ceremony, and Stuart knew that they must wait until he turned to make his offering to the mountain god. The moment came at last. Kumi raised his spear above his head, making a threatening motion as though he meant to kill his enemy. Sensing the tension in Obadiah, Stuart warned him in a harsh whisper.

'Hold your nerve, man! He won't come for you before he has saluted his god.'

Even as he spoke, the Prince fell to his knees, prostrating himself face down. His action was the signal for every other man present to do the same. In the sudden silence, Stuart's command seemed unnervingly loud.

'Now! Come on, man, run for your life!'

Obadiah obeyed instantly, following his rescuer into the shadows, his heart racing as he waited for the shout that would raise the alarm. It came as they reached the stream. A single cry, and then a chorus of shrieks that would freeze the blood of any man.

'Damn!' Stuart muttered. He had hoped for longer. 'Into the stream, Thorne. It gets quite deep beyond those boulders. If they come this way, hold your breath and dip beneath the surface.'

'I can't swim.'

'You won't need to. Just hold your breath and crouch

down.' Stuart cursed softly, realising that he was probably asking the impossible.

The water was cold as they slipped into it, working their way upstream to the pool below the little waterfall. Here the water came half-way up Stuart's chest, and he swam towards the fall, looking for something that he had noticed once when bathing. There was a large boulder with a hollowed-out space big enough for a man to crouch in. He beckoned to Obadiah urgently.

'Hide there. I think I hear them coming . . .'

Although Obadiah obeyed with alacrity, he was only just in time before the first of the warriors burst through the shadows, his spear held aloft. Taking a deep breath, Stuart dipped beneath the water, staying there so long that he thought his lungs would burst. When he surfaced cautiously, he saw that the natives had passed on but were still within earshot. He signalled to Obadiah to stay hidden, waiting until they had finally disappeared into the forest. Even then he waited, shivering as the cold water numbed his limbs. At last he judged it safe to move.

'Come on,' he whispered. 'We'll go back the way we came and circle round the village. They will have searched the beach by then and found no sign of us. No doubt they'll think we fled into the forest.'

Obadiah joined him, looking at him oddly. 'Why are you risking your life for me?'

'Because Jane asked me to,' Stuart replied. 'But I've no intention of getting caught! So stay close to me and do exactly as I tell you.'

CHAPTER EIGHT

'WHERE CAN HE BE?' Jane asked for perhaps the fiftieth time. 'Why did I let him go! Why did I ask him to risk his life!'

'You should be in bed,' Sarah replied, looking at her worriedly. 'Do you want Charles to go and look for him?'

Jane shook her head. The tension had been mounting all evening as they listened to the ominous sound of the drums. Something was going on in the village—but what? The suspense was difficult to bear, but there was no point in making the situation worse by sending Charles into possible danger.

Touching the bruising on her cheek, which was still painful, Jane wondered again why she had begged Stuart to rescue her husband. Silently, she cursed herself for a fool. Why must she always feel concern for others, even those she despised? If anything happened to Stuart, she would blame herself. She half started out of her chair as the door opened, but it was only Charles. As restless as everyone else, he had been pacing about outside the house, feeling frustrated.

'There's no sign of them on the beach as yet,' he said. 'I walked almost as far as the village. They seem to be having another of their feasts.'

'Oh, Charles!' Sarah exclaimed. 'You promised you wouldn't go far.'

'I said I wouldn't get involved.' He smiled at her reassuringly. 'Those damned drums are . . .' He broke off as the drumming ceased abruptly. 'Now what?'

They looked at each other, feeling the tension.

'Something has happened,' Jane declared with conviction. 'Keep a watch by the window, Charles. And it might be best if you had your pistol loaded.'

'Yes, I was thinking the same. I cleaned it earlier, just in case.'

Sarah made a little frightened sound in her throat, and Charles took her in his arms, kissing her brow, but they all felt the same anxiety. The cessation of the drumming could mean one of two things: either Stuart had succeeded in snatching the victim from his guards, or . . . No one dared to contemplate the alternative. Time seemed almost to stand still. In the silence, even the sound of their breathing appeared to be momentarily suspended.

Then a cry escaped Charles's lips as he saw something vaguely through the gloom. 'I can see someone . . . No, there are two of them. I think it must be they,' he said hardly believing his own eyes. 'I can't be certain, but they are running this way. It must be.'

'Is anyone following them?' Jane asked, coming to stand at his shoulder and straining to see through the darkness. 'I can't see anyone else. Can you?'

'No.' He gave her a delighted grin. 'I knew he would manage it! Stuart's a good man to have on your side in a crisis.'

'Yes. Yes, I know.' Jane sighed with relief. She could see the two men clearly now. They were both safe—at least for the moment. 'But we mustn't start celebrating yet, as the islanders are sure to come here soon.'

Even as she spoke the words five or six figures broke from the forest, running swiftly as though to head off the fugitives. It was obvious that Kumi had sent some of his men to watch the mission house, suspecting that they might try to reach it. Now it was simply a question of who could run faster. Unless Charles could frighten the natives off . . .

'Fire at them,' she urged. 'It's Stuart's only chance.'

'Are you sure?' He stared at her uncertainly. 'If we do that, they may attack the house next.'

'We'll have to take that chance. Stop arguing, and do as I say!'

Her tone of command startled him into action. He

emptied his own pistol first, then picked up the one Stuart had taken from the mutineer he had killed. He did not need to fire this, though, for the natives turned and fled into the trees.

'We've routed them!' he cried excitedly. 'They've run for it.'

'I expect they'll come back,' Jane said. 'But not before Stuart is with us.' She hurried to the door, flinging it open as the two men made a last, desperate dash. 'Thank heaven you are safe, Stuart! I had begun to wish that you . . .'

She moved towards him, expecting that he would embrace her, but instead, he turned to Charles with a frown.

'That was a damned stupid thing to do,' he muttered, fighting for breath. 'If I'd wanted to use force, I would have taken the guns with me and shot my way out. I had hoped to persuade Kumi to let us all go peacefully, but there's small hope of that now. Next time they come, it will be with the intention of killing the lot of us!'

'I'm sorry. I—I didn't think.'

'It was my fault,' Jane put in quickly. 'I was afraid they would prevent you from reaching us.'

'As they undoubtedly would,' Obadiah said. He walked across the floor to a side table, helping himself to a glass of brandy from the decanter. 'They are savages. Since the only thing they understand is force, we'll have to show them what Englishmen are made of! You have two pistols, and I have another two in my sea-chest. We can hold them off for a while.'

'We have pistols but not much ammunition,' Stuart replied coldly. 'We may hold them for a while, but not for long. If even one of them succeeds in getting close enough, they could burn us out in seconds.'

Sarah gave a little scream, and Charles put a protective arm about her. 'We shan't let that happen,' he promised.

Stuart did not contradict him, but his face was grim.

'Our only hope is that the Queen still regards Jane with affection,' he said. 'She may force Kumi to bargain with us.'

'Bargain with what?' Obadiah asked acidly. 'My life? They'll not take me prisoner again! Not alive!'

'Then they may have to be satisfied with your corpse,' Stuart retorted furiously. 'If it's a choice between you and the rest of us, I just might break your worthless neck myself!'

'Stuart, don't,' Jane pleaded. 'Don't say things you don't mean. We mustn't quarrel with each other. If Kumi won't listen to you, I'll go to the Queen and beg her to help us.'

'Now that's just what you won't do,' he growled, his eyes flashing with anger. 'Even if you were fool enough to attempt it, I wouldn't let you. With you out of the way, Kumi would simply demolish this place. No, you are our only protection, and you will stay here. Do you understand?'

He was looking at her as though he hated her. Jane felt a tingling in her cheeks almost as if he had slapped her. She blinked hard, holding back the tears that pricked behind her eyes. He had never loved her as much as she loved him, and now he hated her.

'Yes, I understand,' she said quietly, feeling the pain strike into her heart. 'And you haven't eaten all day. I'll bring you something.'

'I'm not hungry,' he replied brusquely. 'Anyway, none of us will eat, except at regular intervals. We have to conserve food—and water. Charles, keep watch while I bring the water-barrel inside. If you see anything, shout. We can't afford to waste a single shot.'

Jane turned aside as he went out, struggling to control her emotions. How could he speak to her so harshly after what had happened between them? Or had that beautiful experience on the beach meant so little to him? Immersed in her private conflict, she was not aware of her husband until he laid his hand on her shoulder. She flinched from him, her mouth hard with distaste.

'Please don't touch me. Don't you ever dare to touch me again!'

His hand dropped to his side, and there was a flicker of shame in his eyes. 'I—I wanted to thank you for persuading Smithson to rescue me. And I want to apologise for all the things I have done to hurt you. I don't know what came over me the other morning, Jane. I must have been mad.'

'Your apology is too late, sir.' She felt the bitterness twist inside her. 'Had I realised what it would mean, I would have left you to your fate! I must have been insane to risk all our lives for yours.'

She saw his face blench, and turned away. She knew he did not understand. He thought she hated him because of what he had done, believing, probably, that she feared for her own life. Her life! What had she to live for now? What did anything matter now that Stuart no longer loved her? She knew it was her own fault, but that did not ease the pain.

As Stuart entered the house, dragging the heavy water-barrel indoors, she found herself freezing inside as she tried to hide her anguish. So that when he glanced at her, her face was cold and stiff.

'You are ill, Ma-Llalla,' Kumi said, kneeling beside her couch. 'Shall I bring the Wise One to you?'

'No, I am not ill, only tired—and saddened at all this suffering our people must endure.' She frowned, reaching out to pat his cheek. 'I was wrong to weaken, Kumi. The missionary's escape is a sign that his god is more powerful than ours. You must not try to recapture him.'

'But the Sleeping One is still angry. Can you not hear him speaking to us?'

'I hear, my brother.' She sighed wearily, feeling his strength beginning to overpower hers. 'But I believe Jane may be right. The Sleeping One is not a god, but a volcano. Like the storms that rage across the ocean, the rumbling is a part of the pattern of life. If the volcano is going to erupt, we cannot prevent this by praying to the Sleeping One. We should build more boats and fill them with food; then our people must leave their homes and be prepared to travel to another island.'

'But we have always lived here.'

'No, Kumi, that is not so.' She raised herself on one arm clutching at his hand. 'My mother told me that there was another island once. It was pleasant, and the food grew in abundance as here. Our people were happy until a warlike tribe drove us away. We came to this place and began a new life.' Her eyes compelled him to listen. 'Perhaps it is time for us to begin again.'

'Is this your wish, Ma-Llalla?'

'Yes. You must warn our people, Kumi. I fear I shall not have the strength.' She smiled at him lovingly. 'Be the man I have always loved so much and put all thought of killing from your mind.'

She was very weak. How could he deny her when she was so near to death? Tears stung his eyes as he bowed his head. 'Your wish is my command, O Gracious One.'

'Thank you,' she whispered. 'Go to Jane in the morning and beg her to come to me. I want to talk with her once more before I die.'

'It shall be as you say.'

He got to his feet, but as he turned away, the Queen recalled something that had worried her.

'Will you send Oona to me?' she asked, vaguely anxious. 'She was crying earlier and her skin was hot. I do not know what ails her—but perhaps Jane will know. I shall ask her when she comes.'

It was impossible to sleep. Jane slipped from her bed, wrapping herself in a coverlet. She could not bear to lie here in the darkness, wondering what was going on. She could hear no sounds from the communal room, and realised that everyone must be relaxing . . . not speaking.

Stuart had insisted that the women go to bed while the men shared the watch. It was possible that they were dozing . . . The idea struck her suddenly. If she slipped out of the window in the darkness and went to the Queen, it might save a lot of anxiety and trouble. She was sure that Ma-Llalla would listen to her. Dressing quickly, she managed to squeeze out of her bedroom window without much difficulty. She crept away from the hut, her heart beating wildly; then, as a figure came swiftly from behind the store hut, she gave a little scream and began to run. She heard the swish of heavy footsteps in the sand and then someone leapt at her, bringing her down. A scream rose to her lips, but it was stifled by a man's hand.

'Be quiet, you idiot!'

Jane stopped fighting as she heard Stuart's voice, looking at him crossly as he rolled her over on to her back. She saw the gleam of fury in his eyes, and shivered. He was very angry with her.

'Where were you going?' he asked coldly. 'Or can I guess?'

'Let me go to the Queen,' she begged. 'I am sure I could get her to see reason.'

'You will end up being locked in a hut . . . and then I'll have to rescue you.'

The bitterness in his voice was like a whiplash, and she felt the sting of tears behind her lids. 'Don't,' she whispered. 'I can't bear it when you're angry with me.'

'Then don't make me angry.' He stood up, giving her his hand to pull her to her feet. She looked at his hard face and drew a sharp breath.

'I was only trying to help everyone. I don't want to be the cause of more bloodshed.'

'Then do as I tell you. Kumi would not hesitate to kill the rest of us if he thought you were out of the way.'

'I can't believe he would kill *you*. You are his friend.'

'Kumi has no friends when it comes to what he believes is right. He loves Ma-Llalla, but he would defy her if he thought it was for the good of his people.'

'You and he are very much alike,' Jane said, her eyes flashing as she became angry. 'You punished Jared harshly because you thought he needed to be taught a lesson. Do you want to beat me for running away?'

'You little cat!' His hands gripped her shoulders and he shook her. 'By God, I know what I would like to do with you!' As his mouth came down to possess hers in a grinding kiss that bruised her lips, she felt her head swimming.

'No . . .' Jane pushed him away, too hurt to give in to the clamouring of her senses. He was not making love to her, he was punishing her because she had made him angry. 'No! I don't want this. You're as bad as . . .' She had been going to say that he was as bad as Obadiah, but the look in his eyes stopped her. 'No, I did not mean that, Stuart. Forgive me.'

Sickness swirled in him as he realised what she had thought. He stared at her in silence, then turned and walked back into the house, leaving her to follow or not as she wished. She stared after him, torn between her hurt and distress at what she had so nearly said.

'Please, Stuart! I didn't mean it.'

'Someone is coming,' Charles's words broke the silence in the mission house. 'I think it's Kumi.'

'Is he alone?' Stuart joined him at the window, frowning as he saw the Prince approaching. 'Now what does he want? I don't trust him, Charles; he has a devious mind. If he's offering a truce, there must be something behind it. I'll go out to him, but keep me covered.'

'Of course.' Charles stared at him. 'Won't you take a pistol?'

'And leave you with one less?' A wry grin twisted his lips. 'I think not, Charles. I'm relying on you to protect the others.'

'Be careful. We need you.'

The brief exchange between them had taken only a few seconds. Jane observed it from her seat in the far corner of the room, though she gave no sign of having done so. Since their quarrel last night, Stuart had hardly looked at her, merely muttering his thanks for the frugal

breakfast he had allowed her to serve. It was clear that
he was still angry with her, and she could hardly blame
him. Yet in a way he had deserved her outburst, for he
had been acting so strangely lately. Only her pride had
kept her from breaking down. She was determined not
to let him see that his indifference was destroying her.
She had caused him too much trouble already, and he
had so much on his mind.

Despite her determination to remain aloof, she was
drawn to the window. Standing beside Charles, she
watched what appeared to be a heated argument
between the two men outside. As their voices rose, she
heard snatches of what they were saying.

'Jane must come now . . .' That was Kumi's voice, and
he sounded very angry.

'She stays here!' I do not forget the feast you gave for
the mutineers . . . Nor what happened to them.'

'They were evil men.' Kumi raised dark, emotional
eyes to his. 'I give you my word that no harm will come to
Jane—or to the rest of you. Even the missionary. The
Queen is ill. She asks for Jane.'

Stuart was silent, torn between his suspicion and
compassion for the ailing Queen. Ma-Llalla had always
treated him well, and if she were really dying . . . His
decision was taken from him as Jane emerged from the
house and came towards them. From the look on her
face, he knew that she had heared the argument—and
this time there would be no stopping her. She paused
beside him, gazing up at him with that stubborn look he
had seen in her face before.

'I must go to her,' she said quietly. 'If Kumi gives me
his word that no harm will come to the rest of you, I shall
go with him.'

'If you have made up your mind, nothing I can say will
stop you.'

She flinched inwardly at the harshness of his tone, but
gave no outward sign as she turned to Kumi. Meeting
her steady gaze, his black eyes glittered with pride.

'I swear that no harm shall come to your people while

you are with me. I swear it by the blood of my ancestors.'

'Then I am satisfied.' He had given his word, and she believed that he would keep it.

She moved towards him. Suddenly the door of the mission was flung open and Obadiah came out. Before anyone knew what he intended, he fired his pistol, the shot passing barely inches above Kumi's head.

'The next one will be in your heart, you heathen savage!' he yelled. 'I'll kill you before I let Jane go to your village.'

'Kumi has given his word that you will be safe,' Stuart said. 'Don't be a fool, Obadiah.'

'A fool, am I?' Obadiah advanced a few paces. 'The moment she's out of reach, his devils will slaughter the rest of us. You said so yourself.'

'Put that pistol away!'

As Stuart took a step in his direction, everything happened at once. Kumi grabbed Jane by the arm, pulling her so that her body shielded him from the missionary's fire. She gave a cry of alarm as Obadiah fired in their direction, his shot going wide; and at the same moment a score of natives broke from the forest, yelling and waving their spears threateningly, while keeping a discreet distance. Stuart cursed aloud, momentarily unsure of what to do. Then he lunged at Obadiah, knocking him to the ground. They struggled desperately for the pistol, Stuart trying to wrest it from his opponent's hand as they rolled over and over. And all the time the natives kept up a weird chanting as they first advanced and then retreated a few paces. Meanwhile, Kumi had begun to drag Jane towards the forest.

'Let me go!' she cried. 'You gave me your word. You promised that no harm would come to my people.'

'The evil one attacked me: he deserves to die. Those who defend him are no longer our friends, but . . .'

What he meant to say was lost. A terrific roaring and whistling sound rent the air, followed by a dull thud as a missile landed in the sand just behind them. Kumi was shocked into silence, as were his warriors. Everyone looked towards the source of the noise. A British naval frigate had anchored in the bay, and her guns were trained directly on the ground Kumi's men would need to cross to reach the mission. Neither the Prince nor his people had ever seen a gunboat before, and they stared at the ship in awe. The first shots had been merely a warning, ploughing harmlessly into the sand, but the intention was obvious. Two boats had put out from the vessel, both packed with armed men wearing the uniform of the British navy. It was an impressive sight.

In the confusion of the moment, Stuart had managed to snatch the pistol from Obadiah's limp hand. He got to his feet, scarcely noticing as his adversary slunk back into the house. Thrusting the pistol through his belt, he walked towards Jane and the Prince.

'There was no need for all this, Kumi. Jane was ready to go with you willingly.'

'I could not be sure,' Kumi said. 'My warriors would not have attacked you unless I was killed.' His mouth twisted with bitterness as he glanced towards the party of armed sailors who had now reached the shore. 'So you have won. Your guns will kill us all.'

'I have never wished you harm, Kumi. No one need be killed if you are sensible. These men are not like the mutineers. They are honourable, civilised men.'

'How can you be sure?'

'That ship belongs to the King of England. Her crew has not come here to murder and plunder.'

'Why has she come?'

'I do not know, but . . .'

'Teddy! It's Teddy Marston,' Jane cried suddenly as she saw the tall man leap from a boat. 'Oh, thank God. Thank God!'

Then she was running down the beach towards the scarlet-coated officer. In his Indian army uniform and with his great height, Lord Edward Marston stood out from the men around him. He was issuing commands to the crew; but on hearing her cry, he spun round, his own weapon dropping as he sprinted to meet her. He caught her up in a welcoming hug, swinging her off her feet in an exuberant manner and kissing her several times.

'It seems we were just in time, Jane,' he said, releasing her at last. 'I was inclined to doubt your cousin when she insisted that you were in trouble, but her intuition was one hundred per cent right!'

'So Morna sent you.' Jane laughed, feeling light-headed from sheer relief. 'I might have known it was her doing! She warned me that my marriage was a mistake, and she was right.'

'I came partly because of Morna's anxiety, but Captain Yorkston is on a more serious mission. It was my good fortune that he was headed for these waters in search of some desperate mutineers.' He looked at her eagerly. 'Will you let me take you back to England, Jane? Will you let me help you to extricate yourself from this unhappy union? You know that I would count it a privilege to serve you in any way I can.'

'Oh, Teddy.' Jane's throat closed with emotion. 'You cannot know how much I have longed to go home!'

'My lord . . .' They both turned as the interruption came. 'What is the situation? Do we attack?'

'Oh no!' Jane cried. 'Please don't let your men fire on the islanders. It really wasn't as bad as it seemed. It—It was a misunderstanding.'

'It looked a nasty affair to us, miss,' the officer said. 'Though things do seem to have quietened since our arrival.'

'Jane, this is Captain Henry Yorkston.' Teddy introduced them with a smile. He glanced towards the mission. Several persons seemed to have gathered outside, while the islanders stood silently watching. 'I believe everything is under control, Henry, but it might be wise to keep the men at the alert for the moment.'

'You must come and meet the Prince—and Captain Smithson.' Jane's cheeks were slightly pink as she saw his brows rise. 'You must have heard Morna speak of her partner who was drowned at sea? Well, it's a long story, but he has been living on the island for some time.'

'Smithson alive?' Teddy glanced at Captain Yorkston. 'You'll want a word with him, I think, Henry?' He frowned as Jane gazed up at him questioningly. 'We believe Stuart Smithson may be able to give us some vital information.'

'About the murder of Captain Ross and the mutiny? Yes, I think you'll find that he can be of help. But it would be best if you heard his story from his own lips.'

'We have already learned a part of it from one of the mutineers. He fell out with his comrades, and was left for dead on an island they visited.' Teddy offered her his arm. 'You are looking remarkably well, Jane. I cannot wait to hear all your news.'

Jane's laughter rang out merrily. He had arrived in time to stop what might have turned into a bloody battle, and here he was on the middle of a South Sea island, offering her his arm and making polite conversation exactly as if they were in an English drawing-room!

'Dear Teddy,' she said, squeezing his arm with affection. 'You will never know how good it is to see you. I shall look forward to exchanging news with you later, but there is something very important that I have to do first.'

His brows rose in mild enquiry. 'Might it have something to do with that proud-faced native who appeared to be dragging you off with him?'

Her mouth quirked again, and she looked up at him with undisguised warmth. 'Yes, it has. He is Prince Kumi, brother of the Queen. I can't explain why Kumi was behaving like that just now, but he really only wanted me to visit Ma-Llalla because she is ill. I must go to her. She is intelligent and warm hearted, and she has been good to us all. None of this need have happened if Kumi had listened to her, but he resents the new religion and tried to placate his old gods by sacrificing Obadiah. He would have succeeded if it hadn't been for Stuart. That incident you witnessed was Obadiah's fault. It's all very involved.'

'I see.' Teddy's eyes glistened with amusement. It was

becoming more and more obvious that there had been a great deal more going on than she was prepared to tell him just yet. 'If you wish to visit this lady, I must certainly not detain you. I shall find it most interesting to meet the Queen—and her brother, of course. I do trust he won't want to sacrifice you?'

'No, he respects me. I shall be quite safe, I promise. Will you be on your best behaviour, Teddy?' Jane looked at him mischievously. 'Poor Kumi's feathers have been sadly ruffled lately. Stuart snatched his victim from under his nose—and your arrival seems to have knocked the breath out of him.'

'I shall accord him all the respect due to royalty, m'dear.'

It was all she could do to keep a straight face as Teddy removed his hat and bowed formally to the Prince. She saw the surprise and dawning admiration in Kumi's face. He had never met anyone quite like the impressive newcomer.

'Your Royal Highness, I bring you greetings from His Imperial Majesty King William the Fourth, Sovereign of England, Ireland, Scotland, Wales and of the British Empire. I am Lord Edward Marston, Marquis of Rossdean, at your service, sir. Forgive the manner of our arrival, due, I fear, to a mistaken notion of my Captain. I can't imagine why, but the fellow seemed to think you were forcing Miss Jane to go with you against her wishes.' Teddy paused for effect, smiling genially. 'She has explained it was all a storm in a teacup, what? So, m'dear chap, apologies are in order. I trust no harm has been done?'

Kumi stared at him in astonishment. 'You come from the King of England?'

'Well, not hot from the throne-room, as it were, but yes, I have the honour to tell you that he is a friend of mine. Would you like me to take greetings to him from your Queen?'

'Queen Ma-Llalla is ill, but on her behalf I am honoured to receive you, friend of King William.' Kumi solemnly knelt before him. 'You are welcome to visit our island.'

'Well, that's very good of you, Your Highness.' Teddy motioned him to rise. 'Please, no ceremony, sir.'

Jane hid a smile as Kumi got to his feet, turning towards him. 'I am ready to go with you now.' She glanced at Stuart, who had been silently standing to one side, watching the proceedings. 'Lord Marston is a friend of Jared, Captain Smithson. Will you look after him and his men while I go to the village, please?'

'Of course.' His face was unsmiling. 'If you would care to step into the house, my lord?'

'Certainly, in a moment.' Teddy's mild manner remained unruffled as he sensed the hostility in him. 'I believe you have much to tell us, Captain, and I am eager to listen. Jane, m'dear, you will return before sunset?'

The look that accompanied his casual question left Kumi in no doubt of the outcome should Jane fail to do so. 'I, Prince Kumi, give my word that she shall be returned to you, friend of King William,' he said proudly.

'Fair enough. Don't forget to pay my respects to Queen Ma-Llalla. I shall be most grateful for an audience with Her Majesty.'

'It shall be as you desire.' Kumi bowed his head. 'Now we must hurry, Jane. Ma-Llalla will be anxious until she sees you.'

'Yes, I am impatient to speak with her.' Jane glanced at Stuart as he walked towards the house, hoping for a smile or a look that would tell her he still cared, but he did not seem to be aware of her. She turned aside, hiding the tears that stung her eyes. 'Let's hurry, Kumi.'

'So you have come! I was afraid you would be angry with me because of what has happened since we last met. I have been weak and foolish, Jane. Many bad things have been done.'

The Queen's cheeks were wet with tears, and Jane felt

her own throat tighten with emotion as she sat on the couch beside her. 'It was not your fault, Ma-Llalla. I know how hard you have tried to protect your people, to teach them of the outside world so that they will be prepared for the future.'

'I was not strong enough.' The Queen sighed, and caught Jane's hand urgently. 'Do not blame Kumi too much. He is a good man, but sometimes he lets his fears ride him him like a demon. I had hoped the new ways would show him how to guide our people, but he cannot turn his face from the past. If only I had been given more time with you, you could have taught me so much.'

'There are other, wiser, teachers than I, Ma-Llalla. You will be well again soon, and . . .'

'No. Do not lie to me or yourself, Jane. Both of us will leave the island very soon. I shall go to the home of my ancestors, and you will begin a new life with the man who cares for you more than his own self. I have seen this. I fought against it, for I wanted to keep you with me. It was selfish and wrong. I know now that my dreams will come to pass—there is nothing you or I can do to stop what must be.'

'Is it the volcano you fear?' Jane glanced towards the mountain. The cloud of smoke seemed to be diminishing and there had been no more rumblings since the previous day. 'Why don't you let us take you and your people to safety? I am sure my friends could arrange that.'

'It is not necessary. Kumi has already begun to build more boats and we shall be ready if the time comes. It is not the volcano . . .' She frowned as the images of pain passed before her eyes. 'I do not know what it is I fear. I only know that it will come soon.'

'You know I would do anything I could to help you?'

'Yes. Your coming has lifted my heart. I shall be ready now.'

Jane felt the tears slip from beneath her lashes and roll down her cheeks. 'Forgive me. I must go now, or my friends will begin to worry. May I visit you again tomorrow?'

'You are always welcome. Tomorrow a great feast shall be prepared on the beach. When the sun reaches its height, bring your friends to sit beneath the shelters we shall build for them and eat with us. You have my promise that it will be a day of rejoicing. No harm shall come to anyone. This time I give you my promise.'

'We shall come, Ma-Llalla.'

'Your heart is good.' The Queen's tears ran down her cheeks. 'Will you look at my Oona before you go? She is restless and her skin burns, but I do not think it is a fever.'

'Of course I'll see her,' Jane replied instantly. 'But I know so little of illness, Ma-Llalla. I might be able to ease her discomfort, but I have no magic to cure her.'

'Then I must pray to your God,' Ma-Llalla said sadly, 'and hope that he will listen to my words.'

'A feast, you say?' Teddy smiled oddly. 'After what Captain Smithson has been telling us, I'm inclined to refuse the lady's offer.'

'Ma-Llalla has given me her word. Everyone will be quite safe. Besides, it is to be held in the middle of the day and on the beach. She has gone out of her way to prove her sincerity.' Jane looked at him appealingly. 'Please don't refuse. I'm very much afraid that she's dying, and—and I'm very fond of her.'

'Then of course I shall attend, though Henry's men will keep a strict watch over the ship. Eh, Smithson?'

Stuart acknowledged his joke with a forced smile. He was feeling jealous, and he did not care for the emotion. It was not something he had experienced in quite this manner before, and he despised himself. Yet he would have to be a blind man not to see the easy comradeship between Jane and the big, bluff aristocrat.

'You would be well advised to do so, sir.'

When Jane glanced at him, Stuart gave a small shake

of his head. Surely she could not imagine that he had told Lord Edward the reason why he had not taken steps to protect the mutineers' ship?

'You will come too, won't you?' she asked. 'Ma-Llalla was asking for you earlier . . .'

'Perhaps.' Stuart found it impossible to smile. He had let her down badly and was not sure what might have happened had her friend not arrived to save them all.

'Well, I'm damned if I'll go to the old witch's feast!' Obadiah cut in, his mouth twisted with rage. 'Those murdering devils killed Saul, and they did their best to get rid of me.'

'You, sir, would be well advised to remain on board the ship until we sail.' Teddy's face was suddenly haughty with pride. 'Had Captain Smithson not disarmed you, you might have precipitated a disaster leading to the deaths of all your comrades. It was by the merest chance that we arrived at exactly the right moment.'

'It was God's work,' Obadiah said piously, glaring at him. While listening to Stuart's disclosures to the newcomers, he had learned the full facts of his brother's death. Although he had suspected something of the sort after Kumi's taunts, he had not really known until now. There was resentment in his face as he looked at Jane.

'Why did you lie to me?' he asked bitterly. 'You told me Saul had left the island.'

'I said he was not here. You were still weak from your illness. I did not want to distress you at the time.'

'It was a deliberate lie. You were protecting those damned savages!'

'Please do not speak to Jane in that manner, sir.' Teddy half rose from his seat.

'I think you forget that she is my wife!'

'A wife you have abused and almost killed. I give you warning, sir, that she is under my protection. I intend to take her back to England and offer her the sanctuary of my mother's house. You have forfeited any rights you had in the matter. Jane will seek a divorce on the grounds of cruelty. No doubt you will fight the case, but I have influential friends who will advise me, and I am confident that we shall win. If you dare to slander her character in court, I shall see to it personally that you go to prison for attempted murder. Your own sister is prepared to testify against you.' Teddy paused for a moment. 'If I were of your own inclination, I should leave you here to await the arrival of the Commissioners' ship. However, that would be little better than murder, since I am aware that you would not survive our departure. I advise you to pack your things and go aboard at once.'

Obadiah's face drained of colour, and for once he was totally speechless. He had no threats that would alarm this man, and he knew Lord Marston's wealth and power made him a formidable enemy. He could not hope to fight him through the courts and win. Standing up, he scowled. 'You're welcome to the cold bitch!'

'Damn you, sir, you'll answer to me for that!'

Now Teddy was on his feet, his face tight with rage. Jane gave a cry of distress and looked to Stuart for help.

'I have a prior claim, Lord Edward,' he said, smiling icily. 'However, I do not believe that there would be the slightest satisfaction for either of us from killing such an unworthy opponent.'

'I'll fight with neither of you over her!' Obadiah sneered. 'I was cursed the day I met her.'

'Please stop this,' Jane said, her distress mounting. 'I do not want anyone to fight on my behalf. Obadiah, I know you hate me, and perhaps you have good reason. For all our sakes, I should be grateful if you will leave now.'

'I shall be glad to quit this accursed island!'

There was silence as he went out of the room, and then Sarah moved to put an arm about Jane's waist. 'I'm so sorry,' she said. 'My brother should be ashamed of himself. You were in no way to blame for any of this. Why, if it were not for you . . .'

'Hush, Sarah.' Jane touched a finger to her lips. 'It is best forgotten. I think we should prepare dinner for our guests now, don't you?'

She smiled at the girl, obliging her to accompany her. It was a relief to concentrate on normal, everyday tasks after the tension of recent days, and despite some tiredness, she realised that she felt much better. Her strength was returning, and it would not be long before she was well again.

Everything had changed so suddenly that she could hardly accept their imminent return to the land of her birth. It was a relief, of course, and yet the island would always hold a special place in her heart. She would never forget the night when Stuart had awakened her as a woman. Stuart . . . She had seen the look in his eyes when Teddy spoke of taking her back to England. For a moment she had thought he was terribly jealous, but that could not be. He knew that she loved him. He could not doubt it after that night. Yet she thought she had glimpsed pain in his eyes . . .

When dinner was served, the six of them sat down to what might have been an English evening party. Captain Yorkston kept Stuart in conversation during the meal, leaving the others to make small talk; and as Sarah's excitement about the journey home was infectious, it made them a merry company. Watching across the table, Jane saw that Stuart's mood was growing ever more distant. He was polite to everyone, responding to his companions' questions fully, but she knew that he was not really with them in spirit. She was not surprised when he made an excuse to leave soon after they had all finished eating.

Sarah helped her to clear the dishes and stack them outside for washing. 'Leave them for now,' she said as the girl hesitated. 'We can do them in the morning.'

'I think I'll just say good night to everyone. I want to pack a few things before I go to bed.'

'You're excited about going home, aren't you?'

'It means that Charles and I can be married. Charles is going to ask Captain Yorkston if he will perform the ceremony for us.'

'I'm sure he will. I'm so glad for you, my dearest.' Jane kissed her cheek. 'Good night.'

After Sarah had gone in, Jane turned away from the house, wanting to be alone for a while. It was a beautiful clear night and she felt like taking a walk on the beach. The sighing of the restless waters of the lagoon accorded well with the beating of her heart. It had been on a night such as this that Stuart first kissed her. Oh, how long ago that seemed now! What had happened? Why had he raised this barrier between them?

'Jane . . .'

She turned, her knees trembling as she saw him. It was as if her longing for him had brought him to her. He stood for a moment, appearing unwilling to come to her. Then, at last, he took the first step. She moved at once to meet him half way.

'Stuart, I hoped I might see you alone.'

'Did you? Why?'

He sounded so bitter that she flinched. Was it because of what she had almost said last night? She had been angry and upset, surely he realised that? She had not meant to hurt him. He must know that she did not regard him in the same light as Obadiah. His face was carved from stone, and her heart sank from the weight of it. She had confessed her love for him once, and he could not be waiting for her to say it again—that would be almost like begging for his attention, and she was too proud for that. No matter how much she loved him, she would not be a clinging vine.

'I—I wanted to thank you for all you have done for me. You must know how grateful I am to you for—for so many things.'

A wry smile twisted his mouth. 'Grateful? I suppose I should have expected you to say that. I exposed you to danger by bringing Thorne back to the mission, and you thank me. God knows what might have happened if your friend hadn't arrived in time to rescue us all!'

'What happened was Obadiah's fault, not yours.'

'I should have anticipated it. The man's a fanatic! Besides, the responsibility was mine.' The harshness in his voice grated on her ears, holding her silent. Was he still blaming her for sending him to what could have been his death? She had tried to call him back, but he would not listen. When he began to speak again, she scarcely heard him, making her responses dumbly because of the tight knot of pain inside her. 'When Obadiah began waving that pistol about I wasn't sure what to do. I believed he was more dangerous than Kumi.'

'I'm sure you were right. Kumi would not have hurt me.' He seemed to be waiting for her to say more—but what could she say? With all her heart, she longed to throw herself in his arms and beg him to love her, but pride held her back. She had given him all of herself. If he wanted her, it was up to him to show her what was in his mind.

'Who can be certain of anything? He is, after all, a savage. We must be grateful that Lord Edward arrived when he did.'

She wondered at the odd inflection in his tone. Could he be jealous of Teddy? It was nonsense—but if he was . . . Her pulses began to race and she moved towards him with hands outstretched. 'Stuart, don't be angry with me, please. I was upset last night. I didn't mean . . .'

'I know that. It was my fault—I shouldn't have . . .' He stared at her, his blood racing in his veins. She looked so lovely in the moonlight and he wanted to hold her in his arms. He wanted to hold her and never let her go—but he had to be sure. 'Why should I be angry? I believed you were angry with me, but I should have remembered that you have a forgiving nature. I cannot so easily forgive myself.'

She met his intent look, staring at him in silence as she

struggled to understand what was in his mind. He was still keeping the barrier in place between them, even though she had tried to break it down. She did not know what more she could say.

'I could never be angry with you, Stuart. Surely you know that? You must know it.'

'Must I, Jane?' He asked softly, a vein cording in his neck as he fought the desire to sweep her into his arms. She was his for the taking—why should he not have what was his? 'What should I know?'

He could not have forgotten her confession of love. He was mocking her by pretending not to understand. She felt hurt by his manner. It was he who had changed, not she.

'What do you want me to say?' she asked. 'I don't understand you.'

'No?' He smiled slightly. 'Then perhaps I am wrong.'

He reached out to touch her cheek, his fingers lingering at the base of her throat. There was something in his face then that made her heart pound madly. She ran the tip of her tongue over her lips, too nervous to speak.

'Last night you pushed me away . . .'

'Last night you were trying to punish me,' she said, her throat tight with emotion. 'I was upset and hurt. I didn't mean what I said about Jared, and . . .'

'Didn't you?' He frowned, his face serious. 'I was angry, too, but I wouldn't have hurt you, Jane.'

'I knew that.'

'Did you? I wonder . . .'

She shivered, feeling a twist of desire in her stomach. Oh, why could he not see that she wanted him to take her in his arms and make love to her the way he had on that wonderful night they had visited the secret cove?

'Stuart, I . . .'

'Jane! Are you out there?'

The door of the mission house opened and Teddy came out, strolling unhurriedly towards them. 'I was worried about you, m'dear. Don't want you disappearing, what?'

'Stuart,' she whispered again, sensing the withdrawal in him.

'Look after your guest, Jane.'

He turned and walked away, his body outlined in silver by the moon's glow.

CHAPTER NINE

SLEEP DID NOT come easily that night for Jane, and when it did, she was troubled by dreams. Strange, haunting dreams that made her wake with tears on her cheeks, remembering clearly the nightmare that had frightened her. She was a child again. Alone and unloved, wandering endlessly through the cold rooms of a vast, empty house . . . Shivering, she dressed quickly and went outside. She had washed the pile of dirty dishes and started to prepare breakfast before anyone else appeared. The first was Sarah, who apologised for being late.

'You are not late.' Jane laughed away her apology. 'I was restless, so I found something to occupy my time.'

Sarah looked at her diffidently. 'What will you do now? Will you marry Lord Marston? He's very fond of you, isn't he?'

'Teddy is a very dear friend . . .' Jane frowned. 'I don't know what I shall do yet. I'm still legally bound to my husband.'

'I know it makes things difficult for you. It doesn't seem fair. I'm so happy. I should like to see you happy, too.'

'Thank you.' Jane touched her cheek. 'I am happy, my dearest. Please don't worry about me. I shall manage. I always have.'

'I—I thought you might be in love with Stuart?' Sarah chewed her bottom lip. 'Have you two quarrelled or something?'

'No, of course not. We are still friends, just as we always were. I . . .'

Hearing a slight sound behind her, Jane turned to see the man who had just arrived, bearing a string of freshly caught fish. He was no more than a few paces away, and he must have overheard their conversation—but how much of it?

'I thought these might come in useful,' Stuart said, sounding a little odd. 'But I see you've already prepared a meal.'

'Only a little fruit.' Jane avoided his gaze, feeling it was accusing. Why was he looking at her in that way? 'But I'm sure everyone will enjoy the fish. Sarah, will you help me to clean them, please?'

'I'll do that for you,' he said.

'Thank you.'

They were treating each other with the politeness of strangers, and it hurt. Yet last night she was sure he had been on the verge of reaching out to her. What had changed? Jane bent her head, concentrating on breakfast, hiding the disappointment she felt inside. Was this how it would be between them from now on? She did not know how she would bear it. It was a relief when the other men came out of the house.

'That fish smells good,' Teddy said. 'Reminds me of army life. Cooking and eating in the open air. Nothing like it.' He looked at Stuart. 'I should like to see something of the island before we attend this feast Jane's friend is giving. Have you the time to spare?'

'Yes, of course. I am at your disposal, sir.'

'Ready when you are.' Teddy turned to Jane. 'I'm afraid that leaves you with the chores, m'dear. I'd send for my valet from the ship, but the silly fellow would turn up his nose. I promise you things will be different when we get home. You'll have servants to pick up your kerchief every time you drop it!'

She laughed and shook her head at him. 'Please don't trouble your valet, Teddy. It would be quite beneath his dignity to do the washing up. Besides, I've always led a busy life. Do you want me to die of boredom?'

'No need for that. My mother will scarcely let your feet touch the ground. She'll have you whisked off to every fashionable seamstress in London in no time, and then life will be too busy even for you, Jane. She's a formidable hostess, and every house in town is open to her.'

Jane was not sure that she wanted to live in the way he was advocating, but it would be ungrateful to say so straight out. She needed time to decide, and Teddy's offer was as generous as the man himself. She could not hurt him by refusing it in front of everyone.

'Please don't lose track of time,' she said as the men began to walk off. 'Queen Ma-Llalla will be expecting both of you at her feast.'

Their only answer was a wave of the hand, a reaction that brought an exclamation of disgust from Sarah. 'Men! I bet they will just forget all about it.'

She was proved wrong, however. By the time she and Jane had changed into their best clothes, the men had returned. It was noticeable that their manner towards each other was several degrees warmer than it had been.

Jane realised that Teddy had deliberately arranged the trip for the purpose of winning over his guide. She looked from one to the other, wondering what had passed between them. Had they discussed her, or was she being vain to think along those lines? At all events, they seemed to have reached some kind of an understanding, and there was no longer any sign of that veiled hostility in Stuart's eyes when he looked at Teddy. If she had hoped that this might lead to a better relationship between her and Stuart, she was disappointed. He was as considerate as ever, but he scarcely looked at her as they all walked to the feast together. Teddy was more forthcoming.

'You look very pretty, Jane,' he said, offering her his arm. 'I think this island has suited you, despite everything. I'm expecting great things of your Queen Ma-Llalla.'

'I did tell you that she's ill—but I don't think you'll be disappointed.' Jane's eyes strayed to where a party of seamen on the beach were standing to attention as they passed. 'Do you think that's necessary?'

'Can't be too careful, you know. Still, they may as well relax for the moment. It is a little warm.' He beckoned to one of the crew, passing on the new orders.

Jane glanced at him with an amused smile. He must be more than a little warm in his uniform, she thought, but he had insisted on wearing the full regalia.

'Mustn't let the side down, what?' he had said with a twinkle in his eyes when she suggested something less formal. 'I shouldn't want to disappoint your friend, m'dear.'

Ma-Llalla had surpassed herself. Shelters of palm leaves had been hastily erected above comfortable couches for the guests, and a sumptuous feast was laid out. A bevy of lovely girls stood guard to wave away any curious insects with more leaves. As the guests arrived, each was garlanded with flowers.

'This is my friend, Lord Edward Marston,' Jane introduced him to the Queen.

Ma-Llalla's dark eyes noted the glory of his crimson and gold coat, moving upwards to his face. She studied him in silence for what seemed to be several seconds, and then nodded.

'You have honour in your heart. You are worthy to be called Jane's friend.'

'Thank you, ma'am,' he said with a smile quirking the corners of his mouth. 'Now I understand why my friend Jane loves you.'

'Please sit beside me. Kumi tells me you come from the King of England. I would hear more of this.'

As Teddy sat beside her and the others sought their own places, Jane found herself next to Stuart. He smiled, and her heart fluttered. She loved him so much. Surely he must be aware of her feelings?

'Lord Marston has impressed the Queen, I think?'

'Yes, I knew they would like each other.'

'A man such as he has few enemies, one would imagine. It is difficult to dislike someone as open and good-natured as your friend, Jane.'

'Teddy rarely becomes ruffled; I've never seen him

lose his temper. Of course I've only known him a short time.'

'He arranged Jared's pardon. I remembered you told me about it. Did he really bring his valet all this way?'

'Yes.' She smiled at his raised brows. 'Teddy never travels without him, but he isn't really as affected as that makes him sound.'

'I believe it's a kind of masquerade he likes to play. He's a good man, Jane.'

'I know.'

Why were they talking like this? Teddy was her friend, but she did not want to talk about him. Stuart's hand lay only inches from hers on the edge of the couch. She longed to reach out and take it. How could he behave as if they were strangers after all that had happened between them? Was he prepared to let her go out of his life without a protest? If so, he could never have cared for her very much. Had it been simply that she was the only woman of his own class available to him? The thought hurt too much to pursue.

The feasting had begun. Dish after dish of succulent food was offered to Jane. She ate sparingly, feeling too choked by emotion to be hungry. When her eyes strayed to the others, she was pleased to see that they all appeared to be enjoying themselves. Especially Charles and Sarah, who were feeding each other with slices of fruit dripping with juice. It was a happy and relaxed atmosphere, all the tensions of the past few days forgotten.

'This is probably our last day on the island.' She did not look at Stuart as she spoke, her nerves tingling. She had to attempt to break down the barrier he had built. 'Captain Yorkston wants to leave as soon as he's completed reprovisioning the ship.'

'You sound almost regretful.'

'In a way, I am.' She could not quite bring herself to meet his eyes. 'Aren't you?'

'I shall take my memories with me.'

Something in his voice made her look up. 'Happy

memories, Stuart? Will they be sweet enough to keep for ever?'

'What do you . . .' He broke off, jumping to his feet with a startled exclamation. 'Damnation! That looks like smoke—and a lot of it . . .'

Jane followed the direction of his gaze, gasping as she saw the thick column of smoke. 'It's the mission—and the church!'

'It's on fire. We have no hope of saving it, Jane.' He cursed aloud. 'Everything you own is in that house.'

'No, a few of my clothes are still in the village. It doesn't matter . . .'

Even as she spoke, he had started running. In another moment he was followed by Kumi and then the other three Englishmen. A silence fell over the islanders, and they looked uneasily at one another, the happy atmosphere turning to suspicion and fear. Then Ma-Llalla turned to Jane, her face creased with worry.

'If this terrible thing was done by one of my people . . .'

'I do not believe it was,' Jane said quietly. 'I think only one man on the island would have behaved so despicably . . .'

Obadiah stared at the island, his resentment growing as he let his thoughts drift back over the past few months. He had believed that his mission to the heathen was a call from God, but now he saw that he had been misled. The Devil's hand was in this. He had tried to break through the barriers of superstition and evil, but he had failed. Yet it was not his fault that his efforts had come to nothing. The evil in this place was too strong. Suddenly he saw his duty clearly. He had built a church in the Devil's stronghold. It must be destroyed before he left the island for good. To allow the disciples of Satan to take over his church would be a terrible sin. He realised that his best chance must be to strike while everyone was at the feast. The house would be deserted; he might as well burn that, too. He would leave nothing for the savages who had rejected his teachings. They were murdering heathen, and he wished he could punish them for their wickedness. Most important was the destruction of the church. When that was done, he would turn his attention to the village.

It was an easy matter to persuade the sailor to row him ashore. He had forgotten a treasured Bible. His excuse was accepted without suspicion, as he had known it would be. He was not a prisoner. He had done nothing criminal, and he refused to be cowed by Lord Marston's threats. Elation gripped him as he strode towards the mission.

'I'll show them!' he muttered, his eyes glittering wildly. 'I'll not be threatened and made to look a fool. When they see what I've done, they'll learn to respect me!'

Just whom he meant to teach a lesson was not clear in his mind. He was possessed by a kind of fever, his thoughts centred only on the task ahead. It was a duty laid on him by God. Now he saw that he had been sent here for a purpose, after all. It was not to convert these savages to the true faith, but to punish them for their sinful ways. They had turned against him, thereby rejecting the religion he had brought them. They deserved whatever punishment he chose to administer. He saw himself as the avenger, a messenger from an angry God. As in ancient times, the Lord's wrath would fall upon the sinners who had turned their faces from him. He was Moses parting the Dead Sea. He was omnipotent. All-powerful. Just as God had brought down fire and brimstone on Sodom and Gomorrah, so he would wreak a terrible vengeance on these savages. When he had destroyed the church, he would set fire to the village.

He was laughing as he lit his torch, carrying it into the church. The dry wood caught instantly, spreading rapidly up the walls to the thatched roof and within seconds it was burning furiously. The mission house took a little longer, but he hurled burning wood from the church into every room, the glow of the fire entering his eyes as he saw the flames shoot into the sky.

*　　　*　　　*

Obadiah had gone mad. He looked like a demon out of hell, his face and hands streaked with soot as he stood watching the flames, and laughing wildly. The church and mission were beyond saving—Stuart realised it at once. He had had a vague idea of saving some of Jane's belongings from the fire, but it was hopeless. Anger stirred in him at the man who had wantonly destroyed the things she had brought with her from England.

'Damn you, Obadiah!' he yelled. 'Haven't you harmed her enough? Why did you have to do this?'

When Obadiah turned towards him, he saw the hysterical gleam in his eyes. It was a kind of temporary insanity. He had seen it happen before, to sailors towards the end of a long, hard journey. He knew then that the missionary was dangerous. The anger left him instantly. It was a tricky situation: somehow Obadiah had to be captured and kept in confinement until the madness passed. Otherwise, he was capable of killing anyone who got in his way. He walked towards him cautiously, knowing that any sudden movement could trigger a violent reaction.

'You've had your amusement,' he said calmly. 'It's time to go back to the ship now.'

'No, not yet.' Obadiah stared at him, hardly registering who was speaking in his mood of elation. 'It's the Lord's work, don't you see? I couldn't let those savages desecrate his house, could I? I had to destroy it. It is a glorious vengeance.'

'You've done what you came to do. Come with me now. You don't want to stay here, do you?' Stuart moved steadily closer as he coaxed. 'Let's go on board together, shall we?'

Suddenly Obadiah seemed to become aware of his proximity. He snatched up a burning brand, holding it threateningly aloft. 'Stay back, Smithson! I've not finished yet. I must burn the village. I have to smite the evil before it becomes an abomination in the sight of the Lord. These people are children of the Devil. I must destroy them!'

He was just mad enough to carry out his threat, Stuart realised in horror. The islanders might now be returning to their homes. Even a small, uncontrolled fire could spread through the forest swiftly, trapping those who were too slow to escape it. He had to stop this crazy fool before he caused a tragedy.

'Put that torch down, Obadiah. You are not going to punish anyone. We are going back to the ship now.'

'Who are you to give me orders? Fornicator! Seducer!' Obadiah's eyes flashed with anger. 'You shall be the first to suffer my vengeance.' He lunged at Stuart, thrusting the burning wood into his face so that he was forced to jerk back and retreat. 'You thought to teach me a lesson once, now I have the advantage. I shall show you who is master!' He advanced on Stuart, slashing from side to side with the torch, and laughing as he pressed forward.

Stuart could do nothing as he dodged the flaming weapon, feeling the heat scorch his skin as it passed too close for comfort. He had no weapon of his own, nothing that he could use to knock the torch from Obadiah's hand. He watched for an opportunity to lunge at him, knowing that his only chance was to disarm him somehow. He could feel the heat at his back, and he knew that he was being driven towards the burning church.

'Oh no, you don't!'

He could not retreat any further. His own attack must come now. He tensed on the balls of his feet, springing forward to try to catch Obadiah's arm in the hope of thrusting it back, but he was not quite quick enough. The missionary had sensed the change and jumped away, pushing the torch into Stuart's side. He felt the instant pain as the burning wood touched his flesh, setting fire to his shirt. Yelling with shock, he threw himself on the ground, rolling desperately as the flames licked through the thin material. As he did so, he heard a terrible crackling sound. Even as he looked up, startled, a part of the church wall broke away and came hurtling towards him. He scrabbled desperately in the sand, trying to escape it.

Suddenly he felt two hands on his shoulders, and he was dragged back out of danger seconds before the burning débris hit the ground, sending out a shower of sparks. Only one man was strong enough to have pulled him to safety so quickly. He glanced up into his rescuer's concerned face.

'The man's gone insane!' Teddy exclaimed. 'Are you badly hurt, Smithson?'

'No.' Stuart ignored the smarting of his scorched flesh and got to his feet, the tatters of his shirt hanging about him in blackened strips. 'We have to stop him! He means to burn the village next.'

'Kumi has gone after him. Look . . .'

Stuart's gaze followed his pointing finger. Obadiah was running towards the forest, still carrying his flaming torch, but Kumi was gaining on him. As the two Englishmen watched side by side, he drew back his arm to launch his spear. It flew straight and true, thudding deep into the flesh between the missionary's shoulders. He fell face down, twitching violently for a few seconds, and then lay still.

'The poor devil.' Teddy crossed himself. 'God rest his soul.'

'Maybe it was for the best. Thorne would have had to be forcibly confined. Better a swift death than an asylum.' Stuart's eyes met his companion's enquiring gaze. 'From what I know of him—and something he told Jane—I think there may be a history of insanity in the family. Thankfully, Sarah seems to have escaped it, and she must never be told the whole truth. It would haunt her and her child, perhaps unnecessarily.'

'She shall hear nothing from me. He attacked you, amd Kumi killed him. No more to be said.' Teddy smiled oddly. 'At least Jane will be saved a great deal of trouble.'

'Yes. Yes, she is free of him at last.'

'And a good thing, too!' Teddy said with feeling.

'Never should have married the rascal. Now, my dear fellow, let me have a look at those burns. My man has a remedy for everything. I'm sure he can fix you up with something to ease the pain.'

Suddenly Stuart threw back his head and laughed. 'Yes, I dare swear he has. I haven't thanked you for saving my life yet, my lord.'

'No need, old fellow. You would have done the same for me. Glad I arrived in time, what? No reason to mention it to the ladies, eh?' Teddy grinned. 'Makes one feel a fool when they fuss over these things.'

'I agree entirely. So I shall leave you to explain my absence, sir. If you will excuse me, I shall avail myself of your valet's skills. I believe he is still on board?' As Teddy nodded, he paused for a moment, then said, 'There's no need for the ladies to know I received these slight burns.'

'I wouldn't dream of mentioning it. We don't want to upset them.' Teddy smiled approvingly. Smithson was clearly a man after his own heart. Ladies were a delicate species, to be cherished and protected.

He watched as Stuart walked unhurriedly towards the boats and spoke to the sailors, who obligingly agreed to row him out to the ship. The burns to his chest, back and arms were more than the slight injury he admitted to, but his pride would not allow him to complain. Shrugging, Teddy went to join the other two gentleman, who were standing to one side. If Smithson wanted this all played down, it was his privilege. All he could do was to ask for the other witnesses' co-operation. He was sure they would agree, there was no point in distressing either of the ladies unnecessarily.

They had left the lagoon, and the island was fast becoming a tiny dot on the horizon. Jane stared at it until it was swallowed up in the endless blue of the sky and sea, feeling a hard lump in her throat. She had taken a tearful leave of Ma-Llalla before being rowed out to the ship, waving to the islanders as they sang their farewell to her.

Despite everything, it had proved painful to leave her friends behind. Even Kumi had seemed sad to see her leave, pressing a gift of a beautiful shell necklace on her at the last moment. She was still clasping it in her hand, and tears stung her eyes as she looked at the delicate colours of the shells.

'You have nothing to reproach yourself for. You could not stay there for ever.'

She turned as she heard Stuart's voice, her heart racing. 'No, of course not. I only wish I could have helped Ma-Llalla more. She's dying, you know. She was very weak when I said goodbye.'

'Yes, I know. I visited her myself. I, too, was fond of her.'

Jane nodded, her brow wrinkling as she recalled something that had been niggling at her subconscious. 'Two of her children are ill. Oona was the first. I can't be sure, but I think they may be sickening for chicken-pox; I saw some spots on Oona's chest when I said goodbye to her. But surely I must be mistaken? How could she have become infected? The islanders have never suffered from that kind of disease.'

'I pray that you are wrong. A disease like that could run through the population like wildfire.' He frowned as he looked at her. 'Let us hope that you have not taken it from her.'

'Oh, I caught all those illnesses as a child from my father's parishioners. Sarah has also had them, so her baby is not at risk. No, it's Ma-Llalla and her people I fear for. What will they do if there is an epidemic?'

'Many of them will die. It is something I have often wondered about. They have been so secure in their island paradise until now.' He was silent for a moment. 'Perhaps her dreams were visions of the future. The disease could have been carried by one of Jack Thorne's men. We shall never know. I doubt if the Commissioners will send another ship there after what has happened.'

Jane's eyelids flickered as if she found it distressing to think about the last tragic events on the island. 'Obadiah must have been ill again. Do you think he was suffering from a recurrence of the fever?'

'I think it likely.' Stuart looked beyond her, watching the white crested waves. 'Kumi thought he meant to set fire to the forest. He acted in defence of his people. If the forest had caught, it could have been a disaster.'

'Yes, Teddy told us how it happened. You mustn't think that I blame you for his death. Obadiah brought it on himself.' She laid her hand on his arm, hiding her hurt as he instinctively shrugged away from her touch. 'I know I had no right to ask you to risk your own life for his. I—I hope you are not still angry with me because of it?'

'I have never been angry with you, Jane. I was angry with myself for exposing you to danger by bringing him to the mission. Until Charles fired those shots, I had had some idea of bargaining with Kumi . . .'

'He did so because we feared for your safety.'

'Well, it is in the past now.' He smiled oddly. 'Your friend arrived in time to rescue us all. To be truthful, I was never more relieved to see anyone as that boatload of sailors.'

'Wasn't it fortunate that Captain Yorkston was on a mission of his own in these waters? Otherwise Teddy might have had to wait for the regular supply ship.' Jane laughed. 'It was all Morna's doing, of course. She was worried about me—and you know how determined she is. She plagued everyone ceaselessly until Teddy said he would visit the island and see how I was.'

'Her cousin can also be stubborn on occasion,' Stuart said, a hint of amusement in his blue-grey eyes. 'So you are to stay with Lady Marston then, Jane? You will become the toast of the town, I think?'

'Please don't make fun of me. You know I am not suited to that kind of life.'

'I know nothing of the sort. You are a lady, Jane, and I'm very pleased that you will be well cared for once we get to England. Lord Marston is a decent man.' Stuart gazed at her steadily, no hint of his thoughts in his expression. 'I want you to know that I wish you every happiness. I shall expect to be invited to your wedding.'

She felt as if he had plunged a knife straight into her heart. This was the first chance she had had of speaking to him alone since Ma-Llalla's feast, and she hoped that he had sought her out so that they could discuss their future together. Seeing the impersonal smile on his lips, her hopes died stillborn. He was wishing her happiness as another man's wife, and that could only mean that he did not want her himself. She blinked hard, holding back her tears.

'You once asked me to be your wife, and I—I thought you cared for me.'

'You know that I care for you deeply, Jane. I respect and admire you more than any woman I know, but . . .' The accusation in her eyes made him falter, but he set his gaze firmly on the horizon, knowing that what he did was for her own good. 'When we were on the island you were in a difficult situation. I knew how desperately unhappy you were, and I wanted to help you to begin again. Anything was better than being tied to that monster. Naturally, I tried to . . .'

'Then those nights we spent together meant nothing to you?'

She gazed up at him, her eyes misted with tears. How could he dismiss what had been between them as if it had never existed? Did he not know he was breaking her heart?

'Of course it meant a great deal to me. I was lonely, too.'

'I—I believed you wanted to share your life with me.'

'It was a pleasant dream—but one I have since realised was never meant to be. I'm not the marrying kind, Jane.'

His words were like a stone in her heart. He did not love her. She had been no more than a passing fancy, someone to help him break the monotony of life on the island. She wanted to give way and weep like a child, but she managed a wobbly smile. She had always been good at hiding her bruised emotions, and now she gave a performance worthy of an actress. On the island she had let him see into her heart, but he had seemed to love her then. Even when she had tried to hide her pain from him, he had refused to let her escape. If he had cared enough now, he would have seen beneath her mask. Instead, he seemed determined to shut her out. She realised that he wanted to be free of the promises he had made her. Her pride told her that she must accept it, but her heart forced her to try one last time.

'Then I shall not break your heart if I marry Teddy?' she asked, and her bright smile was painful to see. 'What will you do when we reach England?'

'I shall look for another ship. The sea has always been my first love, as you know. I doubt that I could be as faithful to another. You'll do better with your Marquis, Jane. Anyone can see that he's in love with you. In two years' time you will have forgotten my name.'

I shall never forget you! her heart cried, but the words remained unspoken. She had come close to begging him to love her, and she could do no more. The pain was twisting inside her, the shame and humiliation of his rejection stinging her cheeks.

'Teddy is very dear to me. I know that I could not hope to find a kinder or more caring husband.' She turned aside so that he should not see how close to breaking she really was. 'I see that he has just come on deck. He must have finished his business with Captain Yorkston. Excuse me, I must go to him.' She walked away, her head high and her shoulders straight.

Stuart watched her, the smile leaving his face as he saw her greet Lord Marston. She would never know just how much it had cost him to send her into the arms of his rival. She must never know, if his sacrifice were to have any meaning! She had to be happy in her new life. He felt the jealousy begin to churn inside him, and the deep, grinding ache he would always carry from now on. Envy was a destroying emotion, but he would conquer it. It was necessary for Jane's sake. He could not expose her to the kind of life his own mother had endured. He could not watch as she grew pale and thin, worn down by worry and hard work. He would never have relinquished his claims to her affection so lightly if he had not been sure that she would be content as Lady Marston. Wealth and security were something he could not offer her, but they would have weighed less in his estimation if he had not liked Teddy. He had tried to hate his rival at the start, but no one could dislike such a generous man. Besides, he had saved his life . . .

For a moment Stuart wondered if he had let pride cloud his judgment. He was indebted to Marston for so much. Damn it! He was even wearing the man's clothes. He had nothing of his own. Nothing to offer the woman he loved. Nothing but his own strength and a life of poverty. He knew only too well how precarious a seaman's life could be. No, he could not marry Jane and risk her future security. He had to give her up for her own sake. Even though the memory of her would haunt him for the rest of his life.

Ma-Llalla had gone to the home of her ancestors. Kumi smeared his body with ashes, prostrating himself at the foot of her couch and wailing his grief. The sun had gone from the sky, never to return, and he felt terribly alone, torn by his guilt and his pain. Had he hastened her death by his actions? He had meant only to protect her, but when the news of the missionary's death had reached her, he had seen the will to live fade from her eyes. She had not blamed him even then, but her cry of despair cut him to the heart. Now she was gone and he did not know what to do. The burden of kingship was heavy without her to lighten the load.

'My lord . . .'

The woman's interruption angered him. He had given orders that he was not to be disturbed during his period of mourning. He rose to his feet and the look on his face was terrible to see.

'Who dares to intrude on me at this time?' he thundered.

'You must come, my lord.' The woman went down on her knees in fright. 'Oona is screaming. She cannot bear the pain—and there are many others like her in the village. We do not know what to do.'

Kumi glowered at her, then nodded, following her from the Queen's hut. At once he became aware of the cries and screams from all parts of the village. It was a scene from Ma-Llalla's dreams. The evil had fallen upon them just as she had foretold. His people were cursed with a strange plague that manifested itself in an unsightly rash on their bodies. Every day more of them showed signs of the illness. They rushed into the sea to try to cool their fevered bodies, but nothing the Wise One suggested helped to ease their agony.

As Kumi hesitated, another woman approached and threw herself at his feet. She was weeping noisily, and he guessed what she had to tell him even before she looked up.

'Oona is dead,' he said, and his face was grey with the grief of it. 'She is the first.'

He stared up at the mountain top. It was free of smoke. The volcano had quietened. It was not a god, only a natural force, as Jane had said. By his stubborness he had brought disaster upon them. He had sent away the strangers who might have been able to tell him what ailed his people. They were waiting for him to speak and he was afraid. He was their leader and he did not know what to do. Then he remembered Ma-Llalla's last words, and he was suddenly filled with a strange peace.

'May the true God's blessing be upon you,' she had whispered as her hand slipped from his.

'We shall care for the sick,' he said, and his voice was strong. 'We shall bury our dead. When the sickness has passed, we shall leave this place and find a new home, and there . . .' He paused, resisting to the last as the pain crushed his breast. 'And there we shall build a church . . .'

*   *   *

It was Sarah's wedding day. The crew and passengers had assembled to watch Captain Yorkston perform the ceremony on deck, and a cheer went up as he invited Charles to kiss the bride. He did so with evident enthusiasm, which brought another round of good-natured smiles and jests.

Jane was the first to congratulate the bride. She kissed Sarah warmly and received a hug in return. 'I'm so very happy for you, my dear.'

'Thank you, Jane.' Sarah's eyes sparkled with excitement. 'I owe it all to you. If you hadn't stood by me, I would never have had the courage to meet Charles after my brother forbade it. You've been the best friend any girl ever had. I do love you so!'

'And I love you, my dearest. I want you to have this.' Jane pressed a small silver brooch into her hand and was hugged again. She smiled as the girl immediately pinned it to her gown. 'Fortunately, I was wearing it on the day of the fire. It isn't valuable, but everything else was destroyed, except for a few clothes I had left in the village. If Morna hadn't sent us both a new gown with Teddy, neither of us would have had a decent dress for your wedding.'

'Your cousin is so kind.' Sarah glanced down at the blue satin of her gown. 'Do you think we shall see her when we reach Sydney harbour? I should like to thank her personally.'

'I expect she will have crossed the mountains by now, but you can write her a letter and the Governor will see it reaches her somehow.'

Jane sighed, her thoughts wandering as Sarah was reclaimed by her new husband. She moved away to the ship's rails, staring out at the foaming water as they ploughed through heavy waves. The weather had become increasingly worse these past few hours and it looked very much as if they might be in for a storm. She hugged her shawl about her as she tried to decide what to do. She knew Teddy expected her to travel on to England with him, and at first she had fully intended to do so. The news that Captain Yorkston could take them only as far as New South Wales, and that they must make further arrangements there, had set her mind churning. Should she go on to England—or make a life for herself in Australia?

It was not as difficult as it might seem. She could join Morna in the Hunter Valley or stay with friends in Sydney Town. She had several good friends who would gladly offer her a home until she found somewhere for herself. Her skills would enable her to find a position as a housekeeper, or she could open her little teashop as she had planned before Sarah and Obadiah came into her life . . .

'That was a deep sigh, m'dear?'

Jane glanced up, smiling as Teddy came to stand beside her. 'I was thinking, that's all.'

'About your young friend? She made a delightful bride. I gave her a trinket-box, but I'll buy her a proper gift when we get to London. Perhaps a silver tea and coffee service. What do you think, m'dear?'

'I'm sure you will pick a suitable gift. You're such a generous man, Teddy.'

'Nothing of the sort. I've taken a fancy to the pair of them. It's good to see a happy young couple, what?'

'Yes.' She smiled at him, feeling a little sad. Why could she not have fallen in love with him? He was kind and generous to a fault, and he deserved to be loved. The last thing she wanted to do was to hurt him. 'I—I think I'll go below for a little while. I have a headache.'

'I'm sorry to hear that.' He looked concerned, and she felt guilty because she had lied. The ache was in her heart, not her head. 'Lie down on your bed for a sleep, Jane. I hope you will soon feel better.'

'Yes, I'm sure I shall. You mustn't worry, Teddy. It's only a little headache.'

She moved away, intending to go below, but as she did so, Stuart left the bride and groom and came towards her. She hesitated, unsure of what to do. He had hardly spoken to her since that first day on board ship, becoming stiff and reserved whenever they met.

'Stay a moment, Jane,' he said, and her heart jerked. 'I wanted to speak to you.'

She waited for him, feeling a strange sensation of breathlessness. There was a serious look in his eyes that made her knees tremble. Oh, why did he not understand that she loved him?

'Yes, Stuart,' she said, her eyes carrying such a look of appeal that he caught his breath. 'What is it?'

He had come to say goodbye. Soon they would be passing Van Diemen's island, and then it would not be long before they reached New South Wales. He had made up his mind to leave the ship there.

'I wanted to say . . .' He faltered as he saw the brilliance of her eyes. Was he right to deny this feeling between them? He believed that what he was doing was for her sake—but when she looked at him like that he wanted to sweep her into his arms and hold her pressed close to his heart.

'Yes?' she asked, holding her hand to her head. 'Was it important? I—I have a headache.'

'No, it was not important,' he replied as the moment of temptation passed. 'It will keep for another day.'

As he turned and walked away, Jane felt close to breaking-point. She had felt so desperate as he looked at her that she had almost betrayed herself. Blinking back her tears, she went quickly below.

Alone in her cabin, she sat down on her bunk, staring into space. The pain inside her was too deep for weeping. She had to accept that there was no future for her with Stuart. Now she must decide what to do about Teddy. She was fond of him, and she did not want to hurt him—but was that the right basis for marriage? Although he had not yet proposed to her, she knew he was on the verge of doing so. She must have her answer ready. She had made one mistake; she could not afford another. Teddy was not like Obadiah, he would always be kind to her—but he deserved to be loved by the woman he married, and her heart belonged to Stuart . . .

CHAPTER TEN

IT WAS THE old nightmare. Jane's head tossed restlessly on the pillow as her dream deepened. A storm was raging about the ship, waves crashing over the sides as they were tossed like a straw in the wind. Stuart was struggling to reach her, but the huge wall of water tore them apart. She heard his voice calling to her . . .

'Jane! Jane, wake up!'

Opening her eyes, she found herself staring into Sarah's terrified face. She started up, throwing back the bedcovers. 'What's wrong? What is happening?' Even as she asked, a huge wave hit the ship, causing her to lurch sickeningly to one side. Her nightmare had come frighteningly alive!

Sarah gave a scream as she was flung forward into Jane's arms and everything in the cabin went sliding across the floor. 'Oh, Jane, I'm so scared! Charles sent me to wake you,' she gasped. 'Captain Yorkston says it is one of the fiercest storms he has ever encountered. He wants everyone to be prepared to abandon ship.'

'You mustn't worry,' Jane reassured her, but her own heart was fluttering. The ship shuddered and shook violently as successive waves thudded against her sides, and she realised they were being driven helplessly before the wind, unable to maintain their course. 'Does the Captain want us on deck?'

'Not yet. All the men are helping to clear the sails. We've sustained damage to the mainmast and they're trying to cut the wreckage clear. Charles told me to stay with you until he comes for us.'

Jane nodded, her arm squeezing the girl's waist to comfort her. 'It won't take me a moment to dress. Sit on the bed while I get ready.' She stepped into her shift as she spoke and pulled on the gown she had worn earlier. 'Perhaps the ship will weather the storm . . .'

As the words left her mouth, there was a tremendous crash on deck and the ship shivered from end to end. There was a moment when the two friends stared at each other in silent horror, and then they were both thrown to one side as the vessel heeled over. Instinctively, Jane knew that this time it would not right itself. They were going to sink!

'We have to get out now,' she said. 'Come on, Sarah, we're leaving.'

She pushed the bemused girl through the cabin door. The ship had turned half on her side, and it was difficult to walk along the tilting gangways to the steps. A trickle of water had already appeared, making the wooden floor slippery beneath their feet, and they had to hold on to each other to keep from falling.

'Go ahead, Sarah,' she urged as another movement of the ship almost flung them over. 'There's no time to waste.'

A light appeared suddenly above their heads as the hatch was opened, and she saw a man's face. He beckoned urgently, reaching down to take Sarah's hands and help her through the opening. The light disappeared for a moment, and another sickening lurch flung Jane to the ground. She heard a strange rushing sound and gasped as she saw the water flooding towards her through the narrow passage. It was a swirling torrent, and she was caught by the full force of it as she struggled to the bottom of the ladder. It whirled about her, dragging at her skirts as she reached desperately for the first rung, and she felt her fingers slipping as it sucked her down.

'Hold on, Jane! I'm coming.'

She heard Stuart's voice as the water rose, engulfing her. It was in her mouth and her nose, choking her and tearing at her so that she was in danger of being swept away. Then his hands grasped hers and she was hauled bodily out of the water, her arms feeling as if they were

being torn from their sockets as her legs bumped and
scraped against jutting wood. She was gasping for
breath, blinded by her long hair that wrapped itself
around her face in a sodden mess. Then she was out of
the ship's belly, lying on her stomach as he panted over
her, fighting to recover his breath; but the deck was
almost vertical and as it was caught by the lash of another
wave, she was wrenched from his grasp, sliding back
away from him towards the sea. She screamed in fear,
grabbing for something to save herself, catching at one
of the ropes the sailors had strung out as lifelines, but she
could not hold on.

'Stuart!' she screamed, her words lost in the howling
wind. 'Don't let me go! I love you! I love you . . .'

'Jane . . .'

She heard his despairing cry and saw him try to battle
his way towards her, using the ropes to pull himself
across the deck. Her nails gouged the wood as she
scrabbled for a hold, finding one at last as she caught at a
metal ring. She raised her head, watching Stuart as he
fought desperately against the tearing gale, his face
agonised by the sheer effort. He was winning his way to
her, his hand outstretched in an attempt to catch hers.

'Hold on, my darling,' he cried. 'Don't let go! I love
you . . .'

She tried to inch towards him. Their fingers touched
momentarily, then, before he could grasp her, a huge
wave crashed across the ship, throwing him off balance
and sweeping her with it. She was carried towards the
submerged half of the deck, disappearing beneath the
water.

'Jane! Oh, no!'

Stuart's cry was wild with agony, his despair smiting
him like a sword. He had been so near to achieving his
goal. Now she had been snatched away by the cruel sea.
He gave a howl of rage like a demented animal, diving
into the water in a desperate attempt to find her.

His cry was the last sound she heard, her head striking
a piece of floating débris. Then she was no longer aware

of the storm or the cold water that dragged her down, down, down . . .

'Stuart . . . Stuart . . . Don't leave me. Don't let me go. I love you . . .' The words came out in a feverish whisper that was hardly audible, except to the man bending over her. He laid a hand on Jane's brow, his expression of concern deepening. As the door opened behind him, he glanced over his shoulder at the girl standing there.

'Is there any change?' she asked.

Teddy shook his head. 'None as far as I can see.'

'But it's weeks since we were picked up. She—She looks so thin and pale.' Sarah came towards the bed, a sob catching in her throat. 'I can't bear it if she dies. She made me go first. You and Charles got me to the boat. She was always protecting me, and now she's going to die.' Tears began to run down her cheeks. 'I don't want her to die . . .'

'She loved you; that's why she made you go first.' Teddy stood up. 'You mustn't give up hope, Sarah. Sit beside her while I speak with the Captain. I don't want her to be alone if the fever should break.'

'Yes, of course I will.' She looked up at him in a desperate appeal. 'What shall I tell her if she asks . . . about him?'

'Nothing for the moment. She was calling for him again just now. If she lives, I'll tell her what happened when I think she can bear it.'

'My poor darling Jane,' Sarah whispered. 'She was more dead than alive when you pulled her out of the water. If only he . . .' A tear slid down her cheek and she stroked Jane's head, her fingers caressing the short, stubby strands that were all that remained of her glorious tresses. 'She'll never forgive us for cutting her lovely hair . . .'

Teddy laid a hand on her shoulder. 'It was at the doctor's insistence. He believed it was sapping her strength. I think she will understand, my dear; don't upset yourself. It was a miracle that so many of us survived. You have Charles and your baby to think of. It can't be long now, I think?'

'A few days.' Sarah swallowed hard. 'Why was I so lucky? What had she ever done to deserve this? She was always thinking of others. It isn't right!'

'Life is seldom fair.' Teddy's eyes were full of shadows, his usual humour weighed down by care. 'All we can do is to pray for her recovery. Then it will be up to her friends to help her through her grief.'

'You love her very much, don't you?'

'Yes.' His smile was gentle as he looked at the woman lying in the bed. 'Yes, I love her very much. If she lives, it will be my privilege to care for her always . . .'

The sun was shining through her window, making little patterns on the pink silk bedcover. It was a very pretty cover, richly embroidered as were the drapes about her bed. Everything in the room was the finest that money could buy. She had never been so pampered in her life. Jane turned her head as a knock sounded at her door, giving permission for whoever it was to enter. She smiled as the maid came in, carrying her breakfast tray. It was beautifully presented as usual with shining silver, delicate porcelain and a posy of flowers. She was being spoilt!

'Good morning, Agnes. How are you today?'

'I'm very well, miss.' The plump-cheeked girl bobbed a curtsy after setting down her burden. 'Her ladyship sends her compliments and asks if you feel well enough to take a drive with her this morning?'

'Yes, I am quite well.' Jane laughed as the girl reached for a quilted wrap, placing it carefully about her shoulders before handing her a cup of hot chocolate. 'You all spoil me so dreadfully! I shall become one of those tiresome creatures who cannot lift a finger to help herself.'

'Not you, miss. You leave your things so tidy that I've hardly anything to do.' Agnes shook her head and smiled. 'Besides, some folk are worth the spoiling. You were ill for such a long time, even after the master brought you home. It's them nasty foreign parts! You suffered so dreadfully that there were times when we all thought . . . Well, that's in the past now. You'll be off to town next week to buy your bride clothes. I've never seen his lordship so happy, and that's a fact!'

'Yes, he is happy.' Jane's hand trembled on the handle of her cup, but she controlled it before the maid noticed anything was wrong. 'I shall get up in a little while, Agnes. I shall ring if I need you.'

'Very well, miss.'

Jane closed her eyes for a moment as the girl went out, her heart catching with a funny little pain. Her wedding was to take place in six weeks. It had taken her many months to give Teddy his answer. He had asked her to marry him when they were still on board the ship that had rescued them after the storm . . . The storm . . . She thrust the terrible memory to the back of her mind, trying to block out the picture of Stuart's face as she was swept away from him, and the agony she had seen in his eyes. His last words were carved into her heart. She would never forget them.

'Hold on, my darling. Don't let go! I love you . . .'

He had loved her after all! It was a bittersweet pain in her heart to know that he had cared for her desperately. He had tried to reach her, but the wave swept her away. Even after the fever had broken, she had not really known if any of it was true. It had all seemed to be a part of the continuing nightmare. Had the storm been real or was she still living in a dream? She had been so weak that she spent most of the following days sleeping, her mind too shocked to accept what had happened. Teddy and Sarah were her constant companions, their love helping her through the painful hours of the long, wearisome journey to England. In the end it was the lusty cries of Sarah's son that roused her from her apathy.

'Let me hold him,' she had whispered, the tears trickling down her cheeks as Sarah laid the fair-haired babe in her arms.

After that, she had begun to recover slowly, making the effort to leave her cabin and stroll on deck. She had known before Teddy told her. She had felt the emptiness inside long before she could bring herself to ask about Stuart.

'We looked for him,' Teddy had said, holding her arm to steady her as she swayed. 'We called to him through-out the night, but in the morning we had drifted away from the wreck. There was no sign of him.'

'He is dead.' She had felt it from the beginning.

'You can't be sure, Jane. He might have made it to one of the other boats . . . There were two others launched. We survived: others could have done so.'

'But the ship that rescued us made a search, and no other boats were found.' Jane shook her head. 'Don't pretend that there's still hope. I know he's dead. I feel it.'

He had taken her into his arms to comfort her as she wept on his shoulder. She did not know how she would have survived the last few weeks of the voyage without his kindness. He asked her to marry him the night before they were due to dock at Portsmouth.

'I know you loved Stuart Smithson,' he said gently. 'When I came to the island that first day, I sensed there was something between you. I asked him if he had a prior claim on your affections the morning we went exploring together. He told me that he cared for you, but was not in a position to marry.'

'We would not have married even if . . .' She faltered, her throat catching. It took a moment or two to recover her composure, then she went on, 'I think he was too proud to ask me to share the hardships of a seaman's life. He—He wanted me to have security . . .'

'He loved you, Jane. He could have saved himself, but he went into the sea after you. Charles saw him once. He tried to signal that we had found you, but he seemed not to be aware of us. He dived beneath the wreck again. No one saw him surface.'

'He would not give up his search, and so he died.'

Jane's eyes were blinded by tears. 'He was a stubborn man. He lived by his principles—and died for them.'

Teddy smiled oddly. 'We were rivals and yet friends. I would give my own life if it would bring him back to you.'

'You mustn't say that!' she cried. 'Stuart wouldn't want that—neither do I. You are my friend, and I love you.'

'Then marry me, Jane. You must know how much I care for you? All I want is to make you happy.'

She blinked away her tears, smiling up at him. 'Oh, Teddy, I don't want to make you unhappy. It wouldn't be right to marry you, feeling as I do.'

'I want to take care of you.' He placed a finger against her lips as she would have spoken. 'Please don't refuse me yet. Think about it, Jane. It would give me great pleasure to look after you. I don't ask you to forget him. We could be friends, sharing our lives in comfort and companionship—couldn't we?'

The picture he presented was a pleasant one. It would mean that she need never worry about being alone. He was kind and generous, and she enjoyed his company, yet surely it was not fair to him. She would gain much, but she had little to offer in return. The love she felt for him was not the same as that she had offered to Stuart.

She had tried to explain, but he brushed her doubts aside, declaring that he was willing to wait until she felt able to start her life again. He had brought her to his mother's house in the autumn, and now it was spring. Finally, she had given way to persuasion. It was impossible to hold out when everyone showered her with kindness and love. Yet, even now, Jane had her doubts. Would Teddy learn to regret the unequal bargain he had made in time?

Lying here would not solve anything. Pushing aside her worries, she got out of bed. She dressed in a fashionable but simple gown of grey silk, one of the many gowns Lady Marston had insisted on buying her, and sat down to brush her hair. It had begun to grow again, and much to Jane's surprise, it waved becomingly about her face.

She had almost made up her mind to keep it short. At least it was easy to manage.

Gathering her bonnet and shawl, Jane made her way to Lady Marston's boudoir, smiling to the butler as she passed him in the hall. She knocked at her hostess's door and was invited to enter. Inside it smelt of lilac, as always, echoing the delicate shades of the furnishings, and she felt a sense of peace. Teddy's mother was a delightful person. Grey-haired and comfortingly plump, she was forever busy, yet she never became flustered or lost her temper. She turned and smiled as Jane entered.

'Ah, there you are, my dear. It's such a beautiful day. I thought we might take a drive to Melbury Park. Lady Amelia has been poorly. It would cheer her up to have company, I think.'

'I'm sure she will be pleased to see you, Ellen. Besides, the drive will be pleasant.'

'That's exactly what I thought.' Lady Marston beamed at her, looking very much like her son. 'That dress suits you, Jane. I've always thought grey such a dull colour, but you can wear it.'

Jane touched the froth of fine white lace at her throat, smiling at the compliment. 'I fear I do not have your elegance, ma'am, but no one could fail to look attractive in the gowns you have given me. They were far too costly.'

'Nonsense! Teddy complains frequently that you will not let him spend his money on you. It will not do, my love. When we are in town, I shall insist on buying you a trousseau worthy of my son's wife.' Lady Marston patted her hand. 'I shall speak to Teddy about it when he comes tonight.'

'Oh, pray do not. The pearls he gave me on his last visit are quire sufficient for my needs.'

'They are well enough for the country, but you will need diamonds in town. After your marriage, you will have a great deal of entertaining to do.'

Jane felt a tingle of unease. As yet she had met only a few of Lady Marston's country friends. They had made her welcome in their houses, and she had enjoyed the small, friendly dinner parties, but she was apprehensive about the large balls she would be expected to give in town.

For the moment, however, Jane was able to subdue her doubts. It was a glorious spring morning, the air softly warm and scented with flowers. The drive through English country lanes was very enjoyable. Lady Marston's carriage was well sprung and luxuriously padded with squashy velvet cushions, and the two ladies spent the time talking and laughing together.

A smart travelling coach drew up outside Lady Marston's country house, and its single passenger alighted. The man's frock coat was of a fine grey worsted and fitted his broad shoulders to perfection. His hessian boots were of good quality leather, highly polished, and his waistcoat was a pale grey watered silk. Opening the door to him, Lady Marston's butler was favourably impressed. He was clearly a gentleman, though there was nothing of the dandy about him, and his skin was tanned as though he had spent much of his life in the open air.

'Good morning, sir. May I help you?'

'I have called to see Miss Jane Blackwood. I understand she is a guest of Lady Marston?'

'Yes, indeed, sir. Unfortunately, Miss Blackwood has gone out with her ladyship.'

'When do you expect them back?'

'I'm afraid I can't say, sir. Her ladyship has gone visiting. It may well be some hours before she returns.'

'I see. It seems that fate is against me.'

'Perhaps you would care to come back this evening, sir?'

The man frowned, then shook his head. 'I have an appointment elsewhere. I shall be occupied for the best part of the week. I may return then.'

'Miss Blackwood will be away, sir. She is going to town to prepare for her wedding . . .'

'Jane is to be married? Then I am too late.' The man nodded grimly. 'I should have expected it. Thank you for your help. Good day.'

The butler stared at him in surprise. 'Who shall I say called, sir?'

'It does not matter. I am sorry to have troubled you.'

'But, sir . . .'

The butler watched as the man walked briskly to his carriage, gave an order to the coachman and climbed inside. He had not noticed until then that the caller had a slight limp. 'Well . . . What an odd way to behave!' The butler's first impression was hastily reviewed. No gentleman would depart without leaving his card, and there had been a very strange look in his eyes when he heard of Miss Blackwood's marriage. Perhaps it would be wiser to say nothing to the ladies of his visit, though he would certainly inform his lordship of the stranger's call.

It was her first evening party in town, and Jane looked at herself in the mirror, feeling nervous. Her reflection showed her an elegantly dressed woman who was past the first flush of youth, but still undeniably attractive. She knew that she had never looked better, yet her heart was fluttering. Tonight was her début under the critical gaze of one of London's foremost hostesses. She was terrified of saying something foolish and disgracing her friends. It had always been an ordeal for her to mix in high society, and tonight everyone would be looking at her, wondering why Teddy had decided to marry at last. Her hands trembled as she reached for her fan.

Leaving her room to join the others in the salon downstairs, Jane found herself wishing that she could spend the evening quietly at home. Yet she knew that it was impossible. Teddy was accustomed to spending much of his life in town. She had agreed to marry him, and that meant sharing his life. She would have to force herself to attend endless balls, dinners and musical evenings. It would be expected of her.

'You look lovely this evening, m'dear.'

As Teddy moved forward to take her hands and kiss her cheek, Jane felt a twist of pain in her heart. He had been so kind to her, and he deserved so much more than she could give. She must not grudge the effort it would cost her tonight.

'Thank you,' she whispered, finding it difficult to smile. 'I hope I shall not disgrace you tonight. I'm so stupid at these affairs.'

'Nonsense,' he said, tucking her arm through his. 'You will have them all at your feet.'

She laughed, forcing herself to appear unconcerned as they all went out to the waiting carriage. Teddy kept up a flow of conversation during the drive, almost as if he had sensed her reluctance. She listened to him and his mother discussing their acquaintances, wondering if she would ever feel as easy in society as they did. It was necessary for her only to smile and answer occasionally, leaving her thoughts free to wander at will.

Finally their carriage drew up outside a very large, grand house. There was a queue of smart vehicles in front of them, and they had to wait their turn. At last Teddy got out to help the ladies down, and they followed behind a stream of richly dressed guests to meet their hostess. It was all a little overpowering, and Jane felt her head swim as she curtsied to a formidable woman in a purple silk gown.

'Ah, Lady Ellen. Lord Edward.' A pair of piercing brown eyes swept over Jane. 'Miss Blackwood. Delighted to meet you.'

'Countess Delvine. I am happy to be here.'

The first hurdle over, Jane breathed a sigh of relief as they all moved into a huge reception-room. Great glistening chandeliers hung from the ornate ceilings, and it was very warm. Jane was offered a glass of champagne from a large silver salver, which she accepted, sipping it cautiously as she watched the company. Jewels flashed from the necks of the ladies, evidence of the wealth of their owners. Everyone seemed to be talking animatedly, and she felt her shyness growing, but made an attempt to hide it as Teddy steered her towards a group of his friends.

Some of them had already visited Lady Marston's house, and she was greeted with warm smiles. Her nerves quieted and she began to relax. They could not eat her, after all! Then a general movement started towards the music-room, where a leading soprano was about to sing for the guests.

'You will excuse me, Jane.' Teddy pulled a wry face. 'Not quite in my line. I'll make my way to the card-room, I believe.'

'Men!' Lady Marston snorted. 'They come to a musical evening and hide themselves in the card-room. Come, my dear, we shall spend our time more pleasurably. I understand Signorina Carlotta has a fine voice . . .'

She went on to describe one of the operas the soprano had recently sung in, but Jane was no longer listening. A man had just entered the room. A tall man in black. He was not looking at her, but her gaze was riveted to his profile. Her heart jerked to a standstill, then raced as the world seemed to fade away and she could see only him. It could not be! It was not possible! She must be imagining the resemblance. Then he turned towards her, and their eyes met. It was he. He had grey streaks in his dark hair and he looked older, but it was he. She gasped, feeling light-headed and shaken.

'Stuart . . .' she breathed. 'He's alive . . .'

'What did you say, my dear?' Lady Marston glanced at her stricken face in concern. 'Are you ill?'

'I think it's the heat.' Jane was trembling from head to foot. 'I need air . . . the gardens . . .'

'I shall come with you.'

'No! No, please let me go alone.'

Jane was aware of her companion's startled look, but she had to escape. Her emotions were churning in a whirlpool of shock, joy and despair. He was alive! He was here! Why? How? She had to be alone for a while.

The other guests became a blur of curious faces as she

hurriedly made her way towards the long windows that opened out on to a terrace and the formal gardens. She could scarcely breathe, her breasts palpitating beneath the thin silk of her gown. Her head was spinning and she felt close to fainting. Reaching the terrace after what seemed an eternity, she ran down one of the rose avenues, not stopping until she knew herself to be out of sight of the house. There was a little stone bench beneath an arch of roses. She sank down on it, covering her face with her hands and shivering, though the night was not cold. She had believed him dead—but he was alive! She tried to come to terms with the knowledge, but her mind was too confused. The tears scalded her eyes, and her shoulders shook with the force of her sobbing.

'Jane! Oh, my dearest girl! I would not have had this happen for the world. If I had known you would be here, I should never have accepted the Countess's invitation.'

It was his voice. He had followed her! She looked up, her face racked with pain, staring at him wordlessly. Then he was beside her on the seat. He reached out and took her into his arms. They gazed into each other's eyes for a moment, seeing what could not be expressed in a thousand words. Then their lips met in a soul-searing kiss that went on for ever.

'Oh, Jane my love,' he whispered huskily. 'Forgive me. I came to Lady Marston's house to find you. I wanted to tell you that I love you—so much that my life means nothing to me without you. They told me you were about to be married, and I thought you had forgotten me. I did not want to complicate matters, so . . .'

'Stuart . . .' She touched his cheek in wonder. Nothing else but the miracle of his survival mattered for the moment. 'Everyone believed you were dead.'

'I was close to death for a long time. I searched for you until my strength was exhausted, and after that I hardly know what happened to me. I must have clung to a spar that had floated free of the wreckage. Mercifully, I was not aware of anything.' He paused to smile ruefully, his eyes glittering in the moonlight. 'I was washed up on

Van Diemen's island. A party of convicts found me. They hid me and cared for me while I was out of my mind with fever, believing I was one of several of their number who had tried to escape. When I finally came to my senses, I had a terrible time convincing the authorities of my identity. In the end, one of the officers recognised me and I got a ship to New South Wales. I worked my passage back to England.'

'I can't believe it,' she choked, her hand trembling. 'I, too, was ill for a while, and when I recovered I felt desolate. I was sure that you had drowned.'

'I believed you were dead,' he said, taking her hand to hold it lightly. 'I wanted to die then, Jane. I cursed God for letting me live—and I cursed myself for being a fool. I had wasted so much time when we might have been together. I love you. I've known I loved you since that day on the island when the tree fell on you, but I had nothing to offer you. My mother married a sailor against her family's wishes. They considered that she had married beneath her, and her father cut her off without a penny. While her husband lived, she endured the hardships of her life without complaint, but he went down with his ship and she was forced to take in washing to support herself and me. I watched her struggle to put food in our mouths, Jane, and I swore that I would never let a woman suffer as she did. I thought you would be better off as Marston's wife. It wasn't until you were lost in the storm that I realised how much I needed you . . .'

'Oh, Stuart.' She touched his cheek, her heart aching. 'What are we to do? I'm promised to Teddy. Our wedding has been announced. He's been so good to me.'

'When I thought you were happy, I meant to go away without seeing you. I have a little money of my own, Jane. My uncle died, and left me his estate. I have just completed the sale. It did not fetch a large sum, but it is enough for what I had in mind. It was my intention to ask for a grant of land in the new territories—perhaps near Morna and Jared, if you wish?'

'Go back to Australia?' Jane's eyes lit up. 'How I should love to go with you . . .'

'Then come with me, my darling . . . as my wife.'

Jane closed her eyes for a moment, the tears squeezing beneath her lashes. 'I can't. How can I?' She looked at him despairingly. 'How can I hurt Teddy now? I waited so long to give him my answer. To change my mind at the last moment would be too cruel . . .'

'It would be crueller to deny our love; you know that, don't you?' He looked into her eyes searching. 'You need not tell him yourself, Jane.' His fingers gripped hers so fiercely that it hurt. 'I shall explain to him. I can't let you go now. I won't! If you didn't care for me . . . but you do. You can't deny this feeling between us. It is too strong. I won't give you up now.'

He pulled her into his arms, his kiss demanding and possessive. She felt her senses swimming as her whole being responded to the passion of his embrace. Trembling, she clung to him, her lips eager for the devouring kisses that wrenched her heart from her body. At last he let her go, and she drew a deep breath.

'You must let me tell him alone, Stuart.'

'No! I let you face another man's anger once before. This time I shall be with you.'

'Teddy is not Obadiah,' Jane said quietly. 'Let me go, Stuart. I must tell him myself.'

Stuart stood up, taking both her hands in his as he helped her to rise. 'We shall find him together. He will understand, because he loves you. Don't argue, Jane. I'm afraid to let you go. You might disappear again —and I couldn't bear it if I lost you now.'

Jane gazed up at him. There was both pain and love in his eyes. She knew that she would never need to doubt his feelings for her in the future. The resistance drained out of her. It was right that they should speak to Teddy together. Nothing must part them ever again.

Lord Edward Marston shook Stuart's hand and wished him good fortune in the future, then he turned to the woman at his side. For a moment he studied her face, then bent to kiss her cheek.

'I wish you every happiness, Jane.'

The wind caught at her cloak and she held it tighter, feeling awkward for the moment. Teddy had insisted on coming to see them off after their wedding, driving them to the harbour in his own carriage. Suddenly, she gave a little sob and threw her arms around him, hugging him.

'You've been such a dear friend, Teddy. I don't know how to thank you.'

'For what?' Teddy grinned. 'It was my pleasure to see you married to the man who can make you truly happy. You mustn't fret about me, m'dear. I never was much in the petticoat line, you know. We might have been comfortable together—but this is much the best. Stuart's a solid man.'

The ship's bell was ringing. She glanced over her shoulder, realising that it was time to go aboard. There was so much she wanted to say, but words were useless in such a case. She reached up on tiptoe to kiss his cheek.

'Goodbye, my dear friend.'

Stuart put his arm round her, understanding her feelings. 'It's time to leave, my love. Goodbye, sir. You have our deep-felt gratitude for everything.'

Teddy nodded, watching as they walked away. He smiled cheerfully and waved as they went on board, his expression never wavering.

The activity was intense on deck. Most of the passengers had gone below, but Jane stood for a moment staring back at the shore and the lonely figure of the man on the dock. She felt Stuart's arm about her waist.

'He told me that he knew you had doubts about marrying him, Jane. It was better to tell him than to live a lie. It would have hurt him far more in the end.'

'I know.' She sighed. 'I always felt it was unfair to him. I pray that he will find happiness himself one day.'

'Amen to that.' Stuart's lips touched her hair. 'Come below now, my love.'

She smiled up at him, her love glowing in her eyes. 'Yes,' she whispered. 'Yes, my darling husband.'

'My wife . . .' he said with a kind of wonder in his voice. He touched her hair. 'Why did you cut it?'

'It was done when I was ill.' She looked anxious. 'It will grow again.'

'It's beautiful as it is,' he said. 'You are beautiful.'

They were alone in their cabin when he drew her into his arms, his lips just touching her forehead as he held her gently, almost reverently, hardly daring to believe that they were together at last. She shivered with delight, a tremor of desire running through her as she slid her arms up round his neck.

'Do you really think I'm beautiful?' she asked shyly.

'Yes,' he said, smiling down at her. 'I was such a fool to think that I could let you go, Jane. On the island I knew that I cared for you, but I did not realise how much you meant to me until the night of the storm. I know now that my life would be meaningless without you.'

He bent his head to kiss her lips, gathering her to him in a crushing embrace that left her breathless and in no doubt of the urgency of his feelings.

'Stuart,' she breathed. 'I love you so much . . . Make love to me now, please?'

His answer was a hungry kiss that sent her senses reeling. 'Jane, my love,' he whispered, his voice caught with passion. 'I have missed you so much . . . So much . . .'

She arched her body against him, her pulses racing as his lips trailed fire down the line of her throat. As he began to unfasten the tiny pearl buttons at the neck of her gown, she felt again the magic of that first night on the island when he had shown her the pleasures of loving, and her body began to quiver in anticipation. As his gentle hands caressed her breasts, her blood quickened with a desire as urgent and hungry as his own. Feeling her response, he swept her up in his arms, carrying her towards the bed. Soon their bodies were entwined as one, lost in the magic of the love that had proved so much stronger than they could have guessed —a love that would give them both so much joy, not just tonight but for all the days and nights of their life.

Carried along on a tide of passion, Jane gave a cry of ecstasy, all doubts and torment gone as she surrendered to the man she loved. It was for this moment she had been born, and all the pain and sorrow meant nothing. She loved, and was loved in return.

At the water's edge, the man stood watching as the ship rode out to sea, her sails billowing in the breeze. He watched until she became a tiny dot on the horizon, then he smiled and turned away . . .

SHE MIGHT BE AN INNOCENT